Sasha Raye

PRODUCER

From Hood to

HOLLYWOOD

From Hood
to
HOLLYWOOD

Sasha Raye

Life Changing Books in conjunction with Power Play Media
Published by Life Changing Books
P.O. Box 423 Brandywine, MD 20613

Library of Congress Cataloging-in-Publication Data;

www.lifechangingbooks.net

ISBN- (10) 1-934230804 (13) 978-1934230800
Copyright ® 2009

Printed in Canada

Acknowledgements

Wow, this is quite amazing. I can't believe I'm writing acknowledgements. Most people said I would never make anything of myself. They said I would never make it in Hollywood, and of course they said I would never succeed in writing a novel. Well to all of those who voted me most likely to fail, kiss my ass. Look for me on the red carpet baby!

Now, on to my real supporters. To my little princess, just trust and believe that Mommy does it all for you. I hope to one day make you proud. To my home-girls, Lisa, Cheryl, Kim, and Shannon…thank you for always having my back. The world is a cold place without the four of you. To my cousin, Daja, thank you for the emergency ends when I needed it. I told you I'd pay you back double plus interest. The L.A. paper smells real good.

To all my LCB family, thanks for looking out; especially Tonya Ridley (Talk of The Town), Danette Majette (Good Girl Gone Bad), and Kendall Banks (Rich Girls). I love the way you check for me even when I'm out filming my new joints. Also, thanks for keeping a hush on who I really am. It's crazy how the book has gotten so much buzz just because they can't figure out my real name. Hilarious!

It is imperative that I thank Virginia Greene and Aschundria Fisher for their editing assistance. I also gotta give thanks to all of my distributors both large and small. Thanks for looking out. I want to give a special shout out to Tyson and Hakim at Black and Nobel books My publisher told me great things about you, so keep doing it! In addition, I'd like to put Nelson on blast from the Bronx, Sidi in New York, and Afrikan World Books in Baltimore.

Last but certainly not least, I'd like to thank the LCB administrative team. Leslie Allen, what can I say? You're rough….damn tougher than nails. Thanks for all the hard work and for turning this book into a masterpiece. To Tasha Simpson and Nakea Murry, I appreciate all that you do for me, and lastly, I'd like to thank my publisher, Azarel. Words can not express my gratitude. I pray my sales will say it all, because I'm bound to sell out.

Lovingly,

Sasha Raye

Prologue

Na, na, na, diva is a female version of a hustla
Of a hustla, of a, of a hustla
Na, na, na, diva is a female version of a hustla
Of a hustla, of a, of a hustla
Stop the track, let me state facts
I told you give me a minute and I'll be right back
Fifty million round the world
And they said that I couldn't get it
I done got so sick and filthy with Benji's, I can't spend

Demi sung along to the tune of Beyonce's new hit *Diva*. As the song blasted through the Ipod speaker in her bedroom, Demi pranced around in front of the full length mirror that showed her body from head to toe. She loved looking at herself on a regular. It was a hobby that many would call conceited, but to Demi, she just loved the reflection that it gave off. Wherever there was a mirror, Demi was in it…admiring herself, and this evening was no different. She continued to sing along with Beyonce, with a paddle brush in her hand, pretending that it was a microphone and that she was performing in front of a make believe audience that existed only in her head, something she also did on regular basis. Ever since the movie, Dreamgirls, Demi loved how Beyonce showed off her great acting skills, and often imitated the superstar whenever possible. She'd seen the movie at least a dozen times and knew it word for word.

Demi glowed in the mirror, dancing like she was on the stage at Madison Square Garden and dressed for a sold-out performance. But in reality she was only dressed for a night on the town with her man. She sported a brand new tightly fitted, strap-

1

less Prada cocktail dress that exposed her 36 C cups and high-lighted every single curve of her body. Her long black, sensuous hair fell down past her shoulders like running water and her long shapely legs were stretched out in a pair of black Manolo Blah-nik rhinestone sandals. Topping it off were her big silver hoop earrings and shiny glossy lips that made her a certified ten. Demi was a mixed beauty, half black half Puerto Rican, and often favored the R&B singer Mya; a stunning beauty, who had men beating down her door growing up. Ever since the ninth grade catching ballers came easy for Demi, an ability that her best friend Michelle envied.

Tell me somethin' where your boss at?
Where my ladies up in here that like to talk back
I wanna see ya, I'd like to meet cha
What you said, she ain't no diva
Na, na, na, diva is a female version of a hustla
Of a hustla, of a, of a hustla
Na, na, na, diva is a female version of a hustla
Of a hustla, of a, of a hustla

Demi continued to sing.

"Oh, so you a hustla now?" a voice called out.

When Demi turned around, she saw Perry standing inside the doorway with a dozen long stemmed red roses and a huge smile.

"Is there somethin' you need to tell me?" he joked plac-ing a Macys' shopping bag on the floor.

Demi returned the expression showing off her newly bleached teeth. "Yeah, I got about ten keys of Blue Magic com-ing in from Thailand. You know like Frank Lucas." She turned down the music.

When Perry started laughing and told her she watched too many movies, Demi quickly walked toward him, stood on her toes, and threw her arms around his neck. She loved his tall six foot one, one hundred and ninety pound frame. She also loved his smooth dark chocolate skin. Most people thought he was too crispy or smoky, but Demi didn't mind, she preferred dark meat anyway.

"Hi, honey," Demi said kissing him on his full lips.

Perry rubbed her back with his free hand. "Hey, gorgeous."

After embracing a few more seconds, Demi stepped back to look at the flowers then grabbed the crystal vase. "These are so pretty. Thanks, but you didn't have to get me anything else for my birthday. The shopping spree on Fifth Avenue was enough."

Demi knew she was lying. She loved the way Perry spoiled her with all sorts of expensive gifts and their lavish lifestyle. She looked around their plush two bedroom apartment in the heart of the upscale Chelsea neighborhood and quietly thanked Perry for her privileged status. Where she came from, not too many people got to live in places with floor to ceiling windows, a fabulous view of the New York City skyline, and a marble tile bath. Perry pampered her and their four-year-old daughter, Aliyah, and never allowed them to ask for anything twice. Perry was a big time hustler, with the matching swagger of Jim Jones; a handsome, confident street niggah who didn't take shit from nobody. A thug type of quality that Demi loved. She'd been head over heels since meeting him at the age of eighteen, and still felt the exact same way. He was addictive like that.

"That dress looks good on you. Turn around."

Demi did a little model spin to show her man how well the dress hugged her huge ass. An ass that gave hip-hop model, Melyssa Ford a run for her money.

"Damn, you look good. You better not let me catch Michelle's ass in that dress either. That shit cost me eight hundred."

Demi sighed. "Come on Perry, don't ruin the moment."

"No, I'm serious. Every time I turn around that bitch got her hand out. Her and yo' connivin'-ass mother."

"Why do you always have to bring this up? My mother is keepin' Aliyah for us tonight so we can go out, ain't she?" Demi asked before placing the vase down on top of the nightstand. "Are you serious? I had to pay her ass a hundred dollars to keep her own fuckin' grandchild. Don't act like she do that shit for free. Michelle charges us, too."

Perry got frustrated every time he mentioned the two closest people in Demi's life. They were money hungry and always wanted to be in his pockets like he was *their* man. "Come on, are you ready? I got a run to make after we get back, so we need to leave."

"So, you're not gonna spend the whole night with me?" Demi asked. "You're gonna work and not help me celebrate my 23rd birthday *all* night?"

Perry shrugged his shoulders. "What you want me to do, Ma? I can't leave that shit in here overnight. It's bad enough I got it up in the crib in the first place." He pointed to the Macy's bag. "Besides, if I don't make runs, how we gon' eat? Shit, did you forget? I gotta pay five thousand dollars for rent every month."

Demi poked out her lips then looked on the floor at the bag. A bag that she knew wasn't for her. Whenever she saw the infamous Macy's or Adidas shopping bag, she knew what it contained, and it wasn't clothes or a new pair of shell toe sneakers. It contained cocaine.

"I know but…it's my birthday."

"I tell you what. If we don't have to beef 'bout this shit, I'll go buy you that Cartier watch you been lookin' at."

"I don't want a watch. What about that new BMW truck? The X6. I been lookin' at that, too."

Perry laughed. "Whatever you want."

Demi took a few steps back away from him. "I got an idea. Fuck going out. Let's stay in. I would rather show you my birthday suit anyway."

When Perry's eyes said that he agreed, Demi didn't waste any time taking off her dress and tossing it on their leather chaise lounge. She then stood in front of her man with a sexy, red Victoria Secret lace bra with the matching thongs.

"Now, come over here so I can show you how much I really want that truck."

Perry didn't waste anytime stripping down to his boxers. He then walked up to Demi, and threw her on top of the bed. He liked rough sex anyway, so it didn't surprise her when he ripped off her thong with one tug. He snatched open her bra, exposing her perfectly round breasts before lowering himself to lick her stiff nipples. Moving his tongue in a circular motion, Perry made sure each nipple got the same amount of attention so the other one wouldn't get mad. From her constant moans, he could tell that it was also a technique that seemed to be turning Demi on, which made his dick stand at attention. With each one of them having high sex drives, their foreplay never lasted too long.

"You want it?" Perry asked.

"Yes," Demi replied in a seductive tone.

At that moment, Perry pulled down his boxers, and plunged his rock hard dick inside her pussy, which was already dripping wet. While Demi lay on her back with her legs in the air, Perry dove inside her nest with quick forceful thrusts. The more he pushed, the more his thick, nine inch shaft rammed her inner walls, causing Demi to immediately talk dirty.

"Oh shit, fuck me...fuck me harder!" she yelled.

As Perry picked up even more speed, the sounds of his balls slapping up against her ass cheeks began to fill the room. However, that sound didn't last long because seconds later they both heard a loud boom coming from the other room.

"What the..." was all Perry could get out before hearing the words "police" being shouted in several different voices.

"Police! Don't fuckin' move!" a white guy with spiky blond hair yelled.

Perry's dick went limp instantly while Demi started shaking underneath him. All he could do was look over at the Macy's bag and shake his head. He always thought that he would be prepared if the police ever rolled up on him, especially since they always seemed to come in the wee hours of the morning. As it turned out, that wasn't the case.

Damn, he said to himself.

One

SIX MONTHS LATER

Harlem

Demi smiled as she saw her five-year-old daughter running out of her classroom at full speed. Except for having Demi's good grade of long beautiful hair and charming smile, Aliyah was the spitting image of her father. Once Aliyah was within arms reach, Demi bent down to hug her daughter, but suddenly stopped. Over the past few months she'd noticed that Aliyah no longer cared for any type of affection, which was strange, and something that she couldn't figure out, especially after Aliyah loved to cuddle as a toddler. Demi sometimes wondered if it was due to her being locked up for a few weeks when all the Perry drama went down. Her mother, Janet, wasn't known for warmth or friendliness, and certainly didn't follow the usual parental guidelines, so it was up in the air how Aliyah was treated during that time.

Demi felt guilty every time she thought back to that horrible time in her life. After the local police, DEA and several FBI agents raided their upscale Manhattan apartment, both she and Perry were taken into custody and eventually charged with a felony drug possession charge with intent to distribute. It didn't matter that Demi had nothing to do with Perry's drug deals. The fact that she was in the house with the one and a half kilos of cocaine found in the Macy's bag was enough to lock her up. However, despite the strict street code of not snitching, Perry ended up ratting out his drug connect to lessen Demi's charges to conspiracy. Once the connect was taken into custody, all of her charges were eventually dropped. Having her freedom taken away was unexplainable, and an experience Demi wouldn't wish on her own worst enemy. Her heart went out to Perry, who wouldn't see the light of day anytime soon, but she was grateful that he cared enough about her and Aliyah to do the right thing.

"Mommy, I had chicken fingers today," Aliyah said spinning around. Keeping still was always something she had a problem with.

Before Demi could reply, she saw Aliyah's Kindergarten teacher, Mrs. Carlin walking toward her with a look of concern on her face. "Hey Ms. Rodriguez, can I talk to you for a second?" she asked.

"Is somethin' wrong?" Demi questioned.

"I just need to speak to you about something. Can we step away from Aliyah if you don't mind?"

Demi looked over at her daughter who'd stopped spinning, but was now clapping her hands. "No, I don't mind at all. Aliyah, Mommy and Mrs. Carlin are gonna talk. Stand here, okay."

"Yeah," was the only thing Aliyah said.

Once the two ladies walked a few feet away, Mrs. Carlin gave Demi another concerned look. "Ms. Rodriguez I want to talk to you about Aliyah's performance in class."

Demi had no idea where the conversation was headed. "Okkkkayyy."

"Since the school year started, I've noticed that Aliyah is a little different from the other students in my class."

"What is that supposed to mean?" Demi asked with an instant attitude.

"Well, I've noticed that she fails to respond to her name when I call her sometimes and she also can't seem to keep up with the other children. Not to mention the constant spinning she does and the hand clapping. She even has outbursts sometimes when we change a normal routine. It's starting to disturb

8

the entire classroom."

"So, what are you tryin' to say? I have a good daughter, not like some of these other bad-ass kids walkin' around here."

"I'm saying that you might want to have her tested. I've been a teacher for twenty-five years and I've seen this kind of behavior way too many times."

Demi placed her hands on her hips then stared at the petite woman. "Have her tested for what?"

"Autism."

"Autism. What the hell is that? Wait…is that when a child is slow or some shit?"

Mrs. Carlin rubbed her slightly wrinkled forehead. "I'm not going to call it slow, but it's when a child has problems with social interaction, language and behavior. I'm sorry Ms. Rodriguez. I wanted to talk to you about this earlier in the school year, but I decided to monitor Aliyah for a while. I wanted to make sure the symptoms were there first."

Demi was heated. Ever since Aliyah was two, she'd noticed herself how hyper she was, but that didn't mean anything. "Bitch, are you a doctor? Huh, do you have a damn medical degree? Hell no. You just some underpaid-ass teacher who don't know what the hell you talkin' about . It ain't nothin' wrong with my child. She's just overexcited sometimes. Mind yo' fuckin' business!" She quickly walked back over to Aliyah, but after grabbing her daughter's hand, she turned back around. "Now monitor that shit!"

After strutting down the hallway, Demi stormed out of PS 154 into the cool March air with Aliyah in tow. Walking down 127th Street, Demi continued to talk to herself about Mrs. Carlin suggesting that Aliyah be tested.

"Lil' stupid-ass woman. Her ass need to be fuckin' tested," Demi ranted. She told herself she would try and get Aliyah in another class first thing Monday morning.

She watched as Aliyah let go of her hand and started twirling around doing a little dance, causing Demi to burst out laughing.

She began to tickle Aliyah on her neck.

"That teacher is the one who crazy. You just silly that's all, and full of damn energy."

As Aliyah began to laugh, Demi noticed how tall she was getting, which was obviously another one of Perry's attributes that her daughter had inherited. Standing at only five foot six, Demi wasn't exactly runway model material, but hopefully her daughter would be.

Shit as broke as I am, gettin' Aliyah into modelin' might not be such a bad idea, Demi thought.

A few minutes later, they both entered building six of the St. Nicholas Housing projects, a place where Demi had grown up her entire life. It was also a place where she hated having to come back to. She hated the garbage piled up on the sidewalk, the pissed filled hallways and the kids spitting curse words and threats at each other all day. After getting a taste of the glamorous life with Perry, moving back in with her mother and two brothers wasn't Demi's idea of a home anymore, and she couldn't wait to make some money so she and Aliyah could get their own place. All of her and Perry's possessions had been confiscated during the raid, so Demi had been left with absolutely nothing except for a few pieces of her wardrobe. She had to start back over, which was gonna be difficult, but certainly not impossible.

"I want a popsicle. I want a popsicle," Aliyah said over and over as she and Demi stepped into the elevator.

Demi pushed the number eight on the wall panel. "Okay, lil' girl. Calm down. I'll see if grandma bought you some from the store when we get in the house."

Aliyah began to scream then hit herself in the forehead. "I want a popsicle. Popsicle!"

Demi's eyes widened. "What in the world is wrong wit' you Aliyah? Stop actin' like that or you ain't getting' nothin'!"

Demi watched her daughter continue to act up during the entire elevator ride up to the 8th floor. She'd spanked Aliyah a few times here and there, but had never been one to punish her

10

on a consistent basis. By Demi getting her ass beat down almost everyday as a child, she often told herself she didn't want to pass on the same child abuse to her own daughter.

When the elevator doors opened Aliyah quickly ran off, which pissed Demi off because she hated chasing after her. "What the hell did I tell you about runnin'?" Demi asked.

Aliyah however never stopped or even turned around. Instead, she continued to run down the hallway and toward their apartment door. By the time Demi caught up, she was damn near out of breath.

"Aliyah…you…gotta stop doin' that shit. These halls are not a playground." When Aliyah started laughing, it pissed Demi off even more. "Okay. We'll see how much you laugh when you don't get that popsicle."

When Demi took out her keys and opened the door, the strong smell of weed hit her in the face like a quick jab. Looking around the room, she saw her brother, Dennis, sitting on the couch with a huge blunt in one hand and talking on his cell phone with the other. The weed along with the stench of the poorly kept house immediately made her skin crawl. Dennis was her older brother and a washed up hustler who laid around the house all day watching soap operas and stupid court T.V. shows. From the looks of the pizza box, powdered donut wrapping and an empty two liter coke bottle, he'd once again been in the same spot all day.

"Uncle D…Uncle D," Aliyah chanted, then threw up her small hand.

"Go in the room and take off yo' uniform," Demi replied. When Aliyah began twirling into the other room, Demi looked at her brother with disgust.

"When the hell are you gonna get a job? This shit is crazy. Yo' ass was sittin' in the same spot when I left for work this mornin'."

"Yo', let me hit you back 'cuz I'm 'bout to curse my sister's ass out," Dennis said, just before closing his small flip phone. "Who the hell you talkin' to?"

Demi looked at her brother who didn't resemble her at all and smirked. With a wide nose, cocoa colored skin and a scorpion tattooed on the side of his face, Dennis looked like the rapper, The Game. Dennis nor her other brother, Donte, who was shot and killed two years prior had the same father, so they all looked more like strangers than siblings.

Demi had only met her father one time on her eighth birthday. He showed up at their apartment, and dropped off a bike, but didn't stay long after him and her mother starting fighting…over money of course. Despite Demi's pleads, her mother sold the bike the next day. Demi hadn't seen her father since.

"Obviously you, niggah. You the only played out hustla I see around here."

He pulled on his blunt, then blew the smoke in Demi's direction. "Yo' don't be comin' up in here messin' up my fuckin' high. It's Friday, bitch. Lighten the hell up."

"How you gon' smoke that shit in front of Aliyah? She might catch a contact or somethin'. Damn be a role model. Ain't you thirty?"

"Girl, get the hell out my face. I didn't know Lee Lee was comin' home. Plus you act like you don't like to get high sometimes."

"I don't get high around my daughter. Besides, don't call her that shit," Demi said throwing her purse along with Aliyah's High School Musical back pack on the floor.

Dennis laughed. "I'll call my niece whatever the fuck I want! You know what…ever since you got wit' that nigga Perry you think you on some different type shit, but guess what, yo' broke-ass back in the hood. She Lee Lee around 'dis muthafucka now!"

Arguing with her brother was a daily routine for Demi, which was another reason she couldn't wait to move out. The arguments also didn't end until they were almost physical. She hated that Donte wasn't around to step in and referee anymore. Opening up her mouth, Demi was getting ready to snap back,

12

but she could see her mother's bedroom door opening. Seconds later, her mother appeared in her doorway, dressed in a dirty wife beater. It was apparent that she didn't have any underwear on by the way her ass jiggled when she walked. At forty-six, Janet Rodriguez was a beautiful Puerto Rican woman who still had the body of a twenty-five year old.

"Would both of y'all shut the fuck up? I'm tryna get that niggah in my room to nut and y'all out her yellin' 'bout stupid shit!"

Her long, jet black hair hung in a stringy mess and fell just past her shoulders.

"Demi started the shit, Ma," Dennis said sounding like a child. "Talkin' 'bout I shouldn't be smokin' weed."

Janet gave her daughter a look of disapproval. "Demi, mind yo' fuckin' business. You don't run shit up in here."

At that moment, a well known young hustler who hung out in front of the building emerged from Janet's room. Dipped in iced out jewelry, and baggy True Religion jeans he walked toward Janet with several bills in his hand.

"No, no. I'm comin' back boo. Go back inside," Janet instructed.

"Yo' B, hit me when the house is empty," he said before handing Janet the money and walking out the door.

Knowing she'd never run after a man, Janet looked down and quickly counted her fee. "Ain't this some shit. I was supposed to get two hundred from that niggah. Now all I got is a hundred! Which one of y'all gon' give me the rest?" she asked holding out her hand toward her children.

Both Demi and Dennis were quiet.

"Don't fuckin' get mute now!" Janet yelled, then looked at Demi. "Since you wanna come up in my house tellin' people what to do, you need to give me my money."

"Ma, come on. You know I don't have a lot of money. I barely get anymore hours at the drug store," Demi replied. She glanced over at Dennis who was pointing at her and laughing. "Dennis why don't you grow the hell up!"

13

"No, you grow up!" Janet barked. "You need to start pulling more weight around here. That two hundred dollars you give for groceries every month ain't working."

"I guess not when Dennis' ass eat up every damn thing!" Demi shot back.

As the two women began to go back and forth, Aliyah ran out the bedroom that she and Demi shared with her hands covering her ears. "Popsicle! I want a popsicle!"

"Lee Lee go sit yo' ass down!" Janet yelled.

Demi was irritated every time she heard the nickname she didn't want her daughter to have. "Ma, did you get the popsicles I put on the grocery list?"

Janet shook her head. "Hell, no. When I got to the register the money was a lil' short, and I still hadn't got my cigarettes so I told the cashier to put them damn high-ass popsicles and those Apple Jacks back."

"What? You know Aliyah acts up when we don't have that cereal," Demi stated.

"Lee Lee needs her ass beat. That's what she needs. She's too damn spoiled anyway," Janet replied.

Demi rolled her eyes and watched as Aliyah continued to run around. "Well, her father used to spoil her, so she's used to that."

"Fuck Perry!" Dennis yelled out after finally putting out his blunt.

"Yeah, fuck Perry. That jail bird can't do shit for her now," Janet added.

"Neither of y'all weren't sayin' fuck him when he was lacin' yo' pockets," Demi said with a smirk.

"Well, his fuckin' money don' ran out, so fuck'em," Janet replied.

Demi wondered why she had to have such a fucked up family. She often wondered through the years how well her father's side of the family would've treated her if he'd stuck around.

"First, the teacher at school tells me that she thinks

14

Aliyah might have Autism or some shit, and now I gotta come home to this. Wow, what a fuckin' day." Demi said out loud.

Janet chuckled. "Why you beefing wit' the teacher? I coulda told you Lee Lee's ass wasn't wrapped too tight. Look at her…running around like she belong in a mental ward. Normal children don't go around hitting themselves. Something wrong wit' her ass. You must've been smokin' some of that shit Perry was selling when you were pregnant."

Janet's words definitely hit Demi below the belt. Even though her mother was known to talk shit, Demi couldn't believe she'd taken it to that level. Walking up to Aliyah, and grabbing her hand, Demi pulled her daughter into their bedroom and slammed the door. Trying to get her mind off of everything, she quickly turned on her T.V. and hit play on the DVD player. Whenever Demi was stressed, she would always turn on Dreamgirls and act out a few parts. This time she had plans on being Jennifer Hudson's character, Effie. However that didn't stop Janet from her tirade.

"Slam all the fuckin' doors you want," she laughed. "Don't get mad at me 'cause your child is special!"

 *Two*

After watching Michelle shop at several stores on 125th street the next day, Demi and Aliyah accompanied her for a late lunch at Slyvia's on Lenox Avenue; a popular soul food restaurant where the barbeque ribs fell right off the bone, the pork chops and collard greens made you lick your fingers, and the corn bread melted in your mouth. Because of the notoriety of the popular spot, busloads of tourists and college students often bombarded the place, which produced long lines. However, with Michelle's undoubting pussy power she was able to convince two women who were at the beginning of the line and obviously gay to let her get in front of them. Whether it was with a man or a woman, Michelle threw her body around to get whatever she wanted, and it always worked.

As the hostess proceeded to show Michelle, Demi and Aliyah to their table, Michelle looked back and gave the two women a wink "Thanks girls. Don't forget, I need somebody's number before you all leave," Michelle said.

Seeing the women damn near blush when Michelle walked away made Demi laugh. As the three of them sat down, the hostess gave them two menus, informed them about their waitress, then walked away. Demi could hardly wait to ask Michelle about her two new friends.

"So, which one of them are you gonna call?" Demi asked before placing a Barbie coloring book in front of Aliyah. She needed something to occupy her daughter's attention because she'd been a handful all day.

Aliyah immediately took a crayon and started marking all over the page like a two year old.

"I guess Aliyah said fuck stayin' inside the lines," Michelle laughed before answering Demi's question. "Girl, please. I ain't callin' 'dem bitches. I just said 'dat to make it look good. I ain't gay, but if I was I would be wit' a Halle Berry type chick, not two Whoppi Goldberg lookin' bitches."

Demi thought back to the dread headed women and smiled. "You might not be gay, but if a paid chick was givin' yo' ass paper, you would be all up on her."

Michelle flashed a sleazy smile showing off her high cheekbones. "True…so true."

Michelle and Demi had been friends since knee high, and were like sisters more than friends. They'd been through everything together, from Michelle's abusive father trying to have sex with her every night to Demi's bad stealing habits. Habits that she'd luckily gotten under control. However, even though they shared each other's darkest secrets, the two women were like night and day when it came to personalities. Michelle was a wild child, who loved to talk shit, fuck every man who crossed her path, and was a get money chick.

Demi on the other hand loved money, too, but didn't feel the need to sleep with every man just to get it. Her mother was already a hoe, so the last thing she wanted to do was follow in her footsteps.

Michelle looked in her H&M shopping bag and pulled out her simple, black spaghetti strap dress. "I'ma work 'dis shit once I put on my leopard print pumps. I might do my thick Betsey Johnson belt wit' it too." Michelle was a risk taker when it came to her style, and rocked a big, curly honey blond weave that looked like Kelis' old hairstyle.

"Damn, I'll be so glad when yo' ass can stop window shoppin' and shit," Michelle said. "It's no fun shoppin' alone."

"Yeah, trust me. I miss shoppin', too. I hate to burst yo' bubble though, boo, because even when I did shop, you didn't catch me in no H&M. I only did Saks and Berdorf Goodman. I wouldn't dare buy that cheap shit you got," Demi said with a huge smile.

"Fuck you, bitch. Those days are over now," Michelle said, picking up a napkin. She balled it up and threw it at her friend as a waitress came over to the table carrying a huge tray. When the woman put down three plates with fried chicken, macaroni and cheese, greens and some silverware on the table, Michelle started waving her hands. "Umm…hold up. We ain't even ordered yet lady."

"Yes, I know, but the two gentlemen over there ordered for you," the waitress replied. She then pointed at two guys who were on the opposite side of the restaurant.

Michelle's eyes narrowed, focusing on the two guys like lasers. "What? Dem two corny lookin' niggahs over there?"

As the waitress confirmed, Aliyah immediately put down the three crayons she had in her hands, and picked up a piece of chicken.

"Wait a minute. Put that down," Demi said, taking the food away.

"I'm hungry!" Aliyah yelled. "Hungry!"

Demi was completely embarrassed. She looked at Michelle. "What are we gonna do? Aliyah is not gonna be able to sit here and wait for some more food."

"Is 'dis shit free?" Michelle asked the waitress.

"Of course. The gentlemen have paid for your meals, drinks, and some rum cake."

"Well shit, in 'dat case, dig in ladies," Michelle replied. She looked over at the two guys and mouthed thanks. "It's so easy bein' me," she boasted.

"How you know they didn't send the food over because of me?" Demi asked.

When Michelle looked at Demi's ponytail and tan colored sweat suit that flushed out her skin tone, she disagreed. "No, I'm sure about 'dis one. It's because of me." Both women laughed as they picked up their forks and began to dig in.

Thirty minutes later, Demi told Michelle that it was time to go. After Aliyah kept having outbursts and wouldn't listen to a word she said, they all got up in an attempt to leave.

19

"Aliyah's ass has always been all over the place, but she really startin' to bug out now," Michelle said.

Demi sighed. She didn't even want to bring up the whole Autism thing. "I don't know why she been actin' like that. I wish Perry was here to help me out. I didn't even want to bring her wit' me today, but my bitch-ass mother wouldn't keep her. Besides, her babysittin' rate is too fuckin' high anyway."

"Damn, well if you need a break, bring her over to my house."

"Bitch, yo' rate is high as hell, too!" Demi laughed.

"And now since Aliyah really can't keep the fuck still, I might double the rate," Michelle joked.

Suddenly, the two guys who'd bought the food came over and introduced themselves. Both men had on baggy jeans, Timberlands, and white-T's; attire that was right up Michelle's alley, but an instant turn off for Demi. In her opinion, both of the guys looked broke and corny.

"I'm sayin' Ma, you lookin' good. You and yo' friend," one of the hoodlums with a Yankee's baseball hat stated to Michelle.

Michelle in turn looked at Demi and gave her an expression that said, "I told you I was the reason they bought the food."

The other guy who had a nicely trimmed goatee was cute. But Demi wasn't impressed. Even though she hadn't had sex since Perry, and had to use a dildo that Michelle bought her for sexual satisfaction, for some reason the guy seemed like a waste of time.

"Thanks for the food, but if you wanted to pay for somethin' you coulda took us shoppin' or some shit. You know, spent some real money," Michelle said, being upfront and gangsta with her attitude.

The young man with the hat smiled displaying a small gap. "Hold up, Ma. I gotta see what yo' head game look like before I wife ya."

Just like I thought, corny... and disrespectful, Demi

20

thought to herself.

Michelle wasn't offended. "So, what you workin' wit', niggah? Cuz you talkin' a little too greasy right now."

"I'm workin' wit' plenty. I stack paper all day, everyday, you feel me, Ma," he said with conviction, eyeing Michelle and Demi with a lustful hunger.

Demi was annoyed and showed it by letting out a huge impatient sigh.

"I'm sayin', what's yo' name, Ma?" the guy with the hat asked.

"Shonte," Michelle lied.

"What's yours?" Michelle asked.

"I'm Malik and this my man, Rasheed," he said pointing to his friend. "What about yo' friend? Why she so quiet?"

"Cuz, she got her tongue cut out." Michelle grinned.

"What? Get da fuck outta here? You lyin' ," Malik said. Even Rasheed began to look at Demi funny.

Demi almost burst out laughing, but she kept her composure and let the lie continue on. Michelle was taking the foolishness to the next level.

"Nah, I'm serious. Her ex-boyfriend was crazy. He caught my friend suckin' the next niggah dick, so he cut her tongue out to make sure it wouldn't happen again," Michelle replied.

Demi looked over at Aliyah who was twirling in circles with her hands covering her ears, which was gaining unwanted attention. Demi was starting to become embarrassed by her daughter's behavior. The best option was to just ignore her, and hopefully everybody else would, too.

"Yo, is you serious? Nah, I ain't believin' that. Yo, let me see that shit!"

"I don't believe it either," Rasheed added.

"Niggah, she ain't tryin' to show you her deformity. She insecure," Michelle responded.

"I don't give a fuck. Yo' friend still look good and shit," Malik said.

21

"And you would still hit that, right?" Michelle asked.

"I ain't even gonna lie to you, Ma…yeah, I would still fuck. Yo' friend is one in a million, body and looks like that, and you ain't gotta worry about her mouth goin' off like a dumb bitch…shit, it's all good," the young hood announced. "If she got her tongue cut out, Shorti must give da bomb-ass head."

Demi couldn't hold it in anymore. "Can you stop fuckin' talkin' about givin' head around my daughter?"

"Oh shit, you can talk. Yo, why y'all tryin' to play a niggah," Malik said loudly.

As arrogant as he was, Michelle liked his style.

Demi grabbed Aliyah's hand. "Michelle, I'll be outside," she said before walking out the restaurant.

"What's up wit' yo' girl?" Rasheed asked.

"She a'ight niggah," Michelle responded.

"Why don't you and yo' girl, come meet us tonight? You know so we can get to know each other a lil' better," Malik said. He looked at Michelle up and down then licked his lips.

Michelle batted her almond shaped eyes. "What's in it for us?"

"Shit, a good-ass time. I'll leave yo' name at the door, Ma. Free liquor and all that," Malik informed.

"Yeah, we'll make sure y'all are taken care of," Rasheed chimed in.

Michelle thought for a few seconds. "Well in 'dat case my name ain't Shonte. It's Michelle and her name is Demi." After exchanging numbers with Malik, she made her way outside and walked toward Demi and Aliyah, who were a few feet away.

"I can't believe you stayed in there, and listened to those clowns," Demi said leaning against an old Buick.

"Girl, you never know. They might have some paper. You be turnin' niggahs down out the gate."

Demi rolled her eyes. "I doubt it."

"Why the hell yo' ass so uptight? You need to loosen up."

"I'm broke, that's why I'm so damn uptight. Shit, I need some money."

Michelle threw her arms up in the air. "Bitch I know 'dat shit. Dats why I don't understand why you be throwin' niggas shade all the time. Look, they invited us to meet them at a club tonight. You down?"

"I don't know, Michelle," Demi hesitantly responded.

Michelle started laughing. "What the fuck else you gotta do? Broke muthafuckas always need to have an empty schedule."

Demi laughed, too. "Shut up."

"Come on girl. Let's go have some fun. Besides, yo' ass ain't been out to a club wit' me in a minute. I know you ain't worried about 'dat nigga, Perry."

"No, not at all."

"Oh, I was gettin' ready to say. Shit, I heard 'dat nigga been sendin' money to some bitch named, Brandy who be up 123rd street anyway."

Demi's eyes widened. "What? Who told you that? Perry ain't got no money. The police took all that shit."

"Hey, I'm just tellin' you the rumor 'dat started goin' around about two months after he got locked up."

"Why the fuck didn't you tell me this before?" Demi asked.

"Man, I ain't wanna get into no rumor type shit, but now 'dat I see you bein' all hesitant about gettin' on wit' yo' life, I'm like fuck it. The shit just might be true."

Demi couldn't believe it. "But how the fuck can he be sendin' her money from jail?"

"Come on, Demi don't act dumb. If a nigga got connects, it's not like the shit can't be done," Michelle replied.

Demi wondered if Perry had been holding out on her all these months. The more she thought about it, the angrier she became. "Fuck it. I'll go to the club wit' you."

Michelle smiled. "Dats what I'm talkin' about."

"What about a babysitter?" Demi asked looking down at

Aliyah.

"Now that's what yo' ass need to figure out. If my moms wasn't on 'dat shit, I could ask her."

Demi agreed. She would rather a hoe like her mother keep her daughter any day as opposed to a junkie. As the three walked down Lenox Avenue, she knew there was only one other person, who would possibly help her out. She just hoped it wasn't gonna take any money to convince him.

 *Three*

As soon as Demi and Aliyah made their way back home, Dennis was on the couch as usual with a Heineken in one hand and the remote in the other. Not in the mood to argue, Demi was about to make her way past him, but got pissed when he didn't acknowledge Aliyah after she called out his name. It was one thing to be nasty toward her, but being rude to her child was unacceptable. Once she sent Aliyah into their bedroom, Demi didn't waste anytime going off.

"How the fuck you gon' just ignore Aliyah like that?" she asked. "That shit is so rude."

When they first came in, Demi didn't bother to look at the television, but when Dennis didn't respond she had to see what had him in such a daze. Looking at the thirty-six inch T.V., her eyes almost popped out when she saw some white girl let a black guy fuck her from behind, with the biggest dick she'd ever seen.

"You nasty muthafucka. You sittin' here watchin' porn in the middle of the damn day."

Dennis took a sip of his beer, but never looked away from the T.V. "Demi, if you don't get the fuck away from me right now I swear."

"I'm just sayin'. When you gon' get a real job or some shit?"

He finally gave her eye contact. "And when the fuck are you gonna move back out? I'm so sick of yo' damn mouth. Watchin' pussy, gettin' high, and drinkin' is my fuckin' job. Now what?" His eyes refocused back on the T.V.

Demi's plans for asking her brother if he could watch

25

Aliyah quickly went out the window. She had to come up with another plan. "Where Ma at?"

"Out…where the hell yo' ass need to be."

"Come on Dennis where she at? I got somethin' to ask her."

"I just said she was out, and don't know if she comin' back no time soon."

At that point, Demi was about to call Michelle and tell her that she couldn't go. Becoming a mother was something she'd chosen to sign up for, and sacrificing was a part of that deal. Even though, it would've been nice to get out for while, she didn't want to ask her brother to do anything for her. However, as Demi went to grab her cell phone, thoughts of getting dressed up in some of her old clothes and having a good time flashed through her head. She decided to bite the bullet.

"Sorry I pissed you off. I just don't want Aliyah seein' that mess," Demi pleaded.

Dennis immediately looked at his sister like he knew she was up to something. "What the fuck do you want? You don't eva apologize."

Demi cleared her throat. "Umm…can you keep Aliyah for me tonight? I mean that's if you not doin' anything." She smiled knowing he didn't have shit to do as always.

"Don't be fake wit' me. Hell no, I ain't watchin' Lee Lee's wild ass. She be twirlin' in front of the T.V. and shit."

"C'mon Dennis, I really wanna go out," Demi pleaded. "I'll even make sure she's sleep before I leave."

"I don't give a shit what you wanna do."

Demi paused for a second. "What if I pay you?" She knew money was the keyword around her house.

"How much?" Dennis asked with a smile.

"All I can afford is thirty."

Dennis burst out laughing. "You must be jokin'. I ain't babysittin' for no thirty dollars. Plus you used to give Ma a hundred."

"Look at what you just said. I used to. Plus Perry gave

Ma a hundred dollars, not me."

"Shit, I need at least fifty," Dennis stated, then took another sip of beer.

Demi began to wonder if a night on the town with two dudes she wasn't even feeling was worth it. However, the contemplating didn't last very long.

"A'ight. I'll give you fifty, but I'm not payin' up until I get ready to leave, just in case I change my mind."

"Fine, but since you not payin' up front, if one of my bitches call and wanna give me some ass, I'm out."

"Niggah, you ain't had a bitch since '98," Demi joked.

However, that was far from the truth. Like mother-like son, Dennis also had his share of women. He used bitches and tossed them out like an old wardrobe.

Six hours later, Demi bobbed her head and turned up the volume on the radio when one of her favorite songs, *Be Without You* by Mary J. Blige came on. As the lyrics to the old school song were heard, she began to sing along to the track and slowly danced around her bedroom. She couldn't wait to get her groove on.

"Bitch, you ain't ready yet. Yo' ass love to sing and prance around in the fuckin' mirror."

When Demi turned around, she saw Michelle standing with her hands on her hips. She was dressed in a short, royal blue mini dress with a plunging neckline, and an overwhelming amount of body glitter.

"Damn, don't you knock? I didn't even hear you open the door. How you know I wasn't in here gettin' dicked down," Demi joked.

"Bitch, please. How you gon' let a dildo dick you down," Michelle shot back. "How many times yo' batteries don' died in 'dat thing since you had it?"

Demi smiled. "Shut up. Yo' ass look rather glittery

tonight."

"I know. Niggahs love 'dis shit. You look good, too."

Demi looked back in the mirror and eyed her old, pink Diane von Furstenberg jersey dress. "Yeah, it's okay. I had a hot Dior one, but I can't find it for some reason." She looked around the cramped space she and Aliyah shared. "It's probably in this damn room somewhere or my mother might've sold it."

"Janet be goin' hard," Michelle said, then looked around the room. "Yeah, 'dis muthafucka is off the chain. So, you good right, ain't no trouble goin' out tonight?"

"Yeah, Dennis is gonna watch Aliyah."

"How much you payin' him?"

"Fifty."

Michelle laughed. "Damn, yo' brother cheap ain't he?"

"Not really. He wanted more, but that's all I claimed I had." Demi began to lower her voice. "Don't get me wrong, I am broke, but I do have a lil' bit of money saved for emergencies. It ain't much, but if my money hungry-ass mother knew I had it, she would have her hand out."

"Hey, you gotta do what you gotto do," Michelle replied.

As soon as Demi started to think about Perry possibly giving some girl money, she got pissed off all over again.

"I wouldn't have to be strugglin' if that nigga, Perry, was givin' me money," Demi announced.

"Yeah, 'dat shit is pretty foul."

Demi looked down at Aliyah and lightly rubbed her closed eyes. "Exactly." She then checked herself in the mirror one last time, making sure she was straight, then followed Michelle out the bedroom.

"Dennis, we out. Aliyah is still sleep in my bed. We good right?" Demi asked then handed her brother the money.

Dennis turned to look at his sister and her friend, seeing them both dressed up with more legs and skin showing than Lil' Kim.

"Yeah, we good. Where the fuck y'all goin' lookin' like some hoes anyway?" he asked.

28

"That ain't yo' business. We goin' out to do us, a'ight," Demi snapped.

"Yeah, whateva…just don't come back fuckin' pregnant, cuz I ain't tryin' to babysit no more of yo' kids, especially for fifty fuckin' dollars," Dennis replied.

"Niggah, shut up. You just mad 'cause I ain't ever let you hit 'dis," Michelle said.

Dennis smiled. "Trust me Michelle, don't nobody want any of that high mileage pussy of yours."

"Muthafucka, *trust me*. I wouldn't want any of 'dat four inch dick of yours either!" Michelle fired back.

Knowing her friend and Dennis could go back and forth all night, Demi began to pull Michelle toward the door.

"Yo', don't be stayin' out all fuckin' night…cuz I may have sumthin' to do, like have a bitch come over. I ain't tryin' to have Lee Lee fuck up no pussy for me!" Dennis shouted from his seated position on the couch.

Demi sucked her teeth and rolled her eyes and continued out the door.

"Yo' family is so fuckin' crazy, Demi. Yo' brother be trip-pin'," Michelle stated.

"Fuck everybody! I swear I can't wait to get the hell away from this place. I'm livin' wit' a professional hoe and a professional loser. What a fuckin' life."

Both girls laughed as they made their way downstairs to the street to catch a cab. Demi was determined to not let any of the drama spoil her night. Besides, with her high-ass babysitting fees, she wasn't sure when she would get another chance to go out anyway.

Club Just, on the lower East side of Manhattan, was pop-ping with tons of people standing out front waiting for entry into the club and dressed to impress. The ladies were hot in their short skirts, dresses, or tight skinny jeans that highlighted their figures and had the guys drooling. The men came in jeans, slacks, some in Timberlands and some in polished casual shoes with button downs shirts. Not to mention, all the long diamond encrusted necklaces, which in turn had the girls drooling.

The street was congested with high end cars and limos, as traffic slowly navigated its way through the dense atmosphere. Demi and Michelle pulled up to the hectic scene in a cab and paid the driver his twenty dollar fare. Demi's eyes lit up when she stepped out the car and looked around. It reminded her of something from a red carpet scene of a movie premiere or an award show. There were so many people out, Demi didn't know where to turn.

"Yo, it's definitely poppin' out here tonight," Michelle said with excitement.

"I know, but damn, look at the fuckin' line," Demi added. She sucked her teeth and observed how the long line snaked around the corner at the end of the block. Demi looked at her watch, and saw that it was only five minutes after eleven and shit was already looking crazy to get inside.

"Malik said he would leave our name at the door."

Demi seemed shocked. "How that corny niggah gon' pull that off?" Demi wasn't trying to play herself and make her way to the front entrance, only to get turned away in front of hundreds of people.

"I don't know and don't give a shit either, so let's go," Michelle replied.

Both women caught all types of attention from the fellows, and caught sneers and glares from a few ladies who were obviously hating as they strutted up to the door. Demi smiled, knowing that the more they hated, the better she looked, which meant job well done.

Once they made it to the front and gave another hating-ass girl their names, a bouncer waved a metal detector over their bodies, checked their purses then gave them permission to enter.

As soon as they stepped inside, the club was jumping to Lil' Wayne's joint, *Lollipop,* and the people on the dance floor were going crazy. Bumping, grinding sweating it out…nothing was off limits. The place was a decent size, having two levels to party on, with a long, full size bar that was constantly over-crowded with paying customers ready to get their drink on.

They weren't in the club five minutes, before Malik and Rasheed walked up to them with huge smiles.

"Yo, Ma, yo' body is killin' that dress," Malik said to Michelle then gave her a slight hug.

"Thanks," Michelle replied.

"Yeah, both of you ladies are gorgeous," Rasheed added. "Especially you," he said to Demi.

"Demi smiled. She still wasn't feeling Rasheed, but didn't want to be rude. "Thank you."

Malik yelled over the music. "Let's go hit da bar!"

"Good idea!" Michelle yelled back.

Demi had lots of attention on her, as she strutted through the crowd in her tightly fitted dress following behind Michelle and their newfound friends. When everyone reached the bar, Malik told the girls to order whatever they wanted. Taking full advantage of his generosity, Demi got herself a Long Island Ice Tea, while Michelle went for the Patron. She didn't have time to fuck around with mixed drinks.

After the drinks came, Michelle kept Malik company, but Demi wasn't giving Rasheed much conversation. He just wasn't her type. He appeared to be Malik's flunky and Demi damn sure didn't want to be rolling with a niggah that had nothing going on for himself. Rasheed didn't have the swagger she was look-ing for, not to mention his gear was off balance. He seemed too timid, always looking down for whatever his boy was getting into. Demi needed an aggressive male that would take her places she would only dream of.

When Rasheed finally excused himself to go to the bath-room, it was the perfect opportunity for Demi to walk around and check out some other options. She took the Long Island to the head, then looked over at her friend who was already hugged up with Malik, and decided to interrupt the two.

"I'll be right back. I'm gonna walk around and see what's poppin'."

"You a'ight?" Michelle asked.

Demi nodded.

"What, you ain't feelin' my boy or somethin'?" Malik asked.

Demi looked at him and then replied with a straight forward, "No."

"I'm sayin', Rasheed cool peoples. He be doin' his thang," Malik tried to persuade.

"I'm gonna be real wit' you, he just ain't my type," Demi responded.

Malik shrugged it off and continued to get his feel on with Michelle. I guess he figured even if his boy didn't score, he would. Demi navigated her way through the thick crowd, trying to weed out the good from the bad, and finally came across a few potential men who caught her eye.

When Ray J's *Sexy Can I*, blasted throughout the club Demi began to move to the beat on the dance floor. She loved the song and knew it from word to word. It didn't take too long for a man to come up behind her trying to get his groove on. Demi turned to get a quick look at him making sure he wasn't ugly or busted, and when she did, she liked what she saw. She continued to dance with him.

Not mad at the slight buzz she'd gotten from her drink, Demi moved with grace and style on the dance floor. But seconds later, she decided to get a bit nasty. She wasn't scared to throw it back on the tall handsome stranger that held her by her hips and twisted and turned with her to the beat. He had rhythm and Demi liked that. He was also respectful, knowing his limits and not moving his hand too far down to private areas.

"What's your name, beautiful," the tall stranger whispered in her ear.

Demi smiled. He wore the fresh scent of Bvlgari cologne and had winter fresh breath.

"What's yo name?" Demi asked him, not ready to give her name out just yet.

"Jorel. Jorel Davis."

Demi gyrated her hips against him, feeling a hard-on growing through his slacks. She smiled at the feel of it. He seemed to be a decent size.

"Well, Jorel Davis, what do you do?" she asked.

"I'm from Cali. I'm a producer."

"Oh, really. I never met anybody from Cali, or a producer," Demi replied.

Just when Jorel was about to respond, another woman came up behind him and starting dancing. Caught by surprise, he quickly turned around and saw another woman grinding up against him. Even though, it felt good to be in between two beautiful women, he was a little caught off guard.

"Baby, I'm way more experienced than she is. You need a real fuckin' woman in your life, not some young chick who can't suck dick to save her life," the woman said.

Hearing the woman's voice, Demi immediately stopped dancing. Turning around, she was heated when she saw her mother, rubbing herself all up against Jorel's backside. It wasn't surprising to Demi that Janet was at the club though because her mother partied more than she did.

"What the hell are you doin' here?" Demi asked.

When she looked at the dress Janet had on, she instantly became infuriated. It was her missing Dior dress, and her mother was fucking it up with a cheap pair of Payless shoes. Janet might've been a hoe, but she wasn't a label hoe. Spending money on designer clothes wasn't her thing. Actually Demi really didn't know what Janet spent her money on.

"I'm dancin' with this handsome man, that's what I'm doin'," Janet replied. Her long hair had been styled into tight spiral curls.

"Why the fuck do you have on my dress?" Demi asked.

However, she couldn't hate. They way her mother's breast sat up and ass stuck out in the dress made her slightly self-conscious.

At that point, Jorel stopped dancing as well and began to look back and forth between the two women.

Janet stopped dancing too, then got within inches of Demi's face. "This dress was in *my* house, so it belongs to me. Besides don't be tryin' to fuckin' call me out in here. I'll fuck yo' ass up!"

Demi was completely embarrassed. "Ma, that was uncalled for."

Jorel's eyes showed that he couldn't believe what was happening.

"No, what's uncalled for is you comin' out yo' mouth wrong. You in here tryin' to be cute. Don't forget I gave you that body in the first place, so if it wasn't for me nobody would want yo' ass."

Demi wanted to snatch her mother bald headed, but thought against it. She could be so loud and ghetto, and obviously didn't care what came out of her mouth, even if it was against her own daughter. She also didn't understand why her mother was so competitive when it came to men. It had been this way ever since Demi started developing into a young woman. She'd even tried to fuck Perry a few times.

"Who keepin' that crazy-ass daughter of yours anyway?" Janet questioned.

Demi was heated. "Don't worry about who's keepin' her. You ain't."

"You absolutely right. Yo' money ain't long enough for me to keep her no more." Janet turned to Jorel. "C'mon honey, buy me a drink and then let me teach you a thing about how I give head. I'm a grown woman, who knows how to satisfy a man," she said seductively.

Jorel was speechless, but managed to speak. "Umm…umm…that's okay. No disrespect, but I kinda had my eye on your daughter."

"Are you sure 'cause that girl got issues?" Janet informed. "Don't you see what I'm workin' wit?" She turned around to show him her ass.

"Yes, I'm sure Ma'am," Jorel replied.

"Don't be callin' me no muthafuckin' Ma'am," Janet

34

said, then turned around to leave.

Both Jorel and Demi were speechless for a minute.

"I'm so sorry about that. My mother is on medication," Demi lied.

"Oh…no it's cool. I go through mother-daughter alterca-tions all the time." When Demi smiled, he grabbed her chin. "Wow, you're beautiful. Has anybody ever approached you about modeling or maybe acting?"

"No, not at all."

"Can I buy you a drink?"

Demi was down for it. "Sure." Moving through the thick crowd on the dance floor, she followed behind him toward the bar, with a huge grin. A grin that hadn't been seen since her and Perry were together .

"Bartender, let me get a…" Jorel began. He then turned to Demi and asked, "What you drinking?"

"I'll take another Long Island Ice Tea."

"Let me get two Long Islands," he called out.

Demi eyed him from head to toe. He wore a nice pair of Ferragamo shoes, black designer slacks, with a crisp white but-ton down under a chic black blazer. He was clean cut and clean shaven, with full thick lips and sported a small diamond earring and a matching diamond pinky ring. He definitely looked VIP, and looked like he was from out of town. He also reminded her of how Perry used to roll which was another plus.

"So, you a producer huh…what movies did you do?" Demi asked. She made sure to use her proper voice, and saved the hood lingo for later when she was back in her own element.

"I've worked on a few movies…mostly independent. But we have good distribution and I'm trying to sign a high-powered deal with New Line Cinema," he stated.

"Oh really…that's what's up. What are you doin' in New York?"

"I needed some time away from L.A. but it's still busi-ness. I had a meeting with a modeling agency earlier about them sending me a few girls to place in the next project I'm working on. Actually the agency is the company who's sponsoring this party," he informed her.

Demi lit up. "Wow, this party is off the hook. By the way, my name is Demi."

"Demi, what a beautiful name," he said as the two shook hands.

Demi stared into his light brown eyes and was floored. When the bartender came back and placed the drinks in front of them, Jorel paid the man with a crispy fifty dollar bill.

"Keep the change," he said.

Even though he hadn't thrown around a lot of cash, Demi was somewhat impressed. They both took a few sips and continued on with their conversation.

"So, Demi, what do you do?" he asked.

Demi didn't want to be upfront with him about her job as a cashier at Duane Reade. A job that she had for about five months and hated with a passion. It helped pay her bills and take care of Aliyah, but for Demi it was a dead end gig.

"To be honest, I'm trying to do my thang like you and start my own business or something," she explained.

"Really, I hear that. You know, you're a beautiful woman. You could go far in the entertainment business," Jorel said with a huge smile.

His smile was contagious and Demi couldn't help but to return it. She took another sip from her drink and peered into Jorel's eyes.

"So, do you think you would be interested?" he asked.

"Meaning?"

"I mean, if you're really interested, I can help you get into one of my films," he stated. "Since you've obviously never acted before, it would have to be a small role to start out with, but if you do well, then I'm sure I'll be able to get you into more films. I can even help you get some head shots done so you can build a portfolio. That's gonna be needed when you go on auditions."

It felt like Demi's heart almost stopped. Her eyes

widened. "I don't know, Jorel. I mean I've acted out a few Dreamgirls' scenes in front of my mirror a few times, but I'm not a professional or anything."

Demi was too embarrassed to say she played the movie damn near every day. She didn't want Jorel to think that she didn't have a life.

"Plus, I have a daughter and…"

"I'm sure you have someone who would support you if they believed you were working for your daughter's future," Jorel said.

Niggah, didn't you just see how my own mother was actin', Demi thought.

She shook her head.

"Well, just think about it. Trust me when I tell you that I don't run across women with natural beauty like yours all the time, so I think you have something special. Even if the acting thing doesn't work out, you could always do music videos or like I said earlier, even some modeling."

Demi was still a little hesitant, but excited at the same time. "Maybe."

"Listen, a few people I know are having another party tomorrow night, in midtown…on Madison Avenue. I would like for you to come." Jorel reached into his jacket and pulled out a white business card. "Here's all my information. Hit me up and I'll put you on the list so you can get in," Jorel added.

"Thanks. I don't know what to say," Demi said overwhelmed.

"Say you'll come tomorrow night, and we can continue our talk then."

"I'm definitely there. Can I bring a friend, too?"

"I wouldn't have it any other way."

Demi knew that Jorel was obviously a once in a lifetime chance and she wasn't trying to fuck it up. She wrote her number down on a napkin, along with her name and email address. Hell, she even wrote down her home address, too. She was that pressed.

As the two talked for a few more moments, Demi loved what she saw even more. Jorel was making her panties moist, and by the way his lips moved when he talked, she was ready to kiss him and shove her tongue down his throat. It was a feeling she hadn't had with a man in a while.

Jorel bought Demi another drink and then excused himself, saying to her that he had to run out on business. The way he wrapped his arms around her before he left, made Demi feel wanted for sure.

She watched him walk away and when he was out of sight, Demi rushed from the bar with her drink in hand, in search of Michelle. She couldn't wait to tell her friend the good news.

She quickly moved through the dense crowd, her eyes scanning the club and the dance floor for her friend. She finally spotted Michelle, still with Malik, near the dance floor. She rushed up to her friend with a broad smile.

"Girl, I need to talk to you, come wit' me to the bathroom," Demi said, pulling Michelle by her arm away from Malik. Rasheed was also standing near the dance floor with a defeated look on his face.

"Damn girl, what's up wit' you? You see me tryin' to get my swerve on wit' Malik," Michelle uttered.

"Well, that niggah can wait."

Michelle followed Demi to the bathroom. Once they were inside, Demi looked at her friend with excitement.

"Bitch, what's up wit' you? You just found a niggah wit' some paper or sumthin?" Michelle joked.

"Better...I met this fuckin' producer from Cali, and the niggah is definitely feelin' me. He invited you and me to an industry party tomorrow night so we can talk more about it. I got his card and everything," Demi informed her friend with enthusiasm.

"Bitch, get the fuck outta here...you serious?"

"Like fuckin' cancer."

"You fucked him?" Michelle asked.

"No, not at all."

"Damn he tryna put you in movies, and you ain't have to fuck. Dats what's up," Michelle said in awe.

"Well, I don't know about all that fuckin' shit anyway."

"Why not? You better fuck him, especially if he talkin' 'bout movies and shit. You want the starin' roll don't you, or you just wanna be one of 'dem people in the background," Michelle stated.

Demi laughed. "You crazy."

"No, I'm serious. Yo' ass been holdin' out ever since Perry been gone. His ass ain't comin' back no time soon. Besides, don't act like you won't a hoe before you hooked up wit' that niggah."

"Well, I wouldn't exactly call it bein' a hoe," Demi said in her defense.

"Yeah, whateva. You in fuckin' denial," Michelle replied. Where 'dis producer nigga at anyway?"

"He had to leave to take care of some business. But yo, you rollin' wit' me tomorrow night, right? You know I need my right hand girl by my side."

"You know I'm there. Shit, especially if 'dat niggah feelin' you like that? Hell, he might have a friend for me."

After deciding to actually use the bathroom, both Michelle and Demi walked out ready to continue partying.

As Michelle looked around for Malik, Demi started teasing. "I see you lookin' around for Malik. Damn, the niggah got you strung like that already?"

"He a'ight," Michelle replied with a huge smile.

"Yeah, whateva. I see it in yo' eyes, you ready to fuck him already."

"You right. I ain't had dick in like two days. You know a bitch need a hit like two to three times a week. I'm a damn fiend right now and want to ride up and down somebody's fuckin' stiff pole."

Demi laughed.

When a Kanye West track began to play, Michelle finally

spotted Malik and quickly made her way over to him, strutting in her tight mini dress that made heads turn in the club. Instead of following her friend, Demi walked back over to the bar. She needed another drink. She moved through the crowd, becoming kind of irate at being bumped into a few times by drunks and haters. But she kept her cool and walked up to the bar and asked the bartender for another Long Island.

As Demi began to wait around for the bartender to return, she heard someone say, "Can I buy you that drink?"

She turned to see Rasheed standing behind her in his cheap looking denim jeans. She hated the fact that he was so cute, because he had absolutely no style. She also loved his smooth cocoa colored complexion.

Demi tried to be on her best behavior. "If you want."

Rasheed took the barstool right next to her and smiled.

"Rasheed," he said extending his hand. "I just thought I'd officially introduce myself this time."

"I'm Demi." She took his hand in hers.

Demi decided to show him a little love, being that she was in a good mood and excited about her talk with Jorel. When the bartender brought her drink over, Rasheed passed him a twenty dollar bill. As Demi thanked him and took a sip, Rasheed ordered himself a Rum and Coke.

Demi thought to herself, *Typical.* A Rum and Coke was the cheapest drink a niggah could get in the club, and it said that he knew nothing about the bar or how to get his drink on.

Rasheed turned to her. "So, Demi, what is it that you do? If you don't mind me asking?"

"I do me, why you ask? You tryin' to pay my bills?"

"Damn, why the attitude, luv…I'm just tryin' to make conversation with you, that's all," Rasheed responded.

"Look, I'm just being nice cuz my friend is feelin' yo' boy. But don't expect anythin' to pop off between us just because my girl might fuck yo' man," she stated bluntly.

Rasheed let out a slight chuckle.

"You think that's what I'm about? You think I'm tryin' to

spit game just to get into yo' pants. Luv, you don't even know me or know what I'm about. You judgin' a niggah already and you ain't even tryin' to take the time out to talk to me in a decent tone. But you sittin' here thinkin' the worse of a niggah already," Rasheed said to her calmly. "I'm probably not like that other niggah you were kickin' it wit' earlier. He seems shady."

Demi looked at him in shock. "Don't go there. You don't know anything about him."

"And you don't know anything about me," he shot back in a calm tone.

"Well, I'm sorry…but I know how y'all niggahs can get," she apologized somewhat.

"Well, I ain't every niggah. I'm Rasheed, and don't put me into that same category of every man that has treated you wrong. I just came over to talk and have a good time."

Demi recanted the attitude she had of him earlier and showed off a minor smile. "I can respect that." She didn't waste anytime taking another large sip of her drink.

"Okay, so let me start over. Hi, I'm Rasheed. Can I get to know yo' name, beautiful?" he asked with a warm smile.

She laughed. "It's Demi."

Rasheed took a few sips from his Rum and Coke. "You're beautiful, Demi."

"Thanks. So, was is it that you do?" Demi asked.

"Well, I know it probably looks like I'm some type of thug because of the way I dress, but that's just my style. I'm actually a writer," he happily responded.

"A writer? What, you write rhymes or sumthin? You a rapper?"

"Nah, I love to write books, poetry…and I just finished a screenplay."

"Oh, so you be tryin' to do yo' thang. That's what's up. You got anything published yet?"

"Nah, but I'm tryin'. Shit, I even been shoppin' my screenplay to a few film makers and even some studios, but haven't had any luck."

"Really. Well, that guy who you said looked shady is actually a producer from California. I got his card and everything. Maybe I can hook the two of y'all up, and get some type of fee," Demi replied.

Rasheed shook his head. "Nah, that's okay, I'll pass. I'd rather take the hard work approach. You appreciate shit more that way."

"Yo' loss," Demi said. "So this screenplay, what's it about?"

"Life. It's about a young man from the Bronx who's kind of misguided and lost in life. He's from the streets, but doesn't know what he wants in life. He was abandoned by his mother when he was young, so he does things that he feels will make him complete…like sell drugs, shoot people and becomes a menace to his community," Rasheed informed.

"Oh, sumthin' like Belly, right? Shit, I love that movie and I love me some Nas."

Rasheed chuckled. "Nah, it's nothin' like Belly. Belly tried to tell the struggles of a young black man, but I feel that Hype Williams didn't do it right. That movie felt rushed to me. The script that I'm workin' on tells the struggles where we suffer from the beginning, from when we come squirmin' out of our mother's womb and how cruel the world can be at birth."

"Oh, so you tryin' to gross out yo' audience. Ain't nobody tryin' to pay to see some shit like that. I mean, I know niggahs like pussy, but damn…you tryin' to fuck it up for niggahs, they ain't tryin' to see child birth on screen," Demi said.

Rasheed smiled. He loved her rawness. There was something about her that he definitely liked.

"Nah, it won't be anything like that. It's gonna be a story about the struggle and love, and how makin' the wrong choices in life can reflect the future for yourself and others around you."

"I'm sorry, but that sounds like some Lifetime channel shit to me. No offense to you, but it sounds boring. See I'm a movie buff. I know about movies and how actors and actresses supposed to make you feel. I'm good at that shit." Demi did a

42

fake pose. "You need to write some shit like the Wire, or Oz. Now them shows right there, pop the fuck off, fo' real. If it ain't on HBO, MTV, BET, or VH1, you know a bitch like me won't be watchin' it," Demi explained.

"You need to expand yo' horizon."

"Expand my what?"

Rasheed took another sip from his drink and then said, "You need to open up to more things that are different for you. Don't be stuck in that same arena of what you're used to, or what you think might work for you. Try sumthin' different for yourself once in a while, you never know…you might surprise yourself in the long run."

Demi sized Rasheed up at the bar and responded with, "Shit, I'm talkin' to you, right, and that's different for me, 'cause under normal circumstances, I would'a been kicked you to the curb."

Rasheed smiled, then took another sip from his drink. "And why is that?"

She went in on him. "Cause, you ain't got no style to you. You ordered a Rum and Coke, and that's lame. You got on a played out long white-T, that's lame. Yo' shoes look old, and that's lame. You ain't got no kind of style to you, so that's whack. But you cute as hell and you cool to talk to, so that's a plus."

Rasheed didn't take offense to her comments. He actually appreciated her honesty. He stared Demi in the eyes. "Luv, don't get fooled by the outer appearance of a man, and forget where he's at on the inside of his heart. That shit you just broke down, don't mean nothin' to me. I get mines and I know where my head is at. I don't need a bunch of jewelry, fashion, and an expensive drink in my hand to make me feel confident. I'm very pleased with who I am and don't need a bunch of unnecessary shit to make me feel good about myself."

Demi didn't want to admit it or show it, but she was taken aback by his reply. She loved the confidence that Rasheed displayed and knew that if he had the type of swagger she was looking for, their night might've turned out differently. Even though Rasheed was cool, she didn't want him to cramp her style.

"You get deep, I like that. But I don't want to waste yo' time any longer. I'm tryin' to get my groove on, baby. It was nice talkin' and thanks for the drink," she said, lifting her body from the barstool.

"It's cool. You're definitely one of a kind. But take in what I said and take care of yourself, beautiful," Rasheed said.

Demi was a bit tipsy. She looked at Rasheed and said to him, "Will do."

Rasheed's eyes followed Demi to the dance floor. He thought about the fact that she had so much potential. She seemed to yearn for more, but he knew that she was trying to find it in the wrong places.

As the night wound down to the wee hours of early morning, Demi found herself in the back of a cab on her way home, drunk and dizzy as hell. Michelle had left with Malik to break her two day dick drought. Demi on the other hand, wouldn't be getting any dick as usual. Instead, she looked at the time and sighed. It was nearing five in the morning and she had to be in front of her cash register at Duane Reade in four hours.

 **Four**

Demi's alarm clock sounded off loudly several times at exactly 7:15 a.m. She never budged. She was sprawled across her bed, still in her party dress and trying her best to recover from the serious hangover. She needed at least another three to fours hours of sleep to attempt recovery, but the alarm continued to ring. Becoming upset with the annoying chirping sound, Demi pushed the clock off the nightstand with a hard shove trying her best to silence it.

"Bitch, you ain't goin' to work today?" her mother asked, standing in the doorway with a cigarette dangling from her lips, and a sheer nightgown covering some of her nakedness.

Demi didn't attempt to move. She remained glued to the bed, eyes still closed and mumbled to her mother, "I'm going in late. Mike will understand."

"So who keepin' Lee Lee while you at work today? Just cuz it's Sunday and I normally only serve two niggas instead of three, don't even ask me. Shit, I got company in my room right now," Janet said. "Besides, my fee don' went up to $150, and I doubt if you got that much."

"Well, I'll just have to think of somethin' else then, a'ight," Demi replied in an irritated tone.

"Don't be gettin' snappy with me. You need to get yo' ass up now. You the one who decided to go get that bullshit-ass job in the first place. I told you, ain't no money in that 9-5 shit. Now, what you need to do is go find you a paid niggah to go lay up wit' and start bringin' back some real cash into this house."

Demi raised her head just enough to see her mother's face. "So, you like yo' daughter bein' a hoe, huh? That makes you feel proud."

Janet took a pull from the cigarette. "Shit, ain't nothin' wrong with being a hoe as long as you a paid one. Broke hoe's are the disgraceful ones. If you don't wanna go get a niggah, go get on a damn pole or somthin'. We need you to have a steady income up in here. Now, get yo' broke-ass up cuz everybody gotta bring some type of paper in this house."

"What about Dennis? All he do is sit on the couch all damn day."

"Oh, trust me. All them bitches he be fuckin', he gets money from them, and pays his dues up in here. Ain't none of y'all livin' off me for free."

After giving her motherly advise, Janet walked away leaving Demi shaking her head.

It was damn near noon when Demi was finally up and running, and when she did, the apartment seemed quiet. She walked into the living room to see her daughter taking a nap on the couch then looked around for her crazy-ass family, but didn't see anyone.

She allowed Aliyah to sleep while she walked lazily into the bathroom to wash up. After jumping into the shower, which was in desperate need of some cleaning solution, Demi let the hot rushing water cascade off her naturally curvy cream colored skin, then began to think about Jorel. Regardless of how much she had to pay for a babysitter, she was definitely going to his party tonight. At that moment, Demi began to get excited about the possibility of breaking into the acting business and hoped Jorel was true to his word and not full of shit. It seemed to be a way out of her mother's fucked up world, and a way to make some real money.

After her shower, Demi quickly began getting ready for work. Demi knew that she was a few hours late, but felt that she had her boss, Mike, wrapped around her finger. He damn near let her get away with anything on the job, so she didn't expect him to say too much.

It was 12:30 when Demi was finally ready for work. She had a good lie prepared for Mike. She knew he would believe her like he always did and let her slide for coming in extremely late and not calling. However, she needed to rush especially since she didn't have a babysitter. As a last resort she ended up calling Ms. Johnson, an older Jamaican lady in the next building who stopped keeping Aliyah when her and Janet got into an argument over a man. Ms. Johnson also didn't normally keep kids on the weekend, so this was really going to be a stretch.

Nervously, Demi picked up the phone to call her, and hoped the lecture wouldn't be too long. After all it was her mother who'd fucked Ms. Johnson's live in boyfriend, not her. Once Demi heard the Jamaican women's thick accent, she immediately started telling the woman a quick sob story. Despite what her mother did, Demi knew Ms. Johnson loved Aliyah, and probably missed her by now.

After listening to Ms. Johnson vent about morals, integrity and values for about five minutes, she finally agreed to keep Aliyah for her usual twenty-five dollar fee. Demi was ecstatic.

Ten minutes later, she hurried her daughter out the door and rushed her off to Ms. Johnson, then jumped on the A train downtown rushing to work.

When Demi finally arrived at work at the downtown Manhattan Duane Reade, it was 1:15 p.m. She rushed into the store wearing her beige khakis that hugged her hips, a white button down, and her hideous blue smock in hand. After quickly clocking in, she made her way upfront to one of the cash registers and put her smock on like she was on time. Her co-workers, however, looked at her with bewilderment.

"Damn Demi, you know what time it is?" her co-worker Vonda asked.

"Yeah, I do actually," Demi spat back.

"Mike is pissed. He's been looking and asking about you

all morning. Damn, what happened?"

"I had a rough morning, that's all."

"But damn, you couldn't call in and let Mike know that you was gonna be late. I'm telling you, he's pissed."

"Forget Mike, I got that niggah wrapped around my finger. Trust me, I already know the routine. He gonna come up in here beefin' at me, talkin' crazy and then once he blows off some steam, he's gonna forget about it like he usually do. Y'all be worryin' too much."

"I don't know, Demi…you like four hours late to work. He had to cover your shift almost all morning," Vonda explained.

Despite her co-workers warning, Demi just blew it off and went to work, taking in her first customer waiting in line. Ten minutes into her shift, Demi noticed Mike coming toward her. His eyes automatically shifted over to Demi with an angry stare. Demi returned the gaze and then heard him shout, "Demi, in my office…now!"

Vonda and a few other co-workers gave off an inquisitive gaze. Demi sucked her teeth and tried to look unfazed by Mike's sudden harshness toward her.

"I don't know why he be trippin. Vonda, I'll be right back. Let me go see what he wants."

Demi stepped from behind the counter with all eyes on her. It was so quiet that you could hear a cotton ball fall. She slowly walked toward the back thinking of what to say to him. She'd perfected her tale. She took a deep breath and slowly opened the door to his back office, which was also used for a supply room. It was cluttered with boxes, containers, store goods, and a few file cabinets.

Mike sat behind a shabby metal desk that was muddled with papers, files, and his lunch. When Demi walked in, he quickly lifted his head, showing a disapproving gaze.

"You wanted to see me, right?" Demi asked.

"You know what time it is, Demi? You parade in four hours after your damn shift starts. You don't call in or nothing, but you walk in here like everything is okay. You think you own this place? Do I look like a fool to you?" Mike barked.

"Mike, let me explain…I tried to call…"

But before Demi could execute her full lie to him, Mike cut her off. "You know, Demi, I don't want to hear it…you're fired!"

Demi couldn't believe what she'd just heard.

"Mike, I know you ain't serious. You gonna fire me just like that," Demi spat back with venom. "I been workin' here for five months."

"You act like five months is a long time. Demi, you come in late constantly. You can be rude to the customers sometimes, and right now, your attitude sucks. You need to go. I'm tired of dealing with your bullshit," Mike stated harshly.

"Come on Mike. I need this job."

"Sorry."

"Oh, so it's like that! You gonna diss me like I'm shit now. Like you haven't been tryin' to take me out since I first started workin' here. Oh, so now I know what this is about. If I had given you some pussy then all of this would be different right?"

"Demi, please, I'm not in the mood for the dramatics. Just get your shit and leave the store. Your last paycheck will be mailed."

Demi was heated. She glared at Mike and wanted to punch him right in his face. Up until now, Mike had always allowed her to come into work a few minutes late or when she needed a few days off, he would oblige without any questions asked. But now he'd flipped the script, which was a total shock.

"Fuck you, niggah! Fuck you!" Demi continued to scream and carry on.

Mike immediately rose from his chair then put a little more base in his voice. "Don't make me call security or the cops if there's gonna be a problem."

"What the fuck did you say? I know you ain't just threaten me!" Demi shouted, stepping closer to Mike with her fists balled. *Damn I wish Perry was still out. All I would have to do is say the word and Mike would be dealt wit.*

Without warning, Demi rushed up to his desk and quickly pushed everything onto the floor, including his lunch and laptop.

"Are you crazy?" Mike shouted.

"Yeah, I am!" Demi spat back. "You just fired me, and I need this job!"

Mike's blood boiled. "Well you should've thought about that before."

"So, you not gonna give me my job back? What about my daughter? I have to take care of her."

"I'm sorry about your little girl, but I'm not giving you your job back."

Demi oozed with anger. After grabbing her purse, she stormed out of the office screaming and attacking Mike's manhood for all to hear. "Fuck you, Mike. You just mad 'cuz I didn't suck yo' little dick!" She was definitely putting him on blast.

Mike rushed out of his office at top speed. He definitely wanted to strangle Demi for talking shit. He watched as his employees snickered and whispered amongst each other.

"Demi, get the hell out my store before I call the police," he warned.

"Hell no!" Demi yelled. She moved down aisle five, and started tossing items off the shelves.

Customers along with all the employees were shocked to see Demi act this way. They stood in silence with their mouths open and watched as she caused disorder in the store.

Mike rushed over to Demi trying to stop her from doing anymore damage. He looked angry, but tried a different approach. "Can you please just leave? Don't you think you've done enough?" In reality he didn't really want to call the police, but had no other choice if she refused to leave.

Demi looked at him with a small smirk. At that point, she figured she'd done more than enough ranting. "I'm out," she ended, then finally walked out. She never gave anyone the pleasure of turning back around.

Everyone just stood around in awe, trying to figure out what had just happened. Mike looked dumbfounded, as customers and the workers looked at him. He didn't know what to say. His intentions were to go back into his office until the day was over.

Demi just wanted to go back home and get ready for the night. For her, it seemed as if Jorel couldn't have come at a better time. She was ready to sell herself tonight to make it happen. Tired of living from paycheck to paycheck, a bigger pay off was what she needed.

 *Five*

The time on the cable box read 9:30 p.m. Demi was in her bedroom getting ready for the party. She begged and pleaded with Ms. Johnson to keep Aliyah all night, which had never been done before. After begging for at least an hour, Ms. Johnson finally said yes. Demi agreed not to tell anyone else. Ms. Johnson didn't want everyone in the hood to think she was expanding her hours to overnight service, which Demi could appreciate. After losing her job, she'd decided not to ask Dennis, which would cost her an extra fifty dollars as opposed to twenty-five. Now that her money was scarce, the babysitting fees definitely needed to be handled.

Demi was ready to turn heads at the club and sprain a few necks in the process. She went into her closet and pulled out a tightly fitted, and very short grey skirt that hugged her figure like paint to walls, and some four inch heels. After flat ironing her hair, and applying just the right amount of make-up, Demi was ready to go. She dialed Michelle's cell number to make sure that she was on her way over, and once Michelle confirmed that she was a block away, Demi breathed a quick sigh of relief. Michelle could be slow sometimes, and Demi wasn't trying to be fashionably late for her chance at stardom.

Before Demi left out of her bedroom, she checked to make sure everything was in place. Not even giving Dennis a chance to say anything, she passed him on the couch doing a swift little stroll, then quickly walked out the door. With the elevators being slow as molasses, she made it downstairs in record time to where Michelle was waiting inside an idling cab. Quickly jumping into the backseat, Demi headed for what she hoped was the start of a new chapter in her life.

The cab pulled up to a fifth floor loft on Madison Avenue fifteen minutes later. After splitting the fare, Michelle and Demi got out in true diva fashion. Demi took in the area quickly and loved what she saw. The high-end cars that were parked on the block and the men and women who were elegantly dressed looked important enough to quickly grab her undivided attention.

Madison Avenue was busy with traffic and people, and Demi wanted to hurry into the building to meet up with Jorel. There was no line outside of the building, and butterflies swam through Demi's stomach as she made her way inside.

There was a nicely dressed doorman standing outside to direct the incoming and outgoing traffic. When Demi and Michelle approached, he nodded courteously and quickly pulled the heavy looking gold plated door wide open.

"What floor is 'dis shit on?" Michelle asked.

"He said the fifth floor," Demi answered.

Demi looked around at the other people and started to think that she and Michelle were dressed too provocatively. Michelle had on a hot pink cropped top with a belt wrapped around it and a pair of black leggings that showed more ass than style. She also popped her gum loudly, which immediately identified them as ghetto-fabulous.

When they got into the elevator with a small group of well-dressed individuals, a few heads turned to look at them and Michelle didn't like it. She suddenly caught an attitude and when the elevator reached the fifth floor and the group began stepping out, Michelle popped her gum even harder.

"Why the fuck y'all lookin' at us?"

Demi turned to Michelle. "Chill girl. This ain't that kind of party. We don't need to be actin' all hood."

"What? Demi, c'mon I know you ain't tryin' to act fake to impress some niggah," Michelle shot back.

"No, but I'm just sayin' Michelle, tone it down a bit. Let's just go in here, do our thang, and feel the crowd out. You my girl and I ain't tryin' to do this without you."

Michelle rolled her eyes and instantly had a nonchalant attitude about the party already. It seemed more pretentious than they expected it to be, but both girls still made their way into the event with their heads held high.

Michelle strutted behind Demi and up to two beefy bouncers at the door, one having a pad and a list in his hand. Demi became nervous, hoping that Jorel was about his word and had their names down.

"Girl, I hope you on 'dis fuckin' list, cuz I ain't tryin' to get embarrassed up in here," Michelle said disbelievingly. When she heard the sounds of Robin Thicke playing from the loft, it was yet another thing to piss her off. "Man, I hope this ain't the music they gon' play all night. I need some shit I can pop my ass to like Busta Rhymes." Michelle started doing a little dance then belted out, "We gettin' Arab money…we gettin' Arab money."

Demi sighed and tried to look confident as she approached the bouncers with Ms. 'I can't take her out the hood,' Michelle right behind. She stared the main bouncer directly in the eyes. "Hello, I believe we're on the list."

"Name," he said.

"Demi Rodriguez and this is Michelle Young. Jorel Davis put us on the list," she informed him.

The man scanned the list quickly searching for both of their last names. At first it felt like he was taking too long, but when he turned the page and still hadn't said anything, Demi began to get nervous. Michelle on the other hand was ready to cause a scene.

"I don't see either one of your names," the bouncer said to them.

"What? Can you please check again? Jorel Davis said that he was going to put us on there," Demi stated loudly and in a professional voice.

"Look, I don't see your name on here. I already double checked the shit," the bouncer barked.

Michelle immediately started pacing back and forth.

"See, why niggahs gotta be playin' themselves…you think we came out here for our fuckin' health. Niggah, what you need to do is run up in 'dat muthafucka and find 'dat faggot niggah who lied to my girl about puttin' us on the list!" Michelle shouted.

"This event is invitation only, and if your name ain't on this piece of paper that's in front of me, you don't get in…it's as simple as that," the bouncer stated with a stern tone.

"Niggah, who the fuck do you think you talkin' to like 'dat?" Michelle blasted. "I'll fuck yo' big punk-ass up!"

"Sssshhh, Michelle chill," Demi said.

"Nah, fuck 'dat, Demi. Don't be tryin' to act all nice and shit cuz you tryin' to get all Hollywood for some niggah!"

Michelle's face fumed with anger.

"Look, I'm being nice, so don't fucking get loud with me," the bouncer warned.

"I'm sorry sir, but it's just that we were told that we would be on that list. You think I would come up here for absolutely nothing," Demi stated.

She felt that pit deepen in her stomach. She was all excited throughout the day, knowing that this was her chance to get into something big; something that could change her life. But as the six-three bouncer stood in front of her, denying her access to the party that might make her career she held her head up, but inside she was dying.

"Fuck 'dis bullshit-ass party, Demi. Everybody lookin' all stuck up anyway!" Michelle yelled.

But Demi didn't want to leave; she was relentless in trying to get into the party. She'd just gotten fired from her job so something needed to come through.

"Look, if you can just go inside and ask for Jorel Davis," Demi began to say.

"Look, I told you, you ain't on the damn list, and you're wasting my time," he shouted.

"Niggah, who the fuck yo' big-ass talkin' to like 'dat?" Michelle shouted in Demi's defense.

When it looked like their night was about to be a total

bust, Demi suddenly heard someone say, "Whoa, whoa, hey what is goin' on out here? It sounds like World War three."

Demi turned to see Jorel standing behind her and Michelle. She smiled widely, but Michelle wasn't so thrilled.

"Niggah, why you ain't put us on the fuckin' list? You got us standin' out here lookin' like assholes," Michelle barked.

Jorel ignored Michelle and stared at Demi. He was taken aback by how beautiful she was. "Damn, you look good," he said.

"Niggah, fuck all 'dat beauty shit. Why we ain't on the list?" Michelle roared, rolling her eyes.

Jorel smiled and returned with, "I'll take care of this, don't worry." He stepped to the bouncer. "Yo, Mitch, they with me."

"They ain't on the list. You know how strict Jimmy can be about his parties," Mitch replied.

"Yeah, but this is me, Mitch. I got them, and plus I made a promise," Jorel said, stepping closer to the bouncer. "Besides, don't make me look like a fool in front of the ladies. You know I always got you." Jorel subtly shoved a fifty dollar bill into the bouncer's hands. "Make it happen for them," he added with a smile.

Mitch looked past Jorel and stared at the two ladies. He had to admit to himself that he loved what he saw. He sighed a bit and nodded.

"They're cool," the bouncer said in a low whisper.

Jorel smiled, and gave him some dap. "My man. You a'ight Mitch. Yo, if you're ever in L.A, give me a call. I might have somethin' for you."

Mitch grinned and nodded.

Jorel turned to the two ladies, held out his arms and announced, "Ladies, your man awaits."

Michelle chuckled. "Shit, you ain't my man."

Demi beamed with joy. She quickly walked up to Jorel and threw her arms around his neck for a quick hug. He returned the affection by throwing his arm around her waist while escorting her inside.

Demi walked into the luxury loft that was big enough to fit her mother's whole apartment inside. More than excited by now, she watched folks mingling about while some were on the dance floor, dancing to the sweet sounds of Mr. Thicke. It was kind of crowded and the atmosphere was a bit diverse, upscale mixed in with a hip-hop crowd.

"Damn, this is nice," Demi said looking around, and searching for the nearest celebrity in her presence.

"You want a drink?" Jorel asked.

Demi nodded. Being amongst such elite people, she was in search for some celebrities to possibly meet. She walked over to the bar with Jorel and ordered a Grand Marnier and pineapple juice, and Michelle got the same.

"So," Jorel started, getting close to Demi. "I'm glad that you made it."

"What happened to my name being on the list?" Demi asked.

"Don't worry about that. It was a minor mistake," he replied. "My assistant obviously forgot. I called and told her to add you, but hey…things happen."

"You know how embarrassed I felt. I thought you played me at first," Demi added.

Jorel looked at her. "A woman as beautiful as you, I would never play games with. Demi, you definitely need to come to L.A., because you can go places just on your looks alone. And with me supporting you, I can take you places that you've only dreamed of."

Demi was all ears. "What can you do for me? 'Cause I'm definitely ready for a change."

"I have a lot of connections, so I can pretty much get you into anything. Like I said last night, videos, movies, modeling, and maybe some commercials. In fact, I know of another producer who's putting this pilot together and they're doing a casting call next week. It's a good show, I read the script, and I can call in a favor and have you in the room with the producer within the week."

"Oh my God, are you serious?" Demi asked.

Jorel smiled. "Beautiful, when it comes to talent and my business, that's something I don't play around with. I like what I see, and with us as a team, we can go places."

Demi felt high off his words. She took a sip from her drink and didn't know how to contain her joyous feeling. She turned to Michelle who was distracted by all the hunks in the room and said, "Michelle, did you hear what he just said to me? He thinks I should audition for this T.V. show. He thinks I have what it takes."

"Seein' is believin'," Michelle replied nonchalantly, downing her drink. She ordered another drink, and after waiting a few brief minutes, she grabbed her glass, and made her way to the dance floor.

Demi sighed, seeing that Michelle was already getting tipsy and acting crazy. Demi waved her off and turned back to Jorel to continue their conversation.

"So, what do you say? You ready to take that first step into stardom and make Halle Berry look like Macy Gray," Jorel said with conviction.

Demi blushed and smiled. "You silly."

"Am I," Jorel responded with a profound smile as he moved in closer to Demi and eyed her from head to toe.

Demi took another quick sip from her drink and felt the heat in the room rising. She stared at Jorel and couldn't help but to be very attracted to him. Her heart raced and her hands became clammy. She locked eyes with him and was ready to get the party popping. She turned to see her friend on the dance floor with a drink in her hand grinding against a guy in a tuxedo.

"You want to get out of here?" Jorel asked.

Demi looked at him with a pure smile and said in a girl-ish manner, "Sure."

Jorel smiled harder and had Demi follow him out of the loft to somewhere more private where they could talk and really get to know each other. Michelle watched her friend leave with

Jorel. She shrugged it off and continued dancing with her unknown friend, and downed the rest of her drink.

Demi followed Jorel into a more secluded area on the floor below the party area. It was an empty space, which was completely dark. The room was quiet and the only pieces of furniture present were a few metal folding chairs and an eight foot folding table with some boxes on top of it.

"What's this place?" Demi asked.

"Well, I'm thinking about renting it out for a year and maybe staying in New York for a while to take care of some business," Jorel informed.

"Really…it's big."

"I know. I need the space."

Jorel soothingly pulled Demi further into the room, unable keep his eyes off her. He loved the way she looked in her tightly fitted skirt and wanted to slide it right off of her. They moved into the darkness, near one of the chairs. Jorel took a seat while Demi stood over him. She gave off a look of innocence, but inside she was burning with hunger to fuck him. She wanted to show him how she got down.

Jorel continued to look up at Demi, as he felt his hard-on growing. He reached for her and moved her closer, forcing her to lean on him with her hands pressed against his shoulders.

"I want you in L.A. with me, Demi. You need to be there, because you can definitely go places," he assured her.

Demi remained silent, but she was feeling radiant on the inside. She continued to stare at Jorel, then moved her lips near his. She began kissing him passionately...wildly…then erotically. Jorel slid his tongue into hers then moved his hands up her skirt gently. Demi positioned herself on his lap and wrapped her arms around his neck before tonguing him down with more force.

At that moment, Jorel became like an octopus. His hands were all over her—cupping her breasts, squeezing her ass, pulling her hair back and sucking on her neck like a vampire. Jorel liked it rough, but his roughness instantly brought back memories of Perry. Demi missed the father of her child, but had to keep it real. He was going to be gone a long time, and there was no way she could hold off from having sex until then. She had to go on with her life, and had plans to start with Jorel.

"Shit, I want you," Jorel panted, sliding her skirt up to her hips.

"I want you, too," Demi replied, her chest heaving up and down from the foreplay and the strong kiss they shared.

Jorel began unbuttoning his pants and sliding them down to his ankles along with his boxers. He was already hard and ready to go. When Demi looked at his size, she was thoroughly impressed.

"I wanna fuck you now," he said, jerking off in front of her.

"Damn...I like."

Demi pulled up her skirt even more and removed her thongs. Her curves were shapely and her shaved mound made her look like a playboy vixen.

"Damn!" Jorel uttered.

Demi moved forward and slowly mounted Jorel as he remained seated against the metal chair with his legs spread apart. Jorel reached for her hips and pulled her down on top of him, inserting his big, black dick deep into her canal.

"Oh, shit!" She bit down against her bottom lip, and panted.

Jorel thrust upward roughly, causing Demi to secure a firm grip around him as the chair began to wobble. He clutched her ass and went to work, fucking Demi like his life depended on it. She pressed her breasts against his chest and felt his thick erection opening her up from below.

"Oh shit, you got some good pussy!" Jorel yelled.

Demi continued to put it on him, gyrating her thick hips against him, and making her walls contract against his shaft with each fuck he threw into her.

Their pants echoed throughout the huge empty room as their bodies began to sweat.

"Fuck me! Fuck me!" Demi screamed.

"Oh, shit, I'm gonna make you a fuckin' star…ooooohhh, yes, I'm gonna make you a fuckin' star!" Jorel chanted.

The two continued to go at it for a few more minutes, until Jorel felt his dick stiffen to the point of no return.

"I'm cummin'…shit, I'm about to cum. Oh, shit, don't stop, oh don't fuckin' stop," he cried out, holding Demi closer to him as he thrust into her harder and deeper.

Demi cried out herself, digging her manicured nails into his back. Jorel rocked back and forth against the chair repeatedly brewing a nut to shoot.

"I'm gonna cum," he repeated loudly.

She began sucking on his earlobes and dug her nails into his back as an orgasm quickly consumed her body. She felt his breath against her neck and his balls slapping against her as his grip around her became tighter.

"I'm cumin', too!" she cried out.

Jorel squeezed her tighter one last time before quickly lifting Demi off of him. The white liquid went in every direction as he stroked his rod of hard flesh while erupting. When it was all said and done, Demi was content and knew that her chances in stardom were in the bag.

Fifteen minutes later, Demi followed behind Jorel pulling down her skirt and collecting herself. She never felt better. She took a quick breather and trotted toward the bathroom to fix her hair and make-up. She didn't want to go back up to the party looking a mess and looking liked she just got fucked.

"I'll meet you back upstairs. I had a great time," Jorel said. "You definitely need to come out to L.A and do your thang. Shit, turn Hollywood the fuck out. Meet me back upstairs in ten minutes so we can continue our talk."

Demi smiled and nodded. She went into the bathroom feeling fortunate and on cloud nine. She quickly fixed herself up and returned to the party, only to see Michelle arguing with security.

"Yo fuck 'dat bitch, and fuck y'all muthafuckas up in here! Y'all don't fuckin' know me!" she heard Michelle yelling.

Demi hurried toward Michelle and asked, "Hey, what's goin' on?"

"Bitch, I'm fuckin' done wit' 'dis fuckin' place. I'll fuck 'dis shit up in here, keep fuckin' playin' wit' a bitch and watch how serious it'll get up in here! Niggahs think they too fuckin ill up in 'dis place!" Michelle shouted. "Fuck y'all!"

"Michelle, what's up?" Demi asked with concern, grabbing Michelle by her arm.

Michelle turned to face Demi with her face in a scowl. "Yo, I'm tryin' to do me and get my drink on, and 'dis skinny white bitch gonna bump into me and gonna look at me like I'm at fault…catchin' an attitude and shit…stank-ass bitch. I'll fuckin' snatch 'dat dirty blond weave off her fuckin' head. Tell 'dat bitch she definitely fuckin' wit' the right one!"

"Michelle, chill…" Demi uttered.

"What, I know you ain't tryin' to act brand new all of a sudden…not for 'dat niggah! He ain't shit either! He playin' yo' ass. Can't you see 'dat?"

"Your friend needs to go. We're not tryin' to allow that up in here," security said to Demi.

"Fuck you, niggah! Who the fuck is you?" Michelle screamed, getting ready to step to him.

"Michelle, please just calm down," Demi pleaded.

"Bitch, what? Yo, it ain't even gotta go down like 'dat. You got my back or do I need to be out?"

Demi knew that Michelle was drunk, and when she got drunk she tended to get loud and violent and any little thing could set her off. As far as Demi was concerned, her home-girl could've been the one at fault and twisted the drama to benefit her.

Demi stared at Michelle. She seemed hesitant to defend her for the first time since they'd known each other. There was an uneasy silence between them.

Michelle finally caught the hint and shouted out, "Oh, so

it's like 'dat now! You just gonna dis me cuz some clown in a suit got you into 'dis weak-ass party and promised you some dumb actress type shit."

"Michelle, it ain't even like that. I'm just sayin', I gotta do me. You know I need to get up out of Harlem and have my own," Demi said tensely. "It's for Aliyah," she pleaded.

Michelle sucked her teeth and caught a serious attitude. "You know what, Demi, it's whateva. Go fuckin' do you, cuz I don't give a fuck!"

Michelle stormed off still cursing and carrying on.

"Michelle...c'mon, it ain't gotta be like this," Demi called out.

"Fuck you, Demi!" Michelle yelled back as she quickly made her way down the hallway.

Demi just watched her friend leave and knew it was probably the alcohol talking. She sighed and let Michelle be. Demi knew that this was finally her night to take her life a step further and she couldn't fuck it up for herself or her daughter. And if that meant allowing her best friend to go home angry and tipsy without her following behind, then so be it. It wouldn't be the first dispute that the two ever had and it damn sure wouldn't be the last.

When Michelle was out of Demi's sight, Demi went back into the party to look for Jorel. She wanted to continue their talk. Tonight was her night, and she wasn't about to let anyone ruin it for her, even if it cost her friendship.

 Six

Two weeks after her rendezvous with Jorel, Demi took Aliyah to see Perry, who was locked up in Otisville Correctional Facility, a federal prison, located an hour and a half from the city. Dr. Jays, on Fulton Street, in Brooklyn was the meeting spot where a private bus, picked up several people from young to old going to see their loved ones. It's had been three months since Demi took Aliyah to see her father, and weeks since she and Perry had spoken. But she knew now was the time for a visit more than ever.

Normally, Demi would've wanted to look good, but this time she had to do a little reverse psychology in order to pull this whole thing off. Normally, she would've rocked a pair of tight skinny jeans and stiletto heels, but this time she pulled the worst thing out of her closet that she could find. Wearing a graphic hooded sweat shirt, baggy jeans, and a pair of white Nikes, Demi wanted Perry to be appalled when he saw her. For Demi, this visit was their most important one yet because she had plans on telling Perry about her moving to L.A. to pursue a career in acting, so she wanted him to think she was doing terribly bad. Not that it was all a lie because without any income coming in, she and Aliyah weren't sitting on top of the world. But she wanted Perry to think she was damn near suicidal. It was gonna have to be a performance of a lifetime. Hopefully she could pull it off.

The bus ride to Otisville was a little over two hours with traffic, so it was twelve o' clock in the afternoon when the bus finally pulled up to the prison in Otisville, New York. Because Aliyah had acted up the first thirty minutes of the bus trip and

worn herself out, she was asleep when they first arrived. However, after Demi woke up her and informed her who she was
getting ready to see, she perked right up.

Despite Demi's boyish attire, the male Correction officers couldn't take their eyes of her as she signed in. She was a
striking sight and a wet dream for many, regardless of what she
had on; an ability that most women probably dreamed of. After
going through a series of custom searches and questions, Demi
and Aliyah finally found themselves in the large visiting hall
with dozens of others, waiting for Perry to appear from the entry
way.

They sat at a small circular table with plastic chairs, with
guards posted nearby along with a few vending machines. The
windows had bars on them, with stale air lingering in the room,
and the chatter echoing off the building walls.

Aliyah sat with her feet swinging from the chair, and
clapping her hands as she waited for her father to arrive, but
soon grew impatient after about three minutes.

"Where's Daddy?" Aliyah asked.

"He's comin', baby. You know yo' daddy can't wait to
see you," Demi said with a smile.

Aliyah smiled and looked around for her daddy while
holding her faithful Barbie coloring book in her hands. Demi too
was starting to become impatient as well. Perry would always be
her first love, no matter what.

Fifteen minutes later, Aliyah's eyes lit up. She stood up
from her seat with a wide smile, shouting, "Daddy, daddy,
daddy!"

Due to her excitement, Demi could tell Aliyah wanted to
run around and twirl, but she was careful to keep Aliyah close to
the table, knowing the regulations of their visit. However,
Aliyah couldn't contain her excitement. She was like a bouncing
ball.

Perry stopped at the entry way to the visiting hall as one
of the C.O's pointed over in his family's direction. After shaking
his head, Perry followed the C.O's direction and slowly moved

his way through the room, navigating through the crowd of other visitors with his eyes fixated on his daughter.

His braids looked freshly done but he had unkempt facial hair that made him look even harder but still handsome. He still looked good, even in his large orange jumpsuit, white tube socks, and brown prison slippers.

When Perry got close, Aliyah ran to him but stopped and started clapping her hands. It was an odd reception for Perry, but he didn't think anything of it.

"There's my baby girl," Perry said, trying to scoop his daughter up in his arms. However, when he did, she started yelling, which prompted him to instantly put her back down. He looked so embarrassed as a C.O. asked him if everything was okay. "Yeah, officer. Everything is fine."

Even though Aliyah didn't want a hug, she kept saying, "Hi, daddy" over and over again. Perry was able to steal two kisses on her forehead, but that was about it.

"I missed you, baby," Perry said with tears in his eyes.

He then walked over to Demi, and this time was able to get a hug. He loved how her soft body felt in his arms. He almost hated to touch Demi intimately like that, because it made him want to have sex and he knew that it wasn't happening. Demi smiled, loving how her baby's father looked even in jail. Her heart began to beat like drums and her hands became clammy. Every time she was around Perry, she became overwhelmed with this unexplainable feeling. But then she hated the predicament he was in—locked away from her for many years because of his violent and treacherous ways on the streets.

Perry took a seat next to Demi, while Aliyah insisted that she sit in her own chair beside him. Perry was confused.

"What's goin' on wit' my princess? Why is she actin' like that? She gotta another daddy or somethin'."

Demi's smiled faded. "No, Perry. Aliyah knows who her father is. She's been actin' like that for a few months now actually. She doesn't like a lot of affection, and she's beyond hyper."

"Well, that's been her damn near since she was born

67

though. All over the place," Perry took his large hand and quickly rubbed it over his daughters head.

"No, it's much worse now. She has all kinds of outbursts, tantrums. It's pretty bad."

"So, what do you think it is?"

Demi's eyes instantly became teary eyed. "She has Autism."

"What? Autism. Who the fuck told you that?"

"Her teacher brought it to my attention about a week or so ago. At first I thought the lady was trippin' so I cursed her out, but to be honest that's when I really started payin' more attention. Like I said earlier, she's been havin' all sorts of issues lately, so I went ahead and made her a doctor's appointment." Demi's tears began falling like rain drops.

"So… what happened?" Perry stared at his daughter, who was tearing the pages out of her coloring book.

"Well, the doctor just basically tested her social, language and behavior skills. After that he told me based on what he saw, that he was almost 100% sure that Aliyah was artistic. He told me I was welcomed to get a second opinion or go to some specialist called a Neurologist, but I didn't think it was necessary."

Perry was pissed. "And why not? We should talk to somebody else. That muthafucka might not even know what he talkin' about."

"Look, I ain't got no money for no specialist. I had to write a bad check just to take her to that doctor. I lost my job, Perry."

"You lost yo' job, Ma?"

Demi shook her head. "Yeah, and right now I don't have any money comin' in."

Perry stared at Demi with his dark brown eyes. "Damn, I was gettin' ready to ask you what's good, and why you ain't been to see me but I see shit been hectic for you."

"Yeah, real hectic. But I bet that bitch Brandy ain't gotta worry about that."

"Who the fuck is Brandy?" Perry asked.

Demi immediately got upset. "Don't try and play me. The bitch on 123rd Street who you sendin' money to. How the fuck you gon' send another girl money Perry, when me and your daughter are barely makin' it?"

"Demi, I don't know what the fuck you talkin' about. I don't know no girl named Brandy on 123rd. How the hell am I supposed to be sendin' her money when I don't have any? Who told you that shit?" Perry questioned.

"Does it matter who told me? Is the shit true?"

"Hell no it ain't true. You know they took all my money. If I had any, you would have it. Demi, when I was out on the street, you and Aliyah didn't want for nothin'. Why would I wait to get locked up to hold out on you? That shit don't make no sense."

Demi hoped that Perry was telling the truth.

"I would never have you or Aliyah out there sufferin'," Perry continued. "Now, tell me who told you that stupid shit?"

"Let's just drop it," Demi suggested.

"Well, whoever told you needs to get their fuckin' facts straight."

Demi decided not to respond.

"So, why haven't you been coming to see me lately?" Perry asked.

Demi hunched her shoulders. "I don't know. I been really busy."

"Too busy to even write a niggah," Perry inquired.

"Well, we're here now, right?"

Perry gazed at her with a hard stare that made Demi a little uncomfortable. He could be very controlling and aggressive at times, but he loved her and knew that his girl had ways about herself that made him furious.

"Demi, watch who you talkin' to like that. I'm still the same niggah in here, that I was out there," Perry said in a calm manner.

"I'm sorry."

69

"It's cool, boo. Let me ask you somethin' though. Why you dressed like that? I ain't never seen you dressed like a tomboy and shit. I mean you still hella fine, but it's just...different."

Demi shrugged her shoulders. "Hey, this is what happens when you broke."

"Daddy. Hi, Daddy," Aliyah interrupted the two, tugging at her father's clothing.

Perry withdrew his mood toward Demi and smiled at his daughter. "What up princess? Daddy loves you."

Despite what might've been going on with her, hearing his daughter's words warmed his heart to the point that he wanted to cry. But he was a man and couldn't show his emotions like that in front of everyone.

Perry turned his attention back to Demi. "So, what's goin' on wit' yo' life?"

Demi sighed. She didn't want to tell him so soon, but it wasn't like the visit was going to last all day, so something told her to get it over with. "Perry...I'm moving to L.A.," she informed him quickly.

"You what?"

"I said I'm movin'...."

"I heard you," he said cutting Demi off. "What you tryin' to take my daughter from me, huh? You gotta another niggah in L.A. or some shit?"

"No, Perry."

He was about to get loud, but had to calm down. "So, why the fuck you goin' all the way out there? Where the hell this shit come from? I ain't even been locked down for a year, and you already tryna roll out on a niggah. Oh, I see you goin' back to yo' old ways, huh?"

"What the fuck is that supposed to mean?" Demi asked.

"You know exactly what it mean. Yo' ass was off the hook when I met you. You and that damn Michelle, fuckin' all types of niggahs. I'm the one who calmed yo' ass down, so don't front."

Demi played with her fingernails before answering. "No, Perry I'm not goin' back to my old ways. It's just that I wanna go try and get into some things like acting or modeling. Maybe some videos. Shit, I ain't gonna be choosy."

Perry burst out laughing. "Acting? Where the fuck that shit come from? I mean I know you like to sing in front of the mirror and shit, but that don't make you no actress."

Demi caught an instant attitude. "Oh, thanks for the fuckin' support!"

"Support? Oh, you wanna bring up support? How are you gonna support me if you move to L.A? How am I gonna see my daughter? Did you think about that shit?"

"I know it's gonna be hard baby, but I don't plan to stay out there long. I just wanna go out there for a year or two, see what I can get into and make some money. I need a good job that's gonna provide for me and Aliyah, especially if she's sick."

Perry looked around the room and then at his daughter. When he saw that she was still occupied with her coloring book, Perry leaned in closer to Demi to say what was for her ears only. "Yo, you know how niggahs are in that fuckin' business, especially wit' that rap video type shit. You wanna play yourself like that? You wanna be a video hoe?"

In a matching tone, Demi replied with, "Why the fuck are you so negative? Don't you get it? I'm tryin' to take care of yo' daughter. You not around anymore, remember?"

Perry finally calmed down a little bit. "You my girl, Demi, and I ain't tryin' to have a niggah disrespectin' you and shit. How that look on me? I can't fuckin' protect you in L.A."

"I'm not lookin' for yo' protection. I wanna do me and right now, I met someone that's gonna help me start a career out there."

"What? You met someone?" Perry asked, falling back in his chair. "Who?"

Demi gave off a look saying, *here we go again*.

"Perry, it's just business." She wouldn't dare mention that she'd fucked him in the process.

71

"Listen, Demi, let's keep the shit real. I'm in this bitch for another ten years…minimal. I know you gonna do you. I ain't gon' be that fuckin' stupid. But don't be lettin' these niggahs fuckin' use you," Perry said sternly.

"I know Perry, but what I got goin' for me in Harlem, besides Aliyah? I need sumthin' better baby. I need to go try this shit out, and see what happens. You never know, I just might blow up." When Perry smiled. Demi grabbed his hand. "Baby, I need to know that you cool wit' this."

"What about Aliyah?"

"What about her? She's goin' wit' me."

"Oh, hell no. Are you crazy? I don't want my daughter all the way out there."

"So, what the fuck am I supposed to do? It ain't like I can leave her wit' yo' family and I'm damn sure not leavin' her wit' mine."

Perry nodded his head in agreement. With his parents dying in a car accident when he was only thirteen, Demi and Aliyah were the only family he had. Perry had a sister, but he hadn't spoken to her in over five years. He hated that she allowed her baby's father to beat her ass into the hospital every week. She hated the fact that Perry was dating somebody half Puerto Rican and half black. Neither seemed like legitimate reasons, but nevertheless it kept the two distant from one another.

"Damn, I wish you could at least leave her wit' yo' moms, but I don't rock wit' her like that anyway," Perry said. "Every time I call the house collect, and she answers, she hangs right up on my ass. I guess she forgot about all that fuckin' paper I used to give her."

"That's why I need to take her with me."

"What about this Autism shit?" Perry questioned.

"Well, if I go make some money, I can take better care of her."

Perry smiled over at his daughter and stared at the picture she was supposed to be coloring. "It's nice, baby girl. You doin' yo' thing wit' that crayon. I'm definitely gonna hang that up in my cell, and when I look at it, I'm gonna always think about you."

Aliyah smiled. She then went back to coloring all over the page. Perry turned to look at Demi. "So, you really serious about this, huh?" he asked.

"How long we known each other Perry? If this is my chance to finally shine in life and get sumthin' better for me and Aliyah, then I need to do it. And wit' you in here, you can't support us. So yes, I'm gonna do me and take it to the next level for myself," Demi explained.

Perry gazed at her for a short moment. He admired her confidence and attitude. He knew she was right, with him locked up, he wasn't able to help. He took Demi by the hand and said gently, "Look Ma, go ahead and do you, and blow the fuck up. But if things get heavy and fucked up out there, you and my daughter better hop yo' ass on the next flight back to N.Y."

That was all Demi needed to hear.

 # Seven

Five days after her visit with Perry, and after confirming with Jorel over the phone that he had a few things lined up, Demi pulled out the small savings that she'd stashed for emergencies and booked a one way ticket on Air Tran to Los Angeles, California. Demi was so nervous that she felt a bit ill once the Air Tran representative confirmed her flight. That was all she needed to hear to realize it was finally happening for her. The rest of the cash she would take with her to use for food and cheap hotel rooms until she got on her feet. The night before the flight, Demi had secretly packed and hid the bag deep in the closet. Even though she tried to block it out, the negative thoughts played with her mind constantly. She wondered if she was doing the right thing, but the more she thought about it she had to tell herself that everything was going to be okay.

This is just temporary, she kept telling herself over and over as the time quickly ticked by. When Demi glanced at the time, and noticed that it was midnight, anxiety began to settle in a little bit, so sleeping was out of the question. She knew that within twenty-four hours, she was going to be three thousand miles away doing her thing. It was exciting, yet frightening at the same time, and Demi had no idea which emotion would out weigh the other.

Deciding to write her family a letter about her decision, she pulled out a piece of notebook paper and a pen, and wrote a short letter.

Dear Ma and Dennis,
I know by now y'all are cursing me out, and I can honestly

understand why. Some people are gonna be mad and call me a bad mother for this...maybe even say I'm selfish...stupid, but the truth is I'm not. Believe it or not, I'm doin' this for Aliyah. To make a long story short, I met this producer name Jorel, who's from L.A. and he's got some things lined up for me out there. So, after talkin' to him a few times, I decided to take an early flight out to California to take advantage of this opportunity. I know it's hard but please try and understand. I feel as if I really need to pursue this. If I don't, I'll probably be mad at myself forever. I will never be truly happy until I can say that I at least tried and gave it my best shot. If it works out for me, I'm gonna make you proud of me Ma, and give you lots of money (smile). Please take care of Aliyah for me. I promise that I'll be back for her real soon. I'm leaving $200.00 for now. I will send more later on as soon as I start makin' money. Trust me I'm tryin' to give Aliyah a better life, and this is the only way I know how. 'I'll call y'all once I get there.
I'm out!

Demi

Looking down at her daughter, who was resting peacefully, tears began to fall down as she thought about how much she was going to miss her. However, Demi felt if she didn't do this, her and Aliyah's life would be miserable. She hated lying to Perry about taking Aliyah with her knowing those were never her intentions, but she just didn't think he would understand. Demi's fear was that her mother wouldn't understand either, but it was an opportunity that she just couldn't see passing up. Acting was nothing more than a silly stress reliever before, but now it was almost a reality.

Demi folded the letter and placed it on the fridge letting one of the color magnets hold it up for all to see. It was titled: *To moms and family, please read.*

At seven thirty the next morning Demi boarded a Los Angeles bound flight at LaGuardia Airport. The only luggage she had was a small roll-on that had clothes, shoes, cash, and a few other things. The flight was semi-crowded and Demi was happy that she had a window seat. She wanted to see L.A. from the sky when the plane began to descend.

"This is it," she said to herself after buckling her seat belt.

She took a deep breath and was ready for the plane to take-off. She had a small wallet size picture of Aliyah clutched in her hand and stared at it for what seemed like forever.

"Yo' mommy loves you, baby girl. This is for you," Demi continued.

Minutes later, the flight attendants began preparations for take-off and the captain announced through the P.A. system the duration of the flight and the estimated time of arrival.

Once the formalities were done, Demi smiled when she felt the plane finally moving. She took a deep breath trying to calm her nerves, and when the aircraft finally took off, her heart sank into her stomach. It was her first time on a plane alone, and without Perry. She closed her eyes and gripped the middle console tightly, embracing herself for the long six hour flight.

"I'm gonna do this," she chanted and took yet another deep breath. The butterflies in her stomach knew that it was too late to turn back.

 *Eight*

Hollywood

Demi's flight touched down at LAX at ten thirty that morning, L.A. time. When the aircraft taxied toward the terminal, Demi's stomach was immediately filled with butterflies. She was finally in L.A. Home of the Lakers, Roscoe's Chicken and Waffles and more importantly the Walk of Fame.

The pilot got on the intercom and announced that they were in Los Angles and that the temperature was seventy-nine degrees. Lastly, he thanked all the passengers for flying with Air Tran airlines, and wished them all a safe trip.

As Demi slowly stood up, she couldn't wait to get off the plane. She'd caught a quick glimpse of the city above in the sky as the plane began to descend toward the runway and remembered thinking to herself how beautiful the city looked. She couldn't wait to bask in the L.A. sunlight.

After patiently waiting for what seemed like eternity for the passengers in front of her to get off the aircraft, Demi was finally able to strut through the crowded terminal trying to pretend like she was a diva in an old pair of Seven jeans, a burnt orange off the shoulder shirt, and open toe sandals. With her roll-on suitcase in hand, she knew that the first thing she needed to do was call Jorel and let him know that she was in town.

Sitting down in one of the airport chairs, Demi reached for her small, flip pre-paid phone from inside her purse, and then pulled out Jorel's card. The phone was another thing she'd bought from New York before leaving. Demi figured by being on a budget, a pre-paid would be cheaper than her old cell phone plan. Not only that, Demi wanted to call her mother whenever she was ready to face the wrath. With all her excitement, she wasn't ready to get cursed out. Demi could only imagine how many times Dennis and her mother had called her old phone. Demi dialed Jorel's number excitedly. The phone rang three times and then it went straight to voice mail. Demi didn't want to leave a message, but as excited as she was she decided to leave one anyway.

"Hey Jorel, guess what, it's me, Demi. I'm in L.A. My flight just landed a few minutes ago and I need to see you. Umm, I'll call you back in a few. Please answer yo' phone, okay. See you soon."

She hung up and sighed worriedly, then looked around the busy airport and suddenly felt lost. With everybody coming and going and walking past like she didn't even exist, she felt alone. But after all she'd sacrificed to get there, Demi was determined to make Hollywood her home for a while. After all, Hollywood was the place where dreams came true.

A part of her wanted to call Michelle, to listen to some of her crazy and loud advice, but Demi decided against it. Even though it hurt that they'd ended on such a bad note, Demi made up her mind to put off any drama from back home for the time being. She didn't want anything negative to interfere with her brand new experience.

After waiting around in the airport for at least thirty minutes with no call back from Jorel, she pulled out his card again, and glanced at his address. Having no idea where South Grand Avenue was, or how far it was from the airport, Demi decided to take a chance. A visit to his office couldn't hurt. Grabbing her suitcase, she proceeded out of the terminal and decided the best thing for her to do was catch a cab.

Demi checked her funds and counted $850 that she'd concealed in a small white envelope stuffed deep into her purse. When she walked outside of the terminal and onto the active streets of L.A., she was somewhat overwhelmed. It reminded her of New York a bit, the way everything was moving in such a rush with the crowds, cars, taxi cabs and security, not to mention all the noise.

Demi began looking for the nearest cab to jump into and found a cab stand nearby that was swamped with other waiting patrons. From the length of the line, she knew it was probably going to be about a half-hour wait, but it was her only option.

Twenty-five minutes later, Demi finally made it to the front of the line, and secured a cab. She tossed her bag into the trunk and slid into the backseat, where there was a black driver at the wheel.

"Miss, where ya going?" he asked, as he adjusted his meter.

"Umm, I'm need to go to this address here, on Grand Avenue. How far is that from here?" she asked the driver, as she passed him Jorel's card.

The driver looked. "That's across town, about thirteen miles. It's a twenty minute drive, but with traffic, ya looking at thirty minutes and the fee is about fifty dollars."

"Fifty dollars!" Demi blurted out.

"Look, we're busy here, either ya going or not. I have other people waiting," he said.

Demi knew she couldn't sit at the airport all day. "No. Just drive, sir."

The driver slowly pulled off en route to her destination, and started the meter. The taxi began heading West on Century Blvd., heading toward Vicksburg Avenue. Demi stared out of the window taking in the view of the city, noticing the tall palm trees that lined the streets. It felt like a different world for her.

Twenty-three years in New York and it was the first time that she'd ever left the city without Perry. The furthest Demi ever traveled without him was from Harlem to Hackensack, New Jersey and that was only because she wanted to go to the Burberry store inside the Riverside Mall.

Demi kept an eye out for the infamous Hollywood sign that overlook the city. She couldn't wait to take a picture of it, but the after riding for a while, the famous landmark was nowhere in sight.

When the cabbie merged onto the I-110 expressway heading north toward Los Angles, he took a quick glance at Demi seated in the backseat, quietly staring out the window. He loved what he saw. She was beautiful.

"So, is this ya first time in Los Angeles?" he asked with nice smile.

"Huh…oh, yeah," Demi responded in a low tone.

"Where ya from?" he asked.

"New York."

"New York," he said excitedly. "Damn, what brought ya out here on the other side of the country, pretty gal?"

"Business."

"Oh, okay. Well, let me be the first to welcome ya to L.A...the city of angels."

"Thank you," Demi replied dryly.

It was obvious that she didn't care for any conversation with the cab driver. She wanted to focus on seeing Jorel, but even after her vague response, the cab driver still kept smiling and looking through his rearview mirror. It was twelve thirty in the afternoon when the cab finally stopped in front of a five story office building on South Grand Avenue right off of 11th street. Demi peered up at the building and knew it had to be it.

The driver turned to Demi and smiled once again. "Welcome to downtown L.A. That'll be $48.50."

Demi reached into her purse and pulled out a fifty dollar bill.

"I wish I could give you a bigger tip, but I'm kinda on a budget," she said.

"Don't worry about it, pretty lady. I understand."

Demi was about to exit the car when the driver suddenly stopped her. "Listen, I know you're new in town, and cabs can become expensive out here. Take down my number, and if ya need a ride anywhere, just give me a call."

Demi looked at him with a deep gaze. She didn't know

what to expect from him. In her eyes, he could've been a pervert, and saw an opportunity to take advantage of an out town girl from New York.

The driver smiled. "Don't worry. I'm a cool dude. I just wanna make sure ya come out all right," he added.

"That's what they all say."

"Well, it's your call. My name is Benny and I'm a married man—ten years and still counting," he said, showing her the tarnished gold wedding band on his left hand.

Demi gave him a quick size up. He seemed cool. But in her eyes and with her experience, she knew that you never could tell who would turn out to be a psycho or not. But then again, besides Jorel, she didn't know one person in the city, and if Benny was willing to help her out with the cab fare, then she knew it probably would be in her best interest to take him up on his offer.

"Okay, give me yo' number, but if you full of shit and turn out to be an asshole, I'll cut you," she warned.

Benny smiled.

"I have teen daughters, pretty gal. Ya look like you might need a friend being in this city."

"Well, if things go right in this building, I'll be on one of those billboards soon," she pointed out.

"Well, I wish ya the best. Good luck and break a leg."

Demi smiled. She took his number and stepped out of the cab. She'd officially met her first contact in L.A., and had a good feeling that things were going to turn out alright.

She waved Benny goodbye and headed toward the building with confidence. When she got near the lobby entrance she stared at Jorel's card, then decided to call him a second time before walking inside.

The phone rang three times again and then just like before, the voicemail came on. She decided to leave him another message, but this time she wasn't so excited. "Hey Jorel, it's me, Demi. I'm in L.A. and actually I'm outside yo' office. I'm on my way inside, but if you get this right away hit me back."

She hung up.

After putting the phone back, Demi looked up at the building and felt those same butterflies swimming around in her stomach again. Her hands started to sweat. She tried to take in a deep breath and relax.

"You can do this," she said to herself. "You ain't fly three thousand miles across the country to get nervous now, Demi. He invited you."

Demi quickly got her nerves together and walked into the quiet and empty lobby where she was greeted by an overweight security guard standing behind an oval desk with a security system positioned behind him.

"Hello Miss, can I help you?"

"Yes, I'm lookin' for this place right here," Demi said, passing the toy cop Jorel's card.

"Okay, it's on the fifth floor, but before you head up, you need to sign in and show me some I.D," he informed her.

Demi reached into her purse and pulled out her driver's license. She then scribbled her name down on the pad and walked toward the elevators.

She admired the lavish, marble decorated lobby with the long chic columns and the stone waterfall which seemed to glisten. After pressing the button for the elevator, she glanced back at the security guard and smiled.

When she reached the fifth floor a minute or so later, she noticed the sign to Jorel's business that read Guild's Casting Agency illuminated in small neon lights behind the receptionist desk.

Demi smiled. She approached the woman sitting behind the counter who was on the phone and busy typing on the computer. When Demi stood in front of her, the receptionist looked up and gestured with her hand for her to hold on. Demi stood there as her heart raced with anticipation.

This is it, she thought to herself.

The lady in the white ruffled button blouse with, her multi-colored braids styled in a bun, finally looked up at Demi.

"Can I help you?"

"Yes, I'm here to see Jorel...Jorel Davis," Demi replied.

"Jorel?" the receptionist asked in an incredulous tone.

"Yes, he gave me his card and told me to visit him when I was in L.A., so, I'm here, and he's expectin' me," Demi told the receptionist trying to sound proper and not ghetto.

"Umm...are you sure that's who you lookin' for?"

"Jorel Davis, yes. We met in New York a few days ago. Here's his card."

Demi passed the lady Jorel's wrinkled card and the woman chuckled unexpectedly.

"What's so funny? He does work here, right?" Demi questioned.

"Oh, yes, he works here."

"So, I'm here to see him. I mean, what's the problem?"

"He's not what you think," the receptionist informed her.

"Not what I think."

"Damn, that Jorel," the lady said with a smile followed by another chuckle. "Let me guess, Jorel promised you a shot at Hollywood, right? He told you that he would be able to get you into a few movie roles and maybe have you star in some music videos and have you become the next big star."

Demi was starting to become nervous. "Yes, he did. Why, is there a problem?"

The receptionist looked at Demi with sympathy. "Look..." she began. But stopped when Jorel came walking out of a nearby room.

When Demi turned around, her mouth immediately dropped when she saw Jorel pushing a huge housekeeping cart, equipped with a broom, mop, a huge trash can, toilet tissue...the whole nine.

"Jorel!" Demi called out.

When Jorel turned, he was shocked to see Demi standing in front of him. He was wearing a wrinkled grey jumpsuit with a name tag that said, Jorel Davis-Custodial Engineer. He looked exhausted and a bit overworked.

In Demi's eyes, he didn't appear to be the same stylish and cool Jorel that she'd met in New York. Now he was a corny looking nerd who was timid and shy. He even had on glasses.

Jorel walked up to her. He threw a worried glanced at Brenda, the receptionist and then stared at Demi. He'd forgotten her name, but definitely remembered who she was. Hell, she'd given him one of the best nights in his life.

"Hey, you surprised to see me. I'm here and ready to get to work with you," Demi said with sarcasm. "My big time producer," she continued.

"Umm…Umm…Mendi, right?" Jorel asked skeptically. "I didn't expect you."

"What…hell no. It's Demi, I know you ain't forget me already."

"Oh no, it's just been really busy around here," he tried to explain to her.

"Why you actin' like that…like you ain't glad to see me." Demi wanted to see how far his little performance would go.

"Look, you being here is so unexpected, that's all," he tried to reason.

"So, what's up wit' you…I mean, in New York, you was all cool and chill, lookin' fresh and shit, talkin' about how I was better than Halle Berry and I definitely needed to come out to L.A. to jump start my career, and now you lookin' like you just a straight fuckin' clown," Demi stated.

Brenda laughed.

Jorel looked lost. "Demi, we can talk, but not now."

"Why not now? Niggah, I flew three thousand miles on a fuckin' plane to come see you. I don't know nobody in L.A. I was feelin' you in New York, so no, I ain't tryin' to talk later. You promised me Hollywood and I came here to get it!" Demi barked. She tried to remain proper and nice, but she quickly became pissed and reverted back to the old Demi.

"Please, lower your voice. I don't need this shit at my job," Jorel replied.

"Niggah what? Don't fuckin' play me, Jorel. I ain't come all the way out here to be played like a muthafuckin' sucka!" Demi screamed.

"Whoa," Brenda uttered. She was shocked by Demi's sudden outburst.

"Demi, you really need to calm down," Jorel tried to plead with her.

"Don't fuckin' tell me to calm down!" Demi shouted. "You a damn janitor! Not a producer, but a fuckin' janitor! Somebody who cleans toilets for a damn livin'!"

Moments later, a tall white man who stood about six-eight came rushing out of his office after hearing Demi screaming. "What's going on out here?" he asked, looking at Brenda then turning to Jorel for an answer.

"I'm sorry, Mr. Guild. It's just a small situation, but I have it under control," Jorel replied.

"You do, huh? Then why is this young woman screaming in my office like this is some concert hall?" he asked.

"Who are you?" Demi asked.

"Do I need to call security?" Mr. Guild asked.

"Security?" Demi spat.

"Mr. Guild, she was just about to leave. I was about to escort her out the building," Jorel informed.

"Please do Jorel, and I need you to hurry and clean the conference room, before the producers of the new reality show, *Dumped* arrive for our meeting. Have this young woman escorted out of my building ASAP, or you can leave with her," Mr. Guild sternly warned. "And Jorel, this office is not a soap opera, so don't bring your drama here, or you'll find yourself out of a job."

"Yes, Mr. Guild, I understand," Jorel replied submissively.

Mr. Guild gave off a serious gaze, and then disappeared into his office. When he was out of sight, Jorel turned to Demi with an angry look. "You need to leave, Demi. I ain't got time for games with you."

87

"Games!" she shouted. "I came here for a new start, and it's niggahs like you who are fuckin' bullshit! Niggahs who always wanna keep a bitch down!"

"Demi, please, just keep your voice down and leave. This is my job," Jorel pleaded.

Demi looked at him with her face twisted with rage but also sadness and disappointment. She felt tears about to form in her eyes, but she refused to cry. Not in front of Jorel anyway.

"Yo' job? Niggah this is my life you decided to play wit'. I believed in you and all you did was fuck me. But you know what, I don't need you. I came out here on my own, and I can make it out here on my own. Fake-ass niggah. I should get yo' ass fired," Demi strongly stated. Just before storming out of the office with her heart crushed, she walked over to a table sitting by the door and pushed all the magazines off the floor. "Now, get to cleanin' muthafucka."

Brenda looked at Jorel and shook her head in disgust.

"This is the eighth one in six months, Jorel. Why do you keep lying to these girls? Are you that hard up for pussy?" she asked with another chuckle.

 *Nine*

Demi stormed out of the office building with tears streaming down her face. She couldn't hold the hurt in any longer. When she got into the elevator, that's when the river really began to flow from her eyes. She rushed past security and out into the city streets. When she reached the corner of 11th street, she stopped and dried her tears. She was then ready to go back into the building and fuck Jorel up for his bullshit. Demi was a Harlem girl and was ready to take it to Jorel. She wanted some compensation for the time and money she put into the trip.

Demi took a deep breath and said to herself, "Fuck this shit! I'm gonna get mines."

However, when she turned around and made her way back to the building, she ran into Brenda coming toward her smoking a cigarette. Demi was ready to get in her face too, but decided against it. She knew Brenda probably had nothing to do with the deception that Jorel had pulled on her. But Demi wanted to know what Brenda had to say about the whole thing, especially since she knew Jorel had pulled the stunt before.

"You okay?" Brenda asked.

"Why the fuck do you care?"

With an attitude of her own, Brenda shot back with, "Look, I know what Jorel did to you was fucked up. He's an asshole, but don't come at me like that. I'm the one who's just tryin' to look out for you."

Brenda took another pull from her cancer stick and continued, "I can't understand why y'all bitches are so fuckin' gullible to niggahs' lies and bullshit. You fly all the way out here for what…some damn dream."

"You don't know me," Demi said.

"Please, you think you the first girl that Jorel done lied to just to get himself some pussy or a blowjob. I seen about eight of y'all dumb bitches come through the office already in the past six months lookin' for that so called dream Jorel done promised, and all y'all are from out of town somewhere."

Demi looked at Brenda with a slight attitude across her face. "I mean, how did he do all that shit if he a janitor?"

Brenda smiled. "Well y'all bitches always comin' to the office, so he must be pretty creative. He obviously don' got some fake business cards printed up, and tellin' ya'll girls a bunch of lies."

Demi frowned. "That asshole. I met him in New York. He said that he was in town meetin' wit' a modelin' agency. We even went to some fancy party and Jorel knew the bouncer."

"Girl, please. Jorel's ass was in New York 'cuz his sister just got married. He flew out there for the weddin'. Now, as far as the party, that don't mean shit either. He probably just took his little business cards wit' him and then started throwin' Mr. Guild's name around like they owned the company together or somethin'. Shit, I have even done that a few times."

"That's why my name wasn't on the list when I got to the damn party," Demi admitted. "I guess those diamonds he was rockin' were fake, too."

Brenda laughed. "You know it. He probably got them muthafuckas from the swap meet. Hey, where you from any-way?"

"Harlem?"

"So you a Harlem girl and you fell for that bullshit. Usually I see bitches from the south or some small town or farm come runnin' to L.A. with that hope. But damn, you would think a girl from Harlem would know better."

"Look, don't stand here and criticize me. You don't fuckin' know me or what the fuck I'm about," Demi hissed.

"Oh, so now you a bad-ass? Well, Ms. Bad ass, since you way out here in L.A, you got some kind of plan for yourself?

You finished dryin' your tears and ready to take on the world, now, right…show this town that you the next fuckin' Beyonce." Brenda snickered, sizing Demi up and then continued. "Bitch, please. L.A. will eat you the fuck up and spit you back out. I've seen bitches like you get tossed out in the town like a fuckin' rag doll."

"Whateva! I don't give a fuck what you think about me. What the fuck do you do, besides being the bosses 'yes' bitch and answerin' the fuckin' phone all day? What you got goin' for yourself?" Demi asked.

Brenda took one last deep pull from her cigarette and tossed it. She looked a bit upset and stepped to Demi like a boxer on fight night. "You don't fuckin' know me or know what the fuck I'm about. I came out here tryin' to look out for a fuckin' sistah, but it's clear you just wanna continue to be a dumb, naïve bitch. What? You got some money saved and think you gonna do somthin' wit' that…please. I'm out. You can rot out here for all I care."

Brenda turned to head back to the building, leaving Demi standing on the corner looking like a lost child. As Demi watched Brenda's backside, she clutched her luggage with a tight grip and honestly didn't know what to do. She sat in deep thought for a moment and then sighed heavily.

"Brenda," she called out. "I'm sorry for the attitude. I'm just upset."

Brenda stopped walking and turned to look back at Demi. This time she made her way back over with a more pleasant look displayed on her face.

"Look, I know Jorel fucked up your situation. He's an asshole. But don't get caught up out here. L.A. is a hard town, and I've seen a lot of girls wit' dreams of becomin' a movie star get turned out in this city because of that desperation," Brenda kindly informed. "You got a place to stay?"

Demi was quiet for a short minute. "I might."

"Look, you don't know me and I don't know you, but I'm gonna give you my number. We can talk later. I get off at six, so if you need a place to lay your head for a few nights, get at me."

"No disrespect to you or anything, but why you bein' so nice to me?"

"Cuz I'm tired of Jorel bringin' these girls through and when he disses them, they ain't got anywhere to go. The last girl he did like that, ended up shot to death in Watts. She was only nineteen," Brenda said.

"Well, niggahs like that are livin' on borrowed time, and best believe, I'm gonna see that niggah soon. But I ain't no charity case. I can handle mines," Demi said with conviction.

"I don't doubt you, but you need to remember that you a long way from Harlem, and out here is a different breed of life. I like you, you're cute. I don't want you to get hurt."

Demi scowled her face a bit. "Hold up. I ain't a dyke, so don't get it twisted."

"Yo, I don't swing that way either. I'm just tryin' to be friendly," Brenda responded with a sneaky grin. "Look, just take down my number and give me a call if you need help with anything."

Demi looked skeptical at first, but knew that she needed some kind of life line out in L.A. She quickly took down her number and hoped that Brenda was a true friend.

Brenda went back to work, leaving Demi on the curb with her bag. It was still early afternoon and Demi didn't know where to go or what to do.

She began walking down the block and suddenly remembered Benny the cab driver. She thought that he seemed nice and probably would know of a place for her to chill, get something to eat, and get a room for the night. She didn't want to seem too eager to call Brenda. Demi had some money, so she figured it would be better for her to get a cheap room for a few nights and go over her options.

Demi refused to come so far, only to fly back home. She didn't want to be embarrassed by her friends and family who would say, "I told you so." So Demi decided to stick it out in

L.A and make it happen for herself.

Demi pulled out her cell phone and called Benny the cab driver. Unlike Jorel, he picked up after the second ring. "This is Benny, speak to me."

"Hi Benny, it's me, Demi. We just met about an hour ago. You picked me up from the airport," Demi spoke softly.

"Hey, pretty gal. I didn't expect a phone call from ya no time soon. Things cool with ya?"

"Umm, not exactly. I need another ride again."

"Oh, well me at the airport again with another passenger. It's gonna be about forty minutes before me able to come through to ya," he informed.

Demi sighed. "That's okay; I'll catch a ride some other way."

"Listen, pretty gal, ya keep a cool head. Ya look like ya goin' through hard times," Benny said.

"What, you don't know what the fuck I'm going through. Mind yo' fuckin' business!" Demi suddenly snapped and hung up the phone.

Demi didn't know why she'd cursed Benny out. He hadn't done anything to her. He was only trying to help. Demi was frustrated, and nothing seemed to be going as planned. She also wondered why the first two people she met in the city were so nice to her. It was way too suspect. She felt stuck.

Pickin' up her phone again, she decided to call Michelle. The one and only person who could probably cheer her up at a time like this, even though they hadn't spoken since the night of the party. When the two friends normally went through their little beefs every now and then, they always gave each other time to breathe and get over it. However, Demi felt as though their time apart had been long enough. She waited patiently as the phone began to ring.

"What up trick?" Michelle said when she finally answered. "You know I'm still mad at you."

"I'm sorry," Demi responded in a child-like tone.

"I can't believe you tried to play me at 'dat whack-ass

party."

"Honestly, I wasn't tryin' to play you. I guess I was just excited about meetin' Jorel, and didn't want to mess things up."

"Shit, it's cool. I done acted up around a niggah sometimes," Michelle admitted. "So, what's up wit' you? You think Dennis will keep Aliyah again so we can hang out? I wanna go check out 'dis new spot in Brooklyn."

"I can't Michelle. I'm in L.A."

Michelle screamed. "What? Bitch yo' ass left New York and didn't even say goodbye? When the fuck did you leave?"

"This morning. I didn't even tell my mother. I just left her a letter and rolled out."

"You lyin'? Where Aliyah at?" Michelle asked.

At that moment, Demi felt bad. "I left her wit' Dennis and my mother."

"Yo' ass is straight trippin'. Yo' moms gon' fuck you up." Michelle started laughing. "I would'a loved to see the look on her face when she read 'dat shit. I should go by there now and see how well they takin' the news."

"Speakin' of goin' over there, please do me a favor and check on Aliyah every now and then. I would ask you to go pick her up and keep her, but I don't have enough money for yo' fees right now," Demi replied.

Michelle sucked her teeth. "I might go get Aliyah's hyper-ass and let her spend the night, but you gotta make sure when you make some paper out there, you break me off wit' some."

Demi's eyes began to water. "I doubt if I'll be makin' money any time soon."

"Why not? Shit, them actin' bitches be gettin' money."

" 'Cause you were right. That niggah Jorel is shady. When I got off the plane, I went to his job, and saw his ass pushin' a fuckin' cleanin' cart. He some type of janitor and shit, not a damn producer," Demi explained as tears streamed down her face yet again.

Michelle wanted to laugh so bad, but knew her friend

was hurt. "Damn, I'm sorry Demi. See, you should'a let me fuck him up 'dat night. So, what you gonna do now?"

Demi began sniffing. "I don't know. Come back home I guess."

"Shit, I don't know why. You out there now. Yo' ass might as well try and get into sumthin'. You want me to come out there? You know me…once I hit the town and fuck a few important people you'll be gettin' all types of movie roles," she laughed crazily. "And don't let me give no head. If 'dat shit go down, you gon' get one of them Oscar statues."

Demi suddenly began to smile. She knew Michelle's crazy personality would take her mind off of what she was dealin' with. "No, I want you to stay in Harlem and check on my baby for me. Even though I don't know what the fuck to do next, I'ma try and work it out."

"Dat's what's up. Do yo' thing, so you can make us some money."

Demi's smiled continued. "Bet. I'll call you later."

After hanging up the phone, Demi wandered around the city for about and hour until she came across a McDonalds on 7th street. Her feet were sore from walking and tugging along her suitcase. She felt sweaty and dirty from the dry heat and haze. She needed a shower, some rest, and a fresh start.

She walked into McDonalds and ordered herself a value meal along with a few apple pies. She sat down and tried to eat her meal peacefully when she noticed a young teen staring at her from a distance. Demi rolled her eyes and gave off an irritated gaze. She didn't want to be bothered.

The young dude got up out of his seat, noticing Demi with the luggage near her side and the tight jeans she wore. He assumed that she was from out of town. He was in mostly red attire, with a red bandanna tied around his head and another one hanging out of his back pocket. He wore lose black khakis and a red and white plaid shirt. He was young in the face, but screamed 'blood gang member' from his wardrobe.

The young gang member stepped to Demi with a hard

gaze. "What it be?"

"Excuse me?" Demi said with an attitude.

Without her permission the young blood slid into a seat across from her.

"Where you from?"

"Look, just leave me the fuck alone, a'ight. Step off," Demi barked.

"Bitch, don't disrespect me, I don't wanna pop your fuckin' head off. They call me Lyfe."

Demi just shook her head in disbelief. *Fuckin' L.A.,* she thought to herself.

Lyfe continued to talk to her. "You look lost, so I'm tryna help you. You need a ride?"

"Oh my God, can you just leave me the fuck alone?" Demi shouted.

A few customers turned to see what was going on when they heard Demi scream. Lyfe looked at Demi and looked unmoved by her outburst.

"Fuck you gettin' loud for? I told you don't disrespect me."

But just when it looked like things were about to get ugly, two cops walked into the McDonalds. When Lyfe turned to see the cops enter the restaurant, he instantly got up and took a few steps away from Demi.

Both officers noticed Lyfe and kept a keen eye on him as they walked toward the food counter. Lyfe looked over at Demi and said to her, "I'll see you around, shorti."

He then walked out of the place leaving Demi sighing with relief. Demi lingered around in the McDonalds for another half-hour, then left to find someplace cheap to stay the night. She was in desperate need of some rest. Taking her best friend's advice, she planned on buying the paper in the morning to search for any gig that would put her on the map.

 **Ten**

Demi found a cheap room at the Knights Inn for two nights. It was in the heart of downtown, and right off the Hollywood Freeway. However, just because it was cheap, didn't mean that it was worth it. From the filthy room, bad smell, holes in the walls, and uncomfortable bed, the hotel was a complete dump. Demi thought about giving Brenda a call, but thought to herself, *fuck that, I don't even know her*. She would rather be on her own and make due with what she had, than to owe somebody her first night in the city. The room was loud and far from cozy, but she had to make it work. Dropping her bag on the raggedy, black iron bed, Demi began getting undressed. After taking a cold shower that was supposed to be hot, she wrapped a dingy towel around her body then sat quietly for a while, contemplating on calling home.

"I'm not gonna cry," she told herself, holding back the tears.

She went into her bag and pulled out her envelope of cash and went through it. With the cab fare she spent, along with food and a two night's stay at the hotel, which was costing her seventy dollars a night, Demi had six hundred and fifty-five dollars left to her name. She tried not to stress over her dwindling cash flow, but knew that if something big didn't come up for her soon, she would be out on the streets and starving.

Once again, Demi thought about calling home. She was missing her daughter heavily already, and California was a whole new world for her.

Trying to block out the stress that dug deep inside, Demi

decided to call it a night. She tried to convince herself that tomorrow would be a better day. However, once she laid down on the unclean sheets, that's when the grief truly hit her. She was all alone, three thousand miles away from home, and couldn't help but to be a little scared.

Her tears stained the pillows as she clutched them close to her, needing to find some kind of comfort and support. She lay fearful and in the fetal position, unable to stop the tears from flowing.

On the exterior, Demi had this bad-ass attitude. She was from Harlem, had been through it all with her friends and family, and knew she could take the world by storm and hold her own, no matter where she rested her head. But in reality, on the inside, she was just a little girl lost, needing some kind of guidance into her future.

Demi glanced at the time and saw it was only eleven at night. She closed her eyes a little and tried to think of happier times and happier places. She thought of Aliyah and knew that she had to continue to push forward for her. With only a high school education, if Demi didn't want to be a stripper or be involved in some dead-end low paying job, she needed a change in her life, and hopefully the entertainment field was the way to accomplish that.

Demi woke up early the next morning around nine, anxious to get her day started. She took another long shower, then pulled out the perfect outfit to start her day. She knew that she needed to be strong and motivated to make it in L.A, but she already knew it was who you knew and not what you knew in order to get your foot in the door. With that in mind, Demi knew that she had to network her ass off; or use what her mama gave her to get to the top.

Demi stared at herself in the mirror and tried to maintain

a positive attitude toward her career. She wanted to start out her day on a positive note. She knew the first thing that needed to be done was to invest in herself; that meant putting together a resume of her previous works, getting some headshots taken, and she probably needed to inquire about getting herself a respectful agent to represent her. She also needed to know the right spots to hang out at; the clubs that were popping, the lounges, restaurants, and the bars that had the prominent producers, moguls and actors hanging out there. She needed to fit in and make a name for herself.

First on Demi's list was getting her headshots done and attaining her comp cards to pass around. She located a photographer that was listed in one of the trade magazines at the front desk. When Demi called him, he mentioned that he had an opening in his schedule. His name was Alex Trend. He recommended that Demi come into his studio the same day. Knowing that this was too good to be true, Demi jumped at the opportunity and told Alex that she would be at his studio in two hours.

Demi got dressed in a pair of J. Brand cropped pencil jeans that highlighted all her curves and a tight fitting v-neck T-shirt that accentuated her breast. She styled her hair with a part down the middle of her head, and flat ironed the rest so it was completely straight.

Sprawled out across her bed were the L.A times, Variety Magazine, and a few other trade papers that displayed information that she highlighted or circled. She wrote down numbers and addresses of other people in the industry, who would more than likely come in handy, then placed the numbers inside her purse.

But now, the problem for her was transportation. It was costly to get around the city, and because she didn't have a car, she regretted like hell cursing Benny out the day before. He was the one person, who'd been friendly to her from the start so it was no excuse for her behavior. She wondered if he was mad at her.

Demi let out a deep sigh and then picked up her phone.

When she dialed Benny's number, he picked up after the second ring as usual.

"Benny speaking," she heard him say in a lively tone.

"Benny…hey, it's me Demi. Look, I'm sorry for my tone with you yesterday. I was just stressed out. The day didn't go the way that I wanted it to," she quickly explained to him.

"Hey, pretty gal," Benny replied freely. "Listen, me didn't take no offense to that. I understand ya under some stress. It's all forgotten."

Demi smiled.

"Thank you, Benny. I'm sorry, though."

"You okay, pretty gal?" he asked.

"I have a lot to get done today, and I need help. Can you come get me?"

"Not a problem, pretty gal. Where are you?" he asked.

"I'm at the Knights Inn on Temple Street."

"Oh, that's not the best place for ya, pretty gal."

"I know Benny, but it was all I could afford."

"Okay. Me understand. I'll be around that way in twenty minutes, hang tight pretty gal," he said.

Demi hung up the phone with a smile on her face, then began collecting the things that she would need for the day. She went into her suitcase, pulled out her stash of cash, and removed three hundred dollars from her stash. Her intentions were to put some of the money toward her headshots, and the rest would go toward paying Benny for driving her around town.

She let out a stressful sigh, knowing that three hundred and fifty dollars wouldn't last her too much longer, and that she needed to get some kind of work, quick. Demi stuffed the remaining money back into the envelope and hid it deep in the bottom of her bag and secured her luggage with a small lock. She picked up the trade papers and magazines that she had across the bed and stuffed a few into her purse.

By ten that morning, Benny was pulling up to her room door, and Demi rushed out clutching her bag with a pair of huge sunglasses, looking like a true diva.

"Hey, Benny," Demi happily greeted as she jumped into the back seat.

"Hey, pretty gal. Ya look amazing," Benny returned. "Where to?"

"I need to go to this place in the city, on Main Street to see about getting some headshots done. Hook me up wit' a good price, Benny. I ain't got a lot of money for cab fare."

"For ya, give me thirty-five and we cool," Benny said.

Demi smiled and paid him immediately plus a five dollar tip this time.

Benny took the 110 freeway heading north. During the ride, the two got to know each other very well. Demi felt that Benny was a nice guy and had a good vibe. He talked about his wife and kids, and Demi learned that Benny was from Trinidad, which explained why he always referred to himself as me. He'd moved to L.A. when he was only eighteen and made a comfortable life for himself. He also had four daughters.

"Damn, you've been busy, Benny. Lots of lovin," Demi joked.

"I love my wife very much," Benny said happily.

Demi chuckled.

"When you find a good woman, you show her how much ya love her everyday, and I've showed how much I love my wife throughout the years," Benny gloated.

"That's good, Benny."

"How 'bout ya, pretty gal, any kids?" he asked.

"Yeah, I have a daughter, her name's Aliyah. She's five."

"I know you miss her."

"Very much. But I'm out here tryin' to make a better life for her. I want my daughter to have the best," Demi admitted.

"I understand. I've been in this area for twenty-two years, and been a cabbie for fifteen. I try to give my daughters everything, cuz in Trinidad; me grew up poor and wore the same clothes weekly sometimes. I saved enough doin' modest jobs in my country and eventually got my Visa and came here. I finally bought my first house five years ago. It's a struggle, but with,

God, hard work and determination, ya can do it. But this city is not easy," Benny warned.

"I'm a tough woman."

"Ya will do it, pretty gal. I see it in ya eyes…that fire. I had that same fire twenty-two years ago, and still do when it comes to my wife and kids."

Demi smiled. "Can I ask you a question, Benny?"

"What is that, pretty gal?"

"Why do you like callin' me pretty gal?"

"Because, I see a woman who came three thousand miles from home to make a better life for herself in film. And when I look at ya, I see my daughters in ya…so young and filled with dreams and hope. I call my youngest daughter, Desha, pretty one. I know that it's good to hear from someone that ya beautiful," Benny proudly stated.

Demi began to glow. Benny made her feel wanted and already loved. She had only known the man for twenty-four hours and already felt a lot of trust for him; like in a family sort of way.

Before noon, Benny pulled up to a four story building on Main Street in the city. At that moment, Demi became a bit nervous. After everything that had been happening to her so far, she hoped that everything would work out well this time.

Before Demi stepped out the cab, she leaned forward and gave Benny a quick kiss on his cheek. "You're a sweetie, Benny, please stay that way," she told him.

Benny chuckled. "Ya have a blessed and wonderful day, pretty gal."

Demi stepped out of the cab and then turned around. "Benny, how do I look?"

"Ya a blossoming flower ready to spread joy and affection to those around ya," he responded with a profound smile.

His comment made Demi blush a little.

"Well, I'm off. Thanks, Benny," Demi said walking toward the building. She strutted in her four inch heels and tight designer jeans.

Demi walked into the lobby and looked at the directory on the wall. She searched for the name Alex Trend. When she found the name, Demi made her way to the elevators and pressed the panel for the third floor. After getting off a short time later, she walked to suite 301, knocked gently and waited for an answer. Seconds later, Demi was soon buzzed inside. She walked into the studio and looked around. The waiting room was empty and decorated with black stylish chairs that were lined against the wall. Previous headshots of Alex's work lined the eggshell colored walls as well. The room had a professional feel to it, with its pied-à-terre décor and the tear-sheets of different models that were positioned throughout the place.

There was a young lady dressed elegantly in a navy silk shirt and a dark tan suit sitting at the front desk. Demi assumed she was the receptionist or some type of assistant.

"Can I help you?" she asked, looking up at Demi.

"I'm here to see Alex Trend. I called earlier. We spoke over the phone."

"Your name?"

"Demi Rodriguez."

"Have a seat Ms. Rodriguez. Alex will be with you shortly," the woman said.

Demi nodded and took a seat in one of the chic chairs. It felt good to be in L.A. seeing about her head shots. It was the first stages of her career and she was proud of it.

Demi sat and waited for Alex to come out of a back room. She didn't have to wait long though, because a few minutes later he came walking down the hallway. He was tall and lean, sporting a few piercings in his tongue and lips and a black tank-top. His right arm was heavily tattooed and his beautiful ice blue eyes made Demi speechless.

For a white guy, Demi found him attractive, but kept her composure.

Alex stood in front of Demi with a smile. He extended his hand toward her and inquired, "Demi?"

She stood to greet him with a matching smile. "Yes."

"Hey, I'm Alex Trend. We spoke over the phone. If I understand correctly you're looking to take some headshots of yourself."

"Yes. See I'm new in L.A, and I'm tryin' to break into some actin'. I saw your ad in Variety and, well, here I am," Demi mentioned.

Alex shook his head. "Well, come…let's talk in my office."

Demi followed Alex toward his office and was ready to get down to business. She wanted to know prices and how soon he would be able to work with her.

When Demi walked into Alex's office, she was floored by dozens of more astonishing photos and tear-sheets of beautiful models that covered his walls. From what she saw, he took great pictures and knew how to capture a woman's glow and character. She even noticed a few pictures of well known celebrities in the mix of photos.

"Have a seat," Alex said, as he took a seat in his leather chair behind his sand granite and charcoal L-shaped desk.

Demi took a seat opposite from him and was ready to get down to business.

"Before I go on, I want you to take a look at a collection of headshots that I've previously done," Alex said, passing her a catalog of photos.

Demi opened the book and began leafing through the pages. She was definitely impressed with his style of work. Majority of the pictures were before and after shots, which Demi loved.

"Finish looking through them and I'll be right back," Alex said.

He got out of his chair and exited the office, leaving Demi alone to examine his work. Demi carefully looked at each photo of men, women and children, and a few elderly were also in the assortment.

"Damn, he's good," Demi muttered to herself.

It took her about fifteen minutes to finish looking

through the catalog. She was already sold. Now, all that mattered to her, was his pricing. She knew attaining headshots would not be cheap.

Alex walked back into his office and took a seat behind his desk again. "So, what do you think?" he asked.

"I love 'em," Demi said.

Alex smiled. "I believe my work can speak for itself."

"How long have you been doing this?"

"Twenty-five years now. I've worked with people from Cameron Diaz, Jessica Simpson, Will Smith, and amateurs who are just breaking into the business, etc. I take much pride and time in my work and believe that headshots ninety-nine percent of the time will get an actor an audition."

Demi nodded, quickly agreeing with him.

"Where are you from, Demi?"

"New York."

"Really. I used to work in Great City, New York. I worked there for ten years actually before coming out here," Alex mentioned. "So what brings you out to L.A.?"

"I just wanted somethin' better for myself and my daughter, so I thought I'd give actin' or even modelin' a shot."

Alex eyed her carefully, studying her features, her skin tone, eyes, lips and character. She was an extremely beautiful woman and he knew it wouldn't be hard for him to capture her in good light and snap some amazing photos of her.

"Well, I must say, you are a very beautiful woman. However you're a little short for runway modeling though. You would strictly have to do print work. Have you gotten any previous headshots done of yourself before?"

"No, not at all."

"Well, with me, I'm not going to lie to you, I'm expensive," he stated.

"How expensive?"

"My going rate, depending on what shots you are looking for and the packaging, can range anywhere from six hundred to fifteen hundred."

Demi's heart sank deep into her stomach. She wasn't ready to hear those kind of numbers.

"But, it's worth it. I come highly recommended. And I ask my clients all the time, how much is your career worth? Being in this business doesn't come cheap, but you can also make it work for you. I understand that we're all not wealthy people coming into this business, so you have to do whatever you think is going to work for you."

"To be honest Alex, that's a little too steep for me right now. I just came into town yesterday and I'm not even settled in yet."

"I see, well what did you come here expecting to spend?" he asked.

Demi was embarrassed to even say. "Maybe two to three hundred."

Alex smiled. "I'm flattered that you came to me, but with what you're looking to spend, you can't even get your foot in the door. Look, your headshots, perhaps, will be the single most important investment in your acting career, and price really doesn't mean much, but quality does, so don't skimp."

"I really need to get this done, but the money is tight wit' me."

"Look, I love your look and I want to shoot you in both natural and studio light, because you have a certain look and glow about you that I'm sure will sell something in this city. But three hundred is kind of insulting. I'll be able to start something with you for at least five hundred." He spread his hands apart. "If you can't come up with that then we can figure something else out," he said in a shady kind of way. He reclined back in his chair focusing on Demi greatly.

"I'm very easy to work wit', Alex," Demi replied as she locked eyes with Alex batting her eyes.

The one thing she learned from her mother was that when it came to dealing with men, they were a sucka for a beautiful woman. Demi seductively crossed her legs in front of him like Sharon Stone in *Basic Instinct*. She wanted to see his reaction.

Alex reclined back in his chair showing off a mischievous smile. The attraction between the two seemed obvious.

"I'm sure we can work something out," Alex said with his eyes glued to every part of her body.

"I'm willin' to do whateva, Alex. I need to get my career jumpin' off and these pictures will be a big help wit' that."

Demi gave off strong sexual vibes, indicating to Alex that if they had to fuck to get her pictures for cheaper or possibly free, then she was down for it.

Her tight jeans rubbed against her clit and her nipples began showing through the tight T-shirt she wore. She was definitely leaving an impression on him.

Alex let out a short sigh, feeling a rise in his jeans. He had a scandalous past with women. He loved his profession as a photographer, and he took advantage of the more desperate ladies that were thirsty to get into Hollywood. He came across women like Demi dozens of times and fucked the majority of them that wanted their headshots done for cheap or free.

But Demi, by far, was one of the most attractive women he came across in the years he'd been shooting. His crave for her made his heart beat like African drums, and the erection in his jeans felt like bricks.

"This is really important to you, huh," Alex said.

"Very."

"Well, let's say we continue this conversation over dinner," he suggested.

Demi smiled, crossed her legs seductively again and returned with, "Just give me the time and place, and I'm there."

"My place…tonight, and wear something sexy."

Alex reached into his desk and passed Demi his business card.

"On there's my personal cell phone number. Call me tonight and I'll tell you where I'm at," he said.

Demi took his card and secured it in her purse. She was ready to leave. But Alex reclined in his leather chair again and said to her, "Do me a favor, stand up and let me see what you're working with."

Demi didn't resist. She stood up, placing her purse in the chair and began modeling for Alex. She did a little twirl for him and then walked around his office in her heels, strutting from wall to wall with her ass twitching in her jeans.

Alex enjoyed the small show that Demi was putting on for him. It was a delight just watching her walk, so he could only imagine what it would feel like to get her into bed with him.

"You like?" Demi asked, striking a small pose.

"You definitely can go places," Alex commented.

Demi smiled. "That's what I need to hear."

Demi picked up her purse and promised to have dinner with him, knowing they would probably do more than just eat. Fucking for pictures or anything else, wasn't what Demi had expected, but with no money, she had to do whatever it took to get ahead. She walked out of his office knowing that with her looks and her charm, her face would be displayed across many billboards in the city real soon.

 *Eleven*

Demi pranced down Sunset Blvd., studying the tall palm trees, busy traffic, stylish shops, well-dressed shoppers, numerous billboards, and thought to herself:*L.A. is the town for me.* She wanted to get to know the city, so instead of a cab, she got on the bus headed to Beverly Hills. It was one of the places that she dreamed of seeing ever since she saw the show *90210*.

But with her funds limited, and her travel restricted, Demi felt like a fish out of water. Sunset Blvd. was for the rich and well-known, and she wasn't there yet.

She spent an hour window shopping and day-dreaming, then spent money on the cab ride back to her nasty hotel. When she got back to the room, it was nearing dusk. Demi was somewhat excited about her dinner date with Alex. She knew that he was the type of man she needed to get to know really well. By his confidence, she knew the man was connected and she wanted what he had; money and fame.

Demi sighed as she stared at herself in the bathroom mirror. She held Alex's card in her hand and stared at the number. She was nervous about calling, but couldn't pin-point the reason why.

She decided to call Alex after taking another ice cold shower. The manager of the hotel had promised her a small discount for the inconvenience of taking cold showers, and for Demi, something was better than nothing. Draping another towel around her body, she pulled out her phone, then dialed Alex's number.

"Alex Trend, speak to me," he answered in a civil tone.

"Alex, hey, it's me, Demi. The girl from earlier," she said courteously, with a school girl smile on her face.

"Hey, I'm glad you called. You ready to meet tonight?" he asked, his tone changing from civil to delight.

"Yes, that's why I'm callin'. What time should I come over?"

"Say about ten. I'll send a cab for you," he stated.

Demi grinned. "Really, wow thank you. I need yo' address."

As Alex gave Demi his home address, she scrambled for a pen and some paper to write down his information. She thanked him again, tossed the phone on the nightstand, then ran back to the bathroom. It was already eight-thirty.

She rushed to put her makeup on, making sure every area was applied properly. She then stared at herself in the mirror. Alex was her first big connect in L.A., so she had to work him with everything she had.

By nine thirty, the cab was pulling up to her hotel door. She wished it was Benny driving her, but she thought that it was late and Benny was probably spending time with his family.

Demi got into the back seat of the cab dressed in a long, turquoise v-neck sweater that she'd turned into a dress and a black pair of peep-toe pumps. She looked fabulous with her sensuous, long black hair falling down to her shoulders, while smelling like an almond cookie, compliments of Carol's Daughter. The cab driver was even stunned by her beauty. He couldn't keep his eyes off of her.

"Where to, Miss?" he asked, staring at her from his rearview mirror.

Demi searched for the address in her purse. "I'm going to this address in Century City."

"Good ways, that will run you about sixty-five dollars," the elderly looking driver with the bushy mustache informed her.

"I'm covered," she replied.

The driver nodded then drove off.

110

The cab drove down Figueroa Street, and it was the first time Demi really got to see the city during the night time. It appeared to be a different city with the streets illuminating from the dozens of billboard signs that lined the street and traffic lights that flooded the blocks. With the thick crowds of people, L.A. was lively like New York to some extent. Demi peered out from the back seat, ready to take on what the city had to offer.

The ride to Century City took about forty minutes with the traffic. The cab drove down W. Olympic Blvd. looking for Alex's place. When she arrived shortly after, Demi was highly impressed. She stared up at the ten story building and knew it had to cost some serious money to live there.

The driver turned to Demi. "That's $66.35."

Demi looked in her purse and pulled out the eighty she brought with her. She passed the driver four twenties and quickly got her change back, hoping Alex would remember that he offered to pay for her ride there.

Demi stepped out the car and walked toward the tall, gleaming glass structure that towered over Olympic Blvd. The brick paved walkway was lined with tall palm trees and small blue lights that illuminated the walkway.

When she walked into the grand lobby with the marble pillars and granite floors, it almost took her breath away.

Damn, this reminds me of me and Perry's old apartment building. Oh, I can definitely get used to this again, she said to herself. Demi strutted to the elevators and pressed the button for the top floor. When she reached the tenth floor, Demi stepped into a 3,000 square feet loft with polished hardwood floors and four large windows facing south. It had an impeccable view of downtown L.A.

"Shit," she muttered with an astonished gaze.

Alex loomed from out of a back room in white pajama looking linen pants and a matching linen shirt. He had a glass of red wine in his hand and smiled when he saw Demi looking absolutely stunning.

"You look beautiful," he complimented.

"Thanks. You look good, too."

"Seriously…I'm so amazed right now," he continued.

Demi began to blush somewhat, loving how refined Alex looked in his casual, but relaxed attire.

"You care for a drink?" he asked.

"I'll take one."

Alex moved closer to her with a smile. He couldn't take his eyes off Demi. She was flawless. He walked over to his makeshift bar and poured Demi a glass of red wine and passed her the glass. "I drink nothing but the best."

Demi nodded and took a few sips. She then said, "You have a beautiful place."

"Thank you. Would you like a small tour?"

"Sure."

Alex took Demi by the hand gently and began leading her through his giant loft. He showed her the two station make-up room, the full kitchen with the marble counter tops, and the four large skylights in the middle of the living room. The décor of Alex's place was chic and impressionable.

"You like?" he asked.

"Yes."

Alex had some baked chicken cooking in the oven, and mashed potatoes with vegetables boiling on the stove. Demi could smell the aroma coming from the kitchen and felt her mouth watering.

"You cook?"

"Since I was ten," Alex replied.

Demi quickly settled into his place and sipped on her wine. They began to talk with the conversation becoming heavy at times. When Alex asked where she was from, she would lie and say that she was from the upper west side of Manhattan.

After a nice dinner and conversation, Demi found herself sprawled out on his leather couch. It had been awhile, but she could've used a blunt. However, Demi didn't know if Alex smoked, so she tried to suppress the craving and talked about business.

Alex walked out of the kitchen sipping on his third glass of wine. He looked satisfied with the meal he prepared and wanted to get into other things. Demi looked up at him and asked, "So, you gonna reimburse me for the cab?"

"Yes, I will. But you have to do something for me first," Alex said.

"And what's that?"

"Let me take some pictures of you."

Demi smiled. She rose up from the couch quickly. She wanted Alex to capture her in her true art form. Alex went to get his black, four thousand dollar Nikon digital camera, while Demi got more comfortable on the couch. When Alex came back, Demi was ready for him. She was already striking a pose.

Alex smiled and snapped a quick shot of her. She loved the flash from the camera and spread out across his couch in a seductive position with her breasts pressed against the soft plush leather, and legs spread looking like she was ready to fuck.

"Damn, I like that," Alex said snapping some rapid pictures of her.

Demi slowly turned and positioned herself on her back and raised her thick thigh in the air letting her short dress fall downward, showing Alex some skin. She arched her back and perched her breasts upward.

"You like it like this?" she asked.

Alex let the camera capture her beauty and approached her closer with the camera aimed directly at her face. Demi was definitely photogenic and the closer he came, the more her beauty showed.

"You're so beautiful," he stated.

"Am I?" she asked.

"Yes…I never lie."

Demi decided to toy with Alex even more, changing her position a third time. She raised herself, gripping the back of the couch and spread her legs in a very enticing position—doggy-style with her sweet ass curved upward and the back of her thighs showing. She turned slightly to get a peek at Alex and stuck out her tongue in an inviting gesture.

Alex sighed and approached her closer with the camera still in his grip, but the rapid picture taking was gradually coming to an end. He took a handful of shots with Demi caught in such a naughty position and then let the camera drop to his side with the strap still caught in his grasp.

"Is this a good enough shot for you?" she asked teasingly.

Alex had his eyes fixated on all of her and couldn't help but to get a hard-on. He ached just to touch her, and felt his heart beating like it wanted to escape from his chest. He was definitely turned on and wanted to ravage Demi sexually.

Demi saw the look in Alex's eyes and knew she was succeeding in seducing him. She turned herself over and sat facing him with a mischievous smile. Her short dress was riding up her thick smooth thighs, almost showing him her goodies underneath. She began licking her lips softly, shifting her head backwards and then began groping herself slowly but surely. She slowly ran her hand up her dress and began to play with herself by parting her sweet thick lips and letting an alluring moan escape from her lips as she dug her fingers inside of her.

Alex stood there for a moment enjoying the show that she was putting on for him. His thick hard-on was showing through his white pajama pants and it made Demi smile. She knew what she came to his place to do, and if she had to trick herself out and give him some pussy to get her career jumpstarted, then so be it, she thought. It wouldn't be the first time for her to fuck a niggah to get something she wanted out of life.

With her seductive gaze still fixated on Alex, she began to spread her legs apart wider and exposed the baby blue thong she was wearing underneath. Even though she'd never had sex with a white guy before, she was ready to fuck. Demi signaled for Alex to come closer. He did without the least bit of hesitation.

"You a nasty little bitch aren't you," Alex said with a lustful grin.

"You willing to see how nasty I can get," Demi continued to tease, as she began tugging at his pants admiring his thick
bulge.

"What you want from me?' he asked.

"A nice break in the price of my pictures."

"How much of a break?"

"For free, maybe," she suggested. She began to fondle
with his bulge for assurance.

Alex chuckled. But then let out a pleasing moan as Demi
began massaging his hard-on through his thin pants. Her touch
began to make Alex quiver a bit, but it brought up a quick satisfaction within him.

"You crazy," he replied faintly, but felt weak in Demi's
touch. "What makes you so fuckin' special?"

Demi showed off a wicked grin and was ready to make
the niggah succumb to his knees with her blessing in sexual favors. She began pulling down his pants slowly and wanted to
see his dick in the flesh. Alex didn't resist, but remained standing still in front of her with some eagerness in his expression.

He was definitely blessed. Demi took his long length in
her grip and began stroking him tenderly, causing another satisfied moan to escape from his lips. She then neared her fleshy
lips toward his goodies and slowly took him into her mouth. She
slowly wrapped her soft rounded lips around the tip of his dick,
having her tongue curl around his shaft. Demi started off simple,
with a small kiss there and a little lick there, and a few sucks underneath his nuts, making Alex whimper like a small animal.

Her sucking increased, and the licks became longer. She
began to play with his balls with her fingers as her blowjob became hurried.

Alex began looking like Alice in Wonderland as Demi
sucked him from the tip to the base of his dick with her tongue
continuing to twist and around his length.

"Ah, shit!" he cried out, not knowing what to do with
himself.

She deep-throated him with perfection and ran her hands

up his chest, pinching his nipples.

"Oh, my God!" he cried out again, as he began to feel weak in his knees.

Demi bobbed back and forth like a jackhammer hitting against concrete and her suction feeling like a power vacuum pulling Alex into her jaws of life. Alex loved her head game, but Demi suddenly pulled away from the dick and stopped.

Alex looked down at Demi with a confused gaze and asked, "Why did you stop?"

"Cuz…we need to talk about my headshots."

Alex looked like he was lost in a maze for a moment. Demi's oral action had him stunned and he wanted her to continue, but the bitch wanted to bring up business.

"What? Shit…," he was lost of words.

"My headshots," Demi repeated.

She stared up at him with a sinful smile, as she continued to stroke him nicely. She felt the veins in his dick pulsating in her grip.

"Fuck it, I'll manage you and do the photos for free. I just wanna fuck you," Alex blurted out.

"I like."

"C'mere!" he shouted, scooping Demi into his arms and tearing into her like a hungry beast.

He threw his hands up her skirt and ripped off her thong. He then pushed Demi down on the couch and came out of his pants. Alex became so hard that it hurt. Demi had her dress pulled up to her thick hips, exposing her shaven mound that stretched across her entrance into paradise.

"You gotta condom right?" she asked.

She wasn't trying to get pregnant or catch some STD and fuck up her chances in L.A. She had her legs spread invitingly for him and wanted it just as bad as Alex. Alex rushed to the bathroom and came back into the room with a magnum clutched in his hand. He quickly tore it open and rolled the condom back against his full length.

Demi peered up at him with her dress wrinkled and tits

116

showing. Alex came closer to her, resting his knees against the couch and grabbing Demi's legs as he was getting ready to position himself between her thighs.

Alex slowly began to sink between Demi's thick bare thighs and tried to thrust all nine inches of dick into her, causing Demi to gasp. She clutched onto Alex like she was holding on for dear life. She straddled him, then felt his big dick open her up like the Grand Canyon.

"Oh, shit, shit!" Alex grunted, feeling how wet and ready Demi was for him.

He was pressed against her, having Demi like a sandwich between him and the plush couch. He danced on top of her, getting into his rhythm as he fucked Demi excitedly—sucking on the side of her neck and cupping her tits. She cried out, running her hands down his back and resting them on his ass as it moved up and down between her thighs like a bouncing ball.

"Aaahhh shit…Aaahhh damn-it!" Demi moaned, closing her eyes and feeling like his large erection was rooted into her.

"I need to take this shit off," Demi said, referring to her dress that was clinging to her looking like a wrinkled turquoise sheet. It was matted and twisted around her waist from the sexing and she wanted to be naked so she could feel Alex's flesh completely against her.

Alex paused for a moment, allowing Demi to remove the rest of her clothing. She tossed her dress to the floor and resumed the position, falling against her back with her legs spread waiting for Alex to continue.

Alex did with a smile, and the two went at each other ravenously...going from the couch to Demi being pressed against the large window that peered out into the city. She had her tits and hands pressed against the glass with Alex fucking her from the back, lifting her legs up from behind, and thrusting into her as sweat discharged from all over him.

Demi's passionate cries echoed throughout the loft and the two finally made it to his bed where Alex continued fucking her on his expensive 18th century mahogany carved post bed. It cost Alex nine thousand dollars, and was one of the ways he impressed the women with his taste in décor. But Demi could've cared less about his old, priceless bed. She wanted Alex to make her cum and then shoot her headshots for nothing. She was on a mission and was determined not to let anything or anyone get in her way.

 *Twelve*

The bright rays of the sun beamed colorfully through the lavish white blinds in Alex's room. Demi felt a soft gentle breeze dance through the room from the open window causing her to snap from her pleasurable sleep. She lay naked under wrinkled, black satin sheets that felt like heaven, then realized she was alone in the king sized bed. It felt good waking up to a nice décor for once, instead of the run-down hotel or her small congested room back in Harlem. A place where she was constantly awaken by her mother fucking some niggah in the next room or her brother arguing with one of his tricks. She wanted to savor the moment, so she stretched out across Alex's bed like a kitten playing with a ball of yarn. It was a beautiful day. Demi had gotten up in the perfect place. She rested her body against the headboard, as she sat in deep thought which caused a warm smile to surface in her expression.

"Good morning, beautiful," she heard Alex say.

She turned to see him standing a few feet away in his blue pajama pants and no shirt. He had a nice body and kept himself fit.

"Hey, you." Demi greeted him with a warm smile.

"You know you're even more beautiful when you sleep, so I couldn't resist."

"Resist what?"

"I took some shots of you while you were asleep."

"Are you serious?" Demi questioned

He nodded. "Hey, I know a good shot when I see one."

Demi climbed out of bed and reached for Alex's silk robe

that was draped on the back of an ottoman to cover her naked body. "I can't wait to see them."

"You hungry?" he asked.

"Very."

The two soon made it into the kitchen where Alex was preparing an omelet and some sausage. Demi felt relaxed around him, and enjoyed the talk that they were having. From his constant smiles, she knew that she'd won him over.

"I enjoyed my time with you," she mentioned, while sipping on some orange juice.

"I did, too," Alex returned.

"So, about my headshots?"

Alex chuckled. "You know what, you're gonna go far in this city."

"And why you say that?"

"You're sexy, beautiful, determined and willing to do whatever it takes to get by. I see it in your eyes, that canny way of doing things and using what you have to get what you want. This town is in for something serious with you in it," he stated.

Demi laughed. "You believe so."

"Yes, that's why I want to manage you."

"Manage me?"

"Yes, you have something that's uncanny about you, an edge," Alex said.

"What kind of edge?"

"That kind of edge where you're willing to take to the next level. Shit… With me, you can become a star under my wing."

"I like what I'm hearin', but no disrespect to you, I heard this shit before," Demi remarked, thinking about the promises that Jorel had promised.

"Well, I'm a different kind of man. Besides, look around you. I have everything to show for it. I'm not gonna bullshit you. I'm a rich man, Demi and very well connected. I can get you into places… places so elite that even the staff need VIP," he joked somewhat.

Alex approached Demi with a look that said he was all about business. "I want to manage you, beautiful."

Demi's smile widened. "So, does this mean I can still get my headshots for free?"

"Just say yes, and it will be all worked out."

"Yes, of course," she replied having her lips just a mere inch from his.

"That's my girl," Alex said, then pressed his lips against hers.

He began kissing her passionately with his hand running between her thighs indicating that he wanted to fuck again before she left.

Demi thought about Alex and his offer during the cab ride back to her hotel room. It was early afternoon and the sun was at its peak. She tried to freshen up before she left his place, but her crumpled dress, disheveled black hair and torn thong underneath made her look questionable as to her previous whereabouts.

The driver had to glance at Demi in his rearview mirror and smile, knowing that she had a wild night out. Demi sat quietly in the backseat watching the city pass her by as the cab driver did sixty on the 101 Freeway.

Even though Demi got a good nights' sleep at Alex's place, she was still exhausted. Alex's pipe game put a spell on her and her pussy still throbbed. She rested her head against the window and closed her eyes. She wanted to take a quick nap in her room before taking care of her business in the city.

When she opened her eyes, the driver was pulling up to her hotel door.

"That'll be $66.39," the driver stated.

Demi reached into her purse and passed the driver the c-note that Alex had given her for the cab ride home. She felt relieved that Alex kept his word and reimbursed her for the ride to his place as well. After giving the driver a reasonable tip, she quickly collected her change and jumped out of the car. However, when she reached the hotel door, an uneasy feeling quickly swept over her. She noticed that the door to her room was slightly ajar and she was sure that she'd locked it last night before she left.

She approached her room with caution. When she pushed open the door to her room, a look of shock spread across her face.

"What the fuck?"

Her room was in chaos. Someone had gone through all of her belongings and dumped her clothing and other personal items out onto the bed and floor. Everything had been thrown around. Demi quickly panicked, remembering that she had her life savings stashed away in her suitcase. She rushed into the room and went ballistic looking for the envelope with the cash.

"Please, please, please…still be here, please still be here," she muttered as she dug through her belongings. She tossed clothes to the side and searched frantically for the cash.

"No, no…please no," she cried out, trying not to give up hope.

But her hopes of finding her money in the room slowly began to deteriorate as she went through everything only to come across a crumpled empty envelope.

"I've been fuckin' robbed!" she screamed.

Demi collapsed on the floor, full of tears, realizing that she had nothing left. She was dead broke. She felt paralyzed in the room, with her stomach churning, aching, and her head spinning. The feeling of numbness took over her body. She couldn't stop the tears from flowing. She wanted to die. She kept thinking to herself, *what now?* How was she going to survive?

"Mutha-fuckas! Mutha-fuckas! Mutha fucka!" she cursed repeatedly, tossing clothes around, and shredding a few of her own items in rage.

Then she started cursing at herself. "How could I be so fuckin' stupid?" Coming from the hood, she should've known better than to leave her money in such a fucked up place. "What the fuck is wrong with me? Why the hell have I been so trustin' lately?" she asked herself thinking about Jorel.

Her pretty face was stained with tears of hurt, treachery and fear. Demi managed to rise to her feet, but felt her knees wobble a little. She gripped the bed for support and sat at the edge of it. She didn't know what to do or who to call. Someone had broken into her room and destroyed her golden opportunity.

Demi tried to wipe the tears from her face, but they kept flowing harder and faster. *Why the fuck is everything goin' so fuckin' wrong,* she thought.

She wanted to call the police, but thought what good they would do, knowing that the thieves were long gone and probably wouldn't be caught anyway. She was an out of town girl with no money and no family around for support.

Demi sat in her room in silence for nearly an hour. She began weighing her options. She thought about calling Alex, then her mind raced to Benny. They were the only two people she knew in L.A. She went to her purse to pull out the prepaid phone, but after searching for a few seconds, realized that it wasn't in there. Knowing that Alex hadn't taken it out of her purse, the only other thing that she could think of was that she'd accidentally left it in the room, and the thieves had taken that as well.

"Shit!" Demi yelled out to the top of her lungs.

Now her only means of communication was gone as well. However, a pre-paid was easy to replace, but her money wasn't. That was the main concern.

She left the room to see the hotel manager or front desk clerk. She'd only paid for two nights and tonight would be her last night unless she came up with the cash to pay for a few other nights.

She approached the front desk and saw a young, scrawny pimple faced black kid behind the desk, who was on the phone and trying to watch an episode of Good Times. She walked up to him heatedly and asked with a menacing attitude, "I need to see

123

the damn manager!"

The kid looked at her with some contempt. But he thought she was so pretty, he softened his manner. He hung up from his call. "Mr. Jones is not here."

"Well, you need to call some fuckin' body, cuz somebody just broke into my fuckin' room and robbed me!"

"They did what?"

"Somebody broke into my fuckin' room and robbed me of everything."

The kid looked surprised. "How did that happen?"

"What the fuck you mean how did it happen? Don't y'all got security cameras and shit around here?"

"Only in the lobby," he informed.

"What the fuck? You need to call yo' boss up and have him come fix this shit. Cuz niggahs took almost four hundred dollars from me and I ain't tryin' to get kicked out. I ain't got no fuckin' money right now!" she screamed.

"Ayyite, just calm down shawty."

"Shawty? I ain't no fuckin' shawty of yours. Niggah you need to do sumthin."

"I'll call 911," the kid said.

"Fuck 911, what they gonna do about gettin' my shit back."

"I have to file this with the police, or I'll get in trouble," he stated.

Demi sighed heavily. She felt like wildin' out on the dude. But she knew it wouldn't get her the money back. Instead, she stood in front of the clerk with a look to kill plastered across her face. She watched him get on the phone to dial the police and then he called up his boss.

An hour later, a sole black and white squad car pulled up to the hotel and two white L.A.P.D. officers stepped out. Demi was seated in the lobby trying to calm her nerves. She couldn't believe that this shit was happening to her. She looked tired…defeated.

"Police are here," the kid said to Demi.

"And?" she spat back.

The young kid rolled his eyes and let out an irate sigh, causing Demi to shoot a murderous look at him. "What the fuck you sighin' for and rollin' yo' fuckin' eyes at me? Niggah, you gonna reimburse me for what they took out my room?"

The kid looked dumfounded and remained quiet. He didn't know what to say.

"I thought so!" she yelled with a serious attitude.

The cops walked into the lobby looking relaxed, barely catching wind of Demi cursing out the young clerk.

"We got a call about a robbery," they inquired, staring at the kid and then over at Demi, who looked uninterested that they'd even showed up.

"Yes, this young lady's room was robbed earlier," the clerk mentioned, pointing to Demi.

"You okay, Ma'am?" the taller officer asked, staring at Demi who still remained seated and indifferent.

"I'm fine," she said.

"Hey, what's with the attitude?" the shorter officer asked with a stern tone.

"I'm just upset and tired," she commented.

"We understand that…but we're here to help you. So don't get snippy with us. You understand?" he continued.

Demi looked the two cops up and down, then said to them dryly, "Yeah, I understand."

They both approached her looking like they could've cared less about her being robbed. The officers knew that the hotel was in a bad area and robberies among other things were frequent.

"What room are you in?" the short cop with the dirty blond hair and blue eyes asked.

"Room 116," she answered.

"What was taken from you?" the taller cop asked.

"They went through my shit and took all my cash."

"You know this is not a nice area," the short cop stated with a smug stare.

125

"And? Y'all gonna take a report or what?" Demi asked, becoming displeased with the interrogation.

"Look, don't tell us how to do our jobs," the short officer shot back.

Demi sighed. She knew that everything was a complete loss. The two officers were a joke.

The officers went through her room with the same less than caring attitudes as before, then told Demi they would file a report. She knew better to believe them.

When the cops left, Demi slammed the door behind them and cursed loudly. "Fuck!"

She looked around her room and tried to hold back her tears this time. But the devastation that her room was in, along with her life, made her burst into tears. With her back against the door, she slowly slid down to the floor and let the tears continue to flow. She pulled her knees close to her chest and gripped herself tightly.

"Why does this shit gotta be so fuckin' hard?" she asked out loud, hoping to receive the answer from somebody.

 # Thirteen

Alex's phone continually went straight to voice mail.
Demi had already left two urgent messages for him, hoping that
he would call her back soon. Becoming frustrated, she cursed
herself for not having a phone on-hand. She had no money and
when the manager finally showed up, he claimed that the hotel
wasn't responsible for her loss. They got into a heated argument
and Demi almost went across his head with her fist. She eventually packed her things and tried to come up with a plan. She was
in a serious squeeze and felt the pressure tightening every hour.
The room was quiet and dusk settled over the cheesy downtown
hotel. She thought about trying to go back to Harlem, but then
thought against it. For her, it would be like giving up, which
wasn't about to happen.

She went into the bathroom to wash her tear stained face
and stared at her reflection in the mirror; a reflection that contained hurt and pain. With her eyes in distress, she suddenly remembered one option that was available to her. She rushed into
the room and quickly searched through her clothing until she re-
trieved Brenda's phone number. Demi was reluctant to call, but
with her failing situation, it was her only option.

After walking to use the payphone outside, Demi slowly
dialed Brenda's number and clutched the phone to her ear with
her heart pounding like a track star's sneakers hitting the pave-
ment. Demi didn't know what to do if Brenda didn't pick up or
worse, if it was the wrong number. But after the fourth ring,
Demi let out a sigh of relief when she heard a voice on the other
end saying, "Hello?"

"Brenda?" she asked incredulously.

"Who callin'?"

"It's Demi, the girl from the other day. Remember, we met outside yo' job after the bullshit wit' Jorel," she reminded.

"Yeah, I remember you. I thought you wasn't gonna call," Brenda stated matter-of-factly.

Demi didn't know how to come at her. She didn't want to seem desperate, so she tried to pick up her attitude and hide the pain in her voice.

"Yeah, can I holla at you about sumthin?" Demi asked.

"About what?"

There was a brief, awkward silence over the phone as Demi tried to get her words together. Her mind raced and her hands started to sweat as she held the phone tightly. She hated asking a stranger for favors, but with only the change she'd gotten back from the cab fare in her pocket, pride would just have to take a back seat.

"Bitch, speak!" Brenda stated loudly, becoming irritated with the dragged out conversation.

"Look, I'm gonna be real wit' you. I need a place to stay right now, and I know you offered me somewhere to lay my head the other day. Is yo' offer still good?" Demi asked straightforwardly.

"Yeah, I still gotta place for you to sleep. My word is always good," Brenda stated boastfully.

For some reason, Demi didn't like her tone. But she swallowed her pride and sucked in her attitude. "Well, can I come through tonight?"

"I offered, didn't I? Take down my address if you wanna come."

Demi hated Brenda's smart mouth. "A'ight hold on, I need to get a paper and pen."

"Hurry, I ain't got all night." She listened to Brenda speak with an antsy tone.

Whateva bitch, Demi thought.

She rushed to get something to write with from the front desk and returned within seconds, ready to take down Brenda's

128

information. "I'm ready," Demi said.

Brenda informed Demi that she lived in Inglewood, which was about twenty minutes from where Demi was staying. When Demi had everything written down, she told Brenda that she would be at her place within an hour or two.

Demi rushed into her room to get her things and called for a cab. She wanted Benny to come get her, because she barely had any cash on her and Benny was a sweetheart. She walked back to the payphone, exhausted from a very trying day and dialed Benny's number praying he would pick up, and more importantly be available.

"It's Benny," he answered.

"Benny, it's me, Demi."

"Hey pretty gal, how ya been?" Benny greeted in his always affable tone.

"Benny, please tell me that you're free. I need you right now."

"Pretty gal, everything okay?"

"No, not really. I need a ride to Inglewood."

"Inglewood?" Benny questioned.

"Yes, I'm goin' to stay wit' a friend out there. I need to get out this hotel room."

"Ya no need to worry, pretty gal. I just dropped off a passenger and I'll come to get you soon," he assured her.

Demi breathed a sigh of relief. "Oh, goodness. Thank you Benny, you're an angel."

She hung up the phone and dashed to her room. After making sure all her belongings were packed, she suddenly felt nervous. Demi could already tell that Brenda was a handful, and definitely wasn't sure if the bitch could be trusted, but it was her only option.

Before Benny arrived, Demi tried to call Alex from the payphone at home and at the office a few more times, but he wasn't answering which was starting to piss her off. Flashbacks of all the drama with Jorel began to invade her thoughts, so she decided to leave him a piece of her mind.

"Niggah, I just left yo' house and now you can't even answer yo' fuckin' phone. What's good wit' that? I need you right now, but obviously it looks like you got what you wanted and now you wanna ignore me. That's real fucked up. I thought you wanted to manage me. Yeah right. Like I said before, I heard it all before. It ain't nothin' but a bunch of bitch-ass niggahs out here in L.A! Fuck you, Alex! Fo' real…FUCK YOU!" Demi cursed loudly.

She slammed the phone down viciously, hoping she broke something that would make the hotel come out their pockets for a new one.

When Benny pulled up several minutes later, Demi was already outside waiting with her bags in hand. She looked dog-tired and crushed, but managed to smile when Benny stepped out the car to help with her bags.

"Hey, pretty gal," Benny greeted with his usual warm smile.

Demi just smiled and walked toward the car.

"Let me get that for you," Benny said, reaching for her bags.

But surprisingly, Demi reached out and hugged him. "You're a good friend to me, Benny. Please stay that way."

Benny hugged her back. "Is the city getting too rough for ya?"

"I'm just tired of the bullshit."

She began to free tears from her eyes as she hugged Benny for some comfort. Being in his grip, Benny felt like the father she never knew. In her short time of knowing him, he was already supportive and caring.

"Why can't I get it right, Benny? Why?" Demi cried out, as she continued to clutch onto him, wetting his shirt with her tears.

"Oh, pretty gal, hang in there. Ya time will come. Hey, if it was easy, then everybody would have it," he stated wisely.

Benny continued to console Demi for a short moment and reassured her that her time in Hollywood would be a tremendous one. He always knew the right words to say. Demi finally let go of her grip and dried her tears.

"Thank you for that, Benny. You're such a blessin'."

"What happened here, pretty gal?"

"Somebody robbed me, Benny. Somebody broke into my room and took every dime I had saved. I don't have any money to pay you."

"Don't worry. The ride is on me. All I ask is when you make it into Hollywood and win your first Oscar, show Benny a little love when you do your acceptance speech on stage."

"Benny, I'm gonna do better than that. You and my daughter are gonna be up there wit' me," Demi said, smiling.

"Hey, what are friends for," Benny said. "Now c'mon, let's get ya to ya destination."

Demi jumped into the front seat of the cab, feeling at ease with her newfound friend.

"Inglewood, huh? Not a nice place to be sometimes," Benny informed her with a concerned stare.

"I know, but right now I don't have any other choice."

 *Fourteen*

Nightfall had come by the time Demi arrived in the notorious Inglewood neighborhood. The streets were bustling with residents going about their business and several young thugs were lingering around the avenues and boulevards; drinking, smoking, or busying themselves by gambling on street corners. A settled, but uneasy mood stirred through the streets, with a handful of gang members enjoying the night with their homies, but were heavily armed knowing that at any given time, anything could quickly pop off on their streets.

Benny slowly navigated his cab through the treacherous streets that were known to be blood territory. He was very familiar with the area and knew to be cautious. He drove down Crenshaw Boulevard with Demi looking closely for Brenda's address.

"I don't like it out here," Benny stated, with his eyes focused on the road. "Lot of gang activity."

Demi knew the risks, but needed a place to stay. She stared at the one story homes that lined the streets with tall palm trees that made the block somewhat look like an urban paradise. An area that immediately reminded her of the street that Tre and Doughboy lived on in the *Boyz n Da Hood* movie.

"There it go…right there," Demi pointed out.

Benny came to a halt in front of a white one story house with blue trim, faded grass, and a silver iron fence. There was also a four door burgundy Benz parked in the driveway. It looked like a decent place to stay. The block seemed quiet and peaceful enough for Demi, but she knew that looks could be deceiving. A block down, Demi noticed several dudes standing on the street corner and observing Benny's cab closely.

Demi sighed. She stared at the house, trying to search for any danger. But it looked all right to her. From a distance anyway.

"Ya cool, pretty gal?" Benny asked.

Demi nodded.

"C'mon…let me take ya bag to the door."

Benny stepped out the cab first, followed by Demi with a troubled look emerging.

"Pretty gal, don't look so down. Things will get better for ya soon, you'll see," Benny said.

"I hope so."

Before they reached the door, Benny passed Demi a hundred dollar bill, saying, "Here's a lil' something to ease ya mind from the troubles."

"Benny, I can't…you have your kids," Demi rejected.

"Pretty gal, ya need it more than me right now. Take the money and put it to good use."

"Benny, I don't know what to say," Demi replied, trying not to become emotional.

"Just stay positive about ya future and you'll be good."

Demi wanted to give Benny a huge hug and kiss, but before she could, the front door opened. Brenda stood in the front doorway, peering at the two with a smirk across her face. She had on a pair of tight, white coochie cutting shorts that hugged her thick thighs, with a pair of tube socks stuffed into a pair of black house slippers, and a tight T-shirt that highlighted her huge tits. She was very attractive, thick and curvy, but could definitely get ghetto and wild.

Benny gave Demi a consoling hug and walked away. As Demi watched him walk to his cab, she told herself that he felt like the father she never had. She was sad to see him leave.

"You comin' in or what?" Brenda asked.

"Yeah," Demi replied with a frown.

Demi picked up her bag and marched inside. When she stepped into the small living room area she was somewhat impressed with the décor. The living room was furnished with a coffee colored leather sectional that was lined against the rustic color walls. There was also a sixty-five inch LCD plasma flatscreen, surrounded by a high-end entertainment system that took up an entire wall. The plush carpet felt like Demi was stepping on clouds.

Brenda's place looked cozy and neat, but for some reason Demi couldn't get rid of the uneasiness that crept through her like an itch that couldn't be scratched.

"So, what happened to you?" Brenda asked, pulling out a cigarette and searching for a lighter.

"Nothin'. I ain't in the mood to talk right now," Demi said with an attitude.

Brenda looked at Demi with a foul glare. "Look bitch, you in my crib, so you respect me and my shit. I'm the one doin' you a fuckin' favor."

"I wonder why?" Demi mumbled under her breath.

"What you say?" Brenda barked back.

"Nuthin…look where do I sleep?"

Brenda lit the cigarette that dangled from her lips and took a long deep pull. She then exhaled a clear thick smoke, while gazing at Demi in an authoritative kind of way.

"For now, you can sleep on the couch, it's comfortable enough. And leave your bag on the side. I keep my crib lookin' nice, so don't be comin' in here fuckin' up my shit. I'm the only bitch who can smoke in my spot, so don't try that shit either. You can use the bathroom down the hall to wash your ass. I'm being nice, cuz I like you, but don't fuck me, Demi, cuz I'm not that bitch to fuck wit'…you hear me?" Brenda stated with conviction in her tone.

"Yeah, I hear you," Demi replied nonchalantly.

"Look, I know L.A. is hard, but I guarantee that you start fuckin' wit me, and you gonna be doin' your thang. I know peoples that can hook you up and put you on. You willin' to make some money?" she asked.

"It depends…"

"Bitch, in this city, you either getting paid or you broke. And look at you, you homeless now, ain't got a fuckin' dime to your name, right? So, what you got goin' for you, huh? A wet pussy and a dry fuckin' purse," Brenda said.

"I'm gonna be an actress or a model...or both," Demi stated with certainty.

Brenda laughed. "An actress? Yo, you know how many wanna-be actresses there are in this fuckin' city...take a number, cuz you like, what, one out of a million. And out of that million or whateva...yo, you only got like a handful that will actually do somthin'. The other failures end up like you, on the curb, still hoping and wondering what the fuck happened. Why they shit went wrong? Bitch, you gotta get yours any way possible. See, I got a job, but I still get mines out there. And see a bitch like you, you cute. You can get money in this city. You ain't gotta be a broke bitch. Plus you from Harlem, too. Shit, you need to be gettin' your ends fo' real."

Demi stood there listening to Brenda's so-called motivational speech. She was from the streets and wasn't naive to what the bitch was talking about. She returned the same hard stare that Brenda gave out and bluntly asked, "Are you tryin' to pimp me? That's why you got me up in your crib?"

"Bitch, don't get it twisted. I don't need no ends from you. I got my own, bitch...look around. Do I look like I need pennies from you? Look, get rid of the fuckin' attitude, cuz this is L.A, not Harlem. Remember, you gonna need a friend in this town, and I'm a good friend to have. I know people and I can put you on to some paper and business. But don't test me, and don't piss me the fuck off, cuz I can fuck your shit up quick and make sure L.A is hell for you," Brenda threatened.

Demi didn't reply. She just stood there with a cool look about her.

"You listening?" Brenda asked.

"No disrespect, but I'm tired, can I get some sleep now?"

Brenda took another pull from her Newport studying Demi's demeanor. "I got pillows and a blanket in the closet."

Demi knew that she was in no position to argue or go against Brenda, with Brenda having the upper hand. Demi knew she had to play her role for now until she came correct with her situation.

Brenda threw two pillows and a blanket on the couch. "Get some sleep, tomorrow is a new day."

Demi stripped down to her bra and panties and tried to get comfortable on the couch under the blanket. She rested her head against the pillows and thought about home and her daughter. She missed her daughter dearly. She closed her eyes and repeated what Brenda had said, "Yeah, tomorrow is a new day."

The lights went off and the room became still and quiet—somewhat like her career move.

 *Fifteen*

Demi woke up the next day to a few dudes, smoking, drinking and talking all around her. She was stunned. She counted six altogether. They were mostly dressed in red, with red bandanas hanging loosely from their clothing, or tied around their heads. Some were swathed with tattoos or wore red fitted baseball caps and other red clothing, obviously indicating that they were bloods.

"Did we wake you up?" one of the dudes said to Demi. He then took it upon himself to sit down right beside her.

He was tall and had on a wife-beater, dark colored jeans and a red bandana around his neck. A bandana that looked like it could be pulled up to disguise his face at any moment.

Demi looked at him before searching the room looking for Brenda. She clutched the blanket tightly to her chest, fully aware that she was still in her bra and panties. She didn't want to appear nervous, but knew that being half-naked in a room full of niggahs wasn't good. The last thing she wanted was to be raped.

"What's your name?" the dude seated next to her asked.

Demi ignored his question. A few dudes, who were taking pulls from the weed being passed around, couldn't help but to stare at her. Demi felt like she was a blood-drenched piece of meat in a lions' den.

"Where's Brenda?" Demi asked, sitting up in a better position with the blanket still pulled closed to her.

"She be back. She went out wit' Nico for a minute to handle some business. But you good," a stocky man stated.

139

He took a pull from the weed and constantly kept gawking at Demi with a look in his eyes that made her uneasy. He had short braids with scruffy facial hair, a wide nose, and was very unattractive.

"What's your name?" the stocky man asked.

"Don't worry about it," Demi snapped.

He chuckled and replied with, "Bitch, you know who I be?"

Demi sighed. She was ready to get up, get her shit and leave. She didn't want to put up with the bullshit that she knew was coming.

"Look, can y'all niggahs leave so I can get dressed?" she asked.

"Damn, shorti, you a feisty lil'…" The man sitting next to her stopped in mid-sentence. "Hold up. I fuckin' seen yo' ass before." He stared at Demi for a few seconds. "What a minute, you that bitch who tried to play me in McDonalds."

Demi looked at the thug, and realized it was indeed the guy who'd harassed her.

"Oh, yeah. I told you bitch, you'd see me again. You remember me? I'm Lyfe," he said in a cocky tone. "Now, let's see what you got goin' on under that blanket."

He tugged at her covers a bit, tryin' to pull it from her chest, hoping to catch a nice view, but Demi held onto it tightly. She tried desperately to come up with a plan to get dressed without the dudes trying to push their dicks into her.

She scanned the room and saw that her bag looked untouched, which was a good thing.

"Leave her ass alone!" the stocky man yelled out.

Lyfe frowned. "Fuck that, Mist. This bitch real disrespectful."

"Well, she'll get hers then," Mist replied.

This time Lyfe smiled. He stared at Demi. "Yeah, my homie is right. What the fuck is your name anyway?"

"Look, can y'all niggahs just leave so I can get dressed?" Demi shouted.

Lyfe looked back at his boy. "See, I told you."

"Damn, you must be naked under that blanket. We seen pussy before. It ain't nuthin' brand new to us," Mist said.

He walked over to Demi with the burning joint in his hand. "You smoke?" he asked, trying to pass Demi the weed.

Demi just sighed and caught a serious attitude. She was about to jump off the couch, sayin' *fuck it,* and grab her shit to change in another room.

The blood members were making her feel uncomfortable, but luckily she was used to being around hood niggahs and knew their demeanor. When Demi was about to get up, the front door opened and Brenda came marching in with a bag in her hand, and a guy following close behind.

Demi sighed with relief.

Dressed like a real hooch on the block, Brenda wore some skin tight, black coochie cutting shorts and a tight cut off T-shirt exposing her pierced belly button.

Brenda swung her long multi-colored braids over her shoulder and looked over at Demi. "Damn, Lyfe and Mist, why the fuck y'all up on my girl like that? Give her some fuckin' room to breathe. Shit, y'all niggahs thirsty like that!"

"What's up wit' your girl? Why she actin' stank?" Mist asked.

"Niggah, she ain't tryin' to have your hot stank breath up in her face. Back the fuck off her Mist," Brenda continued.

From her demeanor with the fellas, Demi knew Brenda was a woman you didn't want to mess with. Mist backed off Demi and reached for the 40oz Malt liquor bottle that was being passed around.

Brenda walked over to Demi. "You good right?"

"I need to talk to you in private," Demi said with a serious look.

"Bitch, what you gotta say now?" Brenda shot back.

Demi looked passed her and focused on the unwanted guests in the room. She didn't want them in her business.

Brenda glanced back and said, "What…you worried

about them?" When Demi didn't respond she started yelling. "Y'all niggahs need to wait outside for a minute, let me and my girl talk."

"Why that bitch actin' all shy and shit, like niggahs ain't never seen tits and ass before?" another blood member stated loudly.

"Man, shorti, if we wanted the pussy, we would'a took that shit from you. Outta respect for Brenda, you lucky you her girl," Mist said, as he slowly exited the room to chill outside.

Demi didn't care about any of their comments. She was happy to see them leave the room. When they were all gone, Demi finally removed the tightly wrapped blanket from around her body and stood up.

"You beefin' 'cuz you ain't want niggahs to see you in your panties and bra," Brenda said.

"Look, why I gotta wake up to find a bunch of dudes around me. What the fuck you runnin' here?" Demi barked.

"Bitch, watch your fuckin' mouth, 'cuz you in my crib. Don't be screaming on me. What the fuck is wrong wit' you?"

"How you gonna leave me here alone wit' those niggahs? I don't fuckin' know them," Demi hissed.

"They wasn't gonna fuckin' touch you, they cool peoples. What the fuck you so worried about anyway? You got fuckin' shelter right?"

Demi sucked her teeth.

"Look bitch, don't forget where you at and who had your back when you ain't had no where to go. So respect me, cuz I will quickly fuck your shit up. Understand?" Brenda barked.

Demi just stood there speechless, without emotion.

"We about to get somthin' to eat, so go wash your ass and get dressed. You need to relax and stop being so uptight," Brenda added.

Demi wanted to leave badly, but felt trapped because she was the new girl in town and had no one else to turn to. But she knew that would all change soon once some doors started to open for her. She would be able to get her own place and wouldn't have to worry about the bullshit that she was putting up with.

Demi grabbed her suitcase and asked Brenda where she could go to freshen up. Brenda pointed her to the bathroom down the hall for her to shower and then informed her that there was a spare bedroom for her to get dressed in.

"How many bedrooms you have in here?" Demi asked.

"Three," Brenda answered coolly.

Demi chuckled with disbelief. "Three bedrooms and you made me sleep on the couch."

"Bitch, I don't know you like that."

Demi shook her head and sucked her teeth again. "Whateva!"

She grabbed a few things from her suitcase and marched toward the bathroom—already having a fucked up day.

She made sure the bathroom door was locked, not wanting any unwanted company while she was showering. Demi didn't trust Brenda at all; there was something about the woman that rubbed her the wrong way. She stripped down and stepped into the warm shower, allowing the lukewarm running water to cascade off her skin. She tried to collect her thoughts and considered the choices she had. She needed to do so much, but her situation pushed her back a few steps almost making it feel like it was impossible for her to continue forward.

Demi spent about ten minutes in the shower until she heard Brenda banging on the door telling her to hurry up. After getting out, she wrapped a towel around her body then went into one of the three bedrooms to get dressed. She decided to wear some Bebe jeans that showed off her thick hips and legs with a green halter top. She looked cute and styled her hair into a side ponytail.

When Demi was finally fresh and ready, she followed Brenda outside where there was a sleek black '08 Escalade sitting on 26" chromed rims with tinted windows parked out front. Demi was impressed. Several other guys were standing around the truck doing the same thing they were doing inside the house—smoking and drinking. When they saw Demi dressed, and looking stunning, they couldn't take their eyes off her.

"Damn shorti. You lookin' nice, what's good wit' that," Lyfe said.

Demi just rolled her eyes.

But the one man who did catch her attention stepped out from behind the driver's side looking like a breath of fresh air, causing her eyes to widen with lust. He was about six-one with a dark complexion and sported long braids that ran down his back. He had a tight chiseled physique and very well-defined, but tattooed arms. In true L.A. fashion he wore a black tank-top, loose fitting khakis, and sported a fresh pair of Converse sneakers. He was blinged out in jewelry and looked like he could be the poster boy for an American Gangsta.

His character alone indicated that he was the head of his set. He looked like a killer, and carried himself like it. Demi locked eyes with him and felt a thrilling chill race through her. She wanted to scream out *Damn*…but kept her composure and tried not to make it seem so obvious that she was attracted to him.

He approached her with a look that said confidence and thug life. "Where you from?" he asked.

"Harlem," Demi replied humbly, knowing he was probably dangerous to her health.

"How you know B?" he asked, referring to Brenda.

"We just met," she answered honestly.

"You know who the fuck I am?"

Demi shook her head no.

"They call me Nico. I run shit out here. Crenshaw Mafia," he said, throwing up his gang sign in front of Demi for show.

Demi was quiet. It amazed her how she'd come to Hollywood to break into the business and ended up in the presence of a notorious bloods gang in a very rough neighborhood.

Nico looked her up and down and loved what he saw. Demi filled out her jeans nicely and Nico shook his head approvingly.

Demi glanced over at Brenda who was surprisingly quiet when Nico stepped up to talk. A clear indication that Nico was definitely the shot caller. It was the first time that Brenda had nothing to say around her.

"I want you to ride wit' me. We rollin' to get somthin' to eat," Nico said.

Demi knew that with her situation, she pretty much didn't have a choice. So she quickly agreed. She got into the passenger side of Nico's sleek Escalade, with Brenda and Lyfe climbing into the backseat, leaving the rest of the gang to go their own way.

Nico drove off and placed an old school Snoop CD into the player. He then glanced over at Demi and asked, "What you hungry for?"

"Whateva," Demi said.

"I gotta place for you," he said and made a U-turn on the block.

The four ended up having lunch at a well known spot on E. Compton Blvd. called D&A Bar-B-Q Pit. The restaurant only had a window in the front to order from, so after getting the food, everybody climbed back inside the truck.

Demi dined on some rib tips, potato salad, baked beans and quickly downed a large black cherry soda. She was hungry. With so much stress and running around, she hadn't had a decent meal since Alex cooked breakfast.

"Damn girl, you keep eatin' like that and you gonna blow up. That shit wouldn't be cute," Nico commented.

"I'm starvin'," Demi admitted.

Nico let out a smile. "Nah, go ahead, enjoy the meal. It's on me."

Demi continued to eat, while Nico looked back at Brenda and verbalized something with his eyes.

She quickly caught on to the hint and said, "I need a fuckin' cigarette. Lyfe, walk with me to the store."

"I'm still eatin'," Lyfe contested.

Nico then shot Lyfe a bothered stare, indicating that he

didn't have a choice. After licking his fingers from the ribs, Lyfe followed Brenda out the car leaving Nico with Demi to talk.

When the two were out of sight, Nico stared at Demi. "So, what you got goin' for yourself? You know comin' out here from New York."

"Well, I know it might sound stupid, but I came out here to try and break into some actin', and maybe some modelin'."

"Really...what you been in so far?"

Demi lowered her head. "Nothin', yet."

"Well, shit everybody gotta start somewhere, right? I wouldn't worry if I were you. As fine as you are, I can see you bein' the next Halle Berry," Nico complimented.

"Halle Berry ain't got shit on me, boo," Demi boasted.

Nico leaned back to get a better look at her. "Damn, so you confident, huh? I ain't mad at ya. But you know you need money to make it out here. L.A can become a very expensive town. You gotta pay to play. You gotta plan for yourself?"

Demi didn't know how to answer him. She had a plan, but it all went to shit quickly, so now she found herself stuck between a rock and a hard place.

She sucked her teeth and said, "I don't know, it's like I take two steps forward before gettin' knocked five steps back."

"You a pretty woman, Demi, fo' real. I see the potential in you. You know you can get money out here with your looks and that body. You would cake off like a muthafucka."

Demi looked at him with a disapproving stare. "Hold up, you, a pimp?"

He laughed. "Nah, shorti...far from it. I'm just a niggah who's tryin' to look out for you, that's all. I know of a good thing when I see it," he returned cooly.

"So, why you comin' at me sideways like that?"

"Look, I'm gonna be real wit' you, I like your style and your looks, you can go places wit' the right management."

Demi sucked her teeth and rolled her eyes, saying to herself, *Oh no not again. I don' heard this shit all before.*

"Why the fuck you rollin' your eyes?"

146

"Look, I've been fucked over before. Besides, the shit you spittin', if I had a dollar for every niggah that done told me that shit, I'd be good right now."

"Well, I ain't every niggah, I'm me…Nico, an O.G up in this muthafucka and I'm tryin' to look out for you, shorti. No disrespect, but look at you…you got the looks and the fuckin' body, but what you got goin' for yourself, huh? You got paper in your pockets right now?"

Demi remained silent.

"You gotta place to stay for the night if Brenda decides to kick you out?"

Demi continued to be silent.

"You gotta job right now?"

There was even more silence from Demi.

"So, that pretty face and nice body is good to look at and maybe fuck, but if you ain't got shit goin' for you right now, then bitch you dead to the world. Like a fuckin' Benz wit' no engine. Just pretty to fuckin' look at, but you can't drive the shit nowhere." Nico stopped to stare at her.

Demi didn't know what to say. He hit buttons on her that no one else had pushed before. All of a sudden, she wasn't hungry anymore.

Nico knew that he had struck some kind of nerve. Demi sat there speechless and somewhat taken aback. In a brief moment, he summed up her life.

"Look, I ain't tryin' to hurt your feelings, but reality…we live in a ugly world, and if you ain't got somebody lookin' out for you and watchin' your back, then you gonna get fucked every time in life. See, a niggah like me, I came up wit' my set, my homies that I ride or die with for life. Nobody fucks wit' us. Crenshaw Mafia for life," Nico called out, quickly flashing his gang's sign again. "Now, if you fucks wit' me, then nobody will fuck wit' you, that's a promise. I got many connects and I'm well-known every fuckin' where in this city. You see this," Nico said, pointing to the ice on his hands and wrist, "I ain't get all this by being stupid. I gets paid out here and got a crew of niggahs comin' up wit' me in this industry shit."

Demi knew a niggah with the gift of gab and knew Nico definitely had the skills to talk. He was a thug, but also was smart and charming. Demi was turned on by him. She listened to him talk and took in everything that he said.

"I feel you, yo. I definitely need to get mines out here, that's what I came out here to do," Demi replied.

"If you feel me, shorti, then let's make some money together," Nico suggested.

"I ain't tryin' to be standing on some dirty ass street corner trickin' for singles."

"Yo, you think that wit' a fine shorti like you, I'm gonna put you on some corner to fuck some trick for a few dollars? You better give a niggah better credit than that. I ain't got time to worry about pennies from a trick. I'm into bigger thangs," he said with conviction.

"Like what?" Demi asked.

"Films, internet, clubs, I'm about that paper. And if you fucks wit' me, I can have you makin' up to two thousand a day," he assured her.

"Two thousand?" Demi questioned. "Doin' what, porn?"

"Its a billion dollar business, shorti. Pussy will never go bankrupt."

"So, you want me to start my film career off by doin' porn?"

"You gotta start somewhere, right? Look, the only people that start off at the top, are the ones diggin' holes."

Demi grinned. "Cute."

"Look at me, Demi," Nico said with authority in his tone.

Demi held Nico's gaze and heard him say, "You want what I got right…the money, the clothes, the fame, the clout in this town. You wanna be a star, right?"

She nodded her head. "I'm tryin."

"Well, tryin' ain't gonna do it for you. You need to start somewhere and get wit' the right people in this city. And I'm the right niggah to get wit'. I look at you, and know you won't be doin' porn for that long, cuz you're too fuckin' cute. You gonna get picked up and do your thang in Hollywood. But let me pull your coat to this, you fucked niggahs before, probably for free right? And was it worth it? Wit' me, you can do what you love and get paid generously from this shit. And when you start stackin' that paper, this fuckin' town is yours to play wit," Nico explained.

Nico had Demi seriously thinking about the idea. For her, he came with some valid points. Not to mention, him being easy on the eyes helped with her decision somewhat. But she was tired of being lied to, abused, and mistreated. She thought that maybe Nico was right. It was who you know and not what you know.

Her mind raced a mile a minute. She was nervous about doing porn. But then she thought about how she'd fucked niggahs for free, and was still nowhere in her life.

She looked at Nico and asked, "I'm gonna be safe doin' this wit' you? I don't need anymore problems in my life."

"I'ma treat you wit' mad love when you fuck wit' me. I like you, so you ain't gotta worry about any troubles."

Nico then reached into his pocket and pulled out a wad of bills, mostly hundreds and twenties. He then peeled off five hundred dollar bills and passed it over to Demi, saying, "Just to let you know how sure I am of you, I'm giving you a small advance on your first film."

Demi took the five hundred. She didn't know what to say.

"Take it and don't stress yourself," Nico said.

Demi took the cash knowing that it solidified her place in the porn industry. She said to herself, *All I have to do is make some quick cash, get paid, then move on to bigger thangs.*

Nico assured Demi of her safety and let her know that she was going to get paid. Demi hoped everything went smoothly; she didn't want anymore mishaps with her career. She wanted to believe in Nico and decided to take that chance with him. She felt like life had been fuckin' her for too long.

Now, it was time for her to do the fucking; this time getting paid in the process.

 Sixteen

Demi all of a sudden got nervous about doing porn, but had already taken the small advance from Nico. She sat on the sofa in Brenda's living room just thinking to herself. She'd come to L.A. to get into film, but adult film was a different playing field. She wasn't a stranger to sex and being promiscuous with men at times, but sometimes a porn star could be typecast in the entertainment business. She wanted to move on to a better career for herself one day.

Brenda's place was finally empty and quiet, leaving Demi with some peace. She sat on the chair going through her suitcase and arranging a few outfits together. She heard Brenda taking a shower in the bathroom. She held the five hundred that Nico gave her in her hand and wanted to stash it someplace safe. She didn't want to make the same mistake twice. But the only place safe enough to hide the money was on her personally. She folded the money in her hand and stuffed it into her bra. It was the best way not to lose it again.

Brenda wanted to go out and hit a popular club. She wanted to take Demi into the city and have her mingle with a few people. Demi was ready. She felt the more people she got to know, the better her chances were in getting some kind of gig or employment for herself. Then she wouldn't have to feel trapped in a dying situation. The night was young, and the warm California weather circulated through the house, causing Demi to feel sticky and somewhat drained. She sat on the couch fanning herself with a leaflet, hoping that Brenda would turn on the A.C. It felt like Brenda was purposely trying to make Demi's stay at her place a living hell.

Demi smiled to herself, like she had a private joke. She remembered how Brenda's whole demeanor changed when Nico was around. Suddenly Brenda became the one who was being told what to do, instead of the bossy, foul mouth bitch that she was. Demi chuckled, thinking about Nico and how good he looked. She was curious about his package and wondered if all of him looked as good in his jeans as he did on the outside. She wanted to fuck him, but knew that he and Brenda probably had a little thing between the two.

Demi noticed the sudden glare in Brenda's eyes when Nico got real close to her and showed more interest in her instead of Brenda. But she knew she didn't need any problems with Brenda, because the bitch was her life line and Demi couldn't jeopardize her temporary residence for a piece of dick; even though it was tempting.

Brenda came walking from the bathroom wrapped in a white towel and looking fresh from her shower. She looked over at Demi seated comfortably on the couch and said, "You need to start gettin' ready. And wear somthin' cute and sexy tonight. I'm takin' you around a lot of good people."

"Where we goin' anyway?" Demi asked.

"Bitch, why you ask so many fuckin' questions? We goin' out, that's all you need to know," Brenda retorted.

"Why you gotta have an attitude all the time?"

"Cuz you think you cute. Bitch, I saw the way you had Nico starin' at you today. Yo, let me tell you somthin'. It's just business wit' y'all two. Don't take his nice words and charmin' attitude toward you personal. I fucked wit' the niggah fa a minute, and I'm his main bitch in this city. So don't think just because you bat your eyes at him and stick out your chest, that you doin' somthin'…cuz you ain't." Brenda rolled her eyes. "You just a bitch he about to put into one of his porno movies and have you get fucked by some big dick blood niggah and make him some money."

From that statement alone, Demi already knew that Brenda felt threatened by her. It was the hate talking, and Demi had been through it all before.

"Yo', can I ask you somthin'? Why the fuck you got me here? You the one that brought him around me," Demi returned.

"Bitch, don't get it confused. You only here for the money and your looks. I saw some potential in you and knew the business could work wit' you, a'ight."

Demi just sighed, knowing Brenda had issues of her own and was insecure about her position with Nico. But Demi couldn't deny that Brenda did have it going on from head to toe. She was a bad bitch, shapely with a raw appeal, and if she had some class, then she would probably give Demi a run for her money.

At times, Demi needed to hold her own around Brenda, even though she knew Brenda had the upper hand…for now anyway. But Demi needed to constantly remind herself that her condition would only be temporary and that she was the badder bitch in the house.

Swallowing her pride and ego, Demi stood up from the couch, looked over at Brenda who stood by the end of the hallway and asked, "Can I least get a bedroom tonight, Brenda? I mean, you got three in here."

Brenda sucked her teeth, turned away from Demi. Before walking down the hall, she uttered, "Just make sure you look nice tonight."

Demi rolled her eyes and wanted to shout out, *"Fuck you, bitch!"* But she kept her composure and went into the bathroom to shower.

An hour later, both ladies left the house looking like two Hollywood divas. Brenda looked remarkable in a money green strapless dress that hugged every one of her curves like a glove. She also rocked a pair of black sandals that laced up her ankles and tons of MAC lip gloss. Her braids were also done up in a high ponytail, which gave off an exotic appeal. Demi followed behind Brenda to the car, dressed in an old Marc Jacobs silk dress which showed off her cleavage. She'd even taken the time to wet her hair, and applied some mousse on it, so her good strands could curl up nicely. Whenever she wore it that way, it always brought out her Puerto Rican heritage.

Demi got into Brenda's E-class Benz and sat back, admiring how the butter soft leather felt against her skin. Brenda quickly backed out the driveway and sped off, maintaining a heavy foot on the gas pedal. She did at least sixty down the block.

The ladies ended up at some stylish club in downtown Los Angeles twenty-five minutes later. The atmosphere looked posh and fashionable, with valet parking out front. Demi was impressed, because the entire time, she'd been thinking that they were going to end up at some hood spot in the ghetto. But with the high-end cars lining the streets, and the people not wearing gang colors, it appeared to be a pretty reputable place.

Brenda pulled up to the valet and stepped out, where a young black man in a bright red vest jogged over to her. Demi jumped out and followed Brenda's lead.

"Take care of my baby," Brenda said to the valet as she walked toward the club.

The outside was crowded with a diverse ethnicity of people, and there was a long line to get in, but the way Brenda moved about, it looked as if she wasn't the least bit worried. She moved straight to the front entrance where three burly bouncers watched the door and handled the crowd outside. Brenda strutted to the entrance, walking like she had major clout, then smiled when she saw the three men.

"Hey, B," one of the bouncers greeted.

"What's good, Derrick," Brenda replied, sneaking a folded fifty into his hand.

"Not much baby," the man said. He lifted the rope, giving her easy access into the posh looking club.

"Good lookin' out," Brenda said, then pranced past him with Demi right on her heels.

The dance floor was popping once they stepped inside, and everybody else looked like they were mingling or getting their drink on. Looking around, Demi liked the atmosphere of the place, but questioned how Brenda had so many connects. They couldn't even walk ten steps without her stopping to give somebody a kiss or a hug. It was almost as if she was a superstar.

As Demi followed Brenda through the thick crowd, she caught compliments and praises from damn near every man they passed, but she ignored them all.

"What you drinkin'?" Brenda asked when they got to the bar.

"Give me a Grand Marnier with pineapple juice."

"And let me get a white Russian," Brenda told the bartender.

"Nice club," Demi said, looking around again.

"Well, don't get too comfortable. We here on business," Brenda stated.

Business, Demi questioned herself. She thought that they were out to have a good time. But knowing Brenda, there was always something with money involved.

The bartender passed the ladies their drinks, and Brenda passed him a fifty, telling him to keep the change. Demi raised an eyebrow at her, thinking, *damn this bitch is ballin' like that?*

Brenda took a heavy sip from her white Russian, while Demi began to drink hers slowly. The DJ had a Young Joc song blaring in the club, causing Demi to do a little bounce to the beat. She had the urge to dance, but decided to wait before she started socializing.

"Brenda, what's up," a well dressed man in a three piece suit, greeted them. He was tall and handsome and looked to be wealthy.

"Hey, Chauncey," Brenda replied with a huge hug.

Chauncey looked Brenda up and down and stated, "Damn, boo. You killing it tonight. Green is your color."

"You know it," Brenda said in a cocky tone. "I'm 'bout that paper, boo."

Chauncey then turned and noticed Demi. He smiled widely while staring at her from head to toe. "Who's your

155

friend?" he asked.

"Chauncey, this is Demi…Demi, Chauncey."

Chauncey reached over for a handshake. When he took Demi's hand into his, her touch felt so soft and inviting, he almost didn't want to let her hand go. Demi didn't either, especially when she noticed the platinum, princess cut diamond pinky ring.

"You're truly beautiful," he complimented.

"Thank you," she returned.

"So, Chauncey, are the others here?" Brenda asked.

"We're all waiting," Chauncey replied.

Brenda smiled. She then turned her attention over to Demi and said, "Demi, let me talk to my homeboy for a minute in private."

Demi looked at Brenda and then to Chauncey, before walking away. When Demi was out of earshot, Brenda looked at Chauncey with an expression that said she was about her business.

"Damn, where you find her?" he asked.

"Forget all that shit. Let's talk business. I want five thousand for everything."

Chauncey smiled. "B, you were always a high price hoe."

"But I'm worth it, cuz I'm nice wit' mines. Plus I'm gonna always bring somthin' new to the table."

"Yeah, well, it's the something new that's always gonna keep you paid," Chauncey returned.

"And you know it, my transaction is still cash upfront."

"The money is waiting for you downstairs," he said. "But is she ready? We don't want any problems like before."

"Nah, Demi, she's more experienced…been in the game before and she's from New York…Harlem, ya know. That last bitch was country, only seventeen and fresh out the lake, and didn't know how to fuck. But you still got yours, right? I mean you damn near raped the bitch. And besides, Nico wants me to break her in, she's about to do films wit' us."

What Brenda told him was partially true, she was about to do porn, but Nico didn't know that Brenda was side hustling and pimping his bitches to her high price clientele.

"You sure Nico down with this?" Chauncey asked with concern.

"Look, you ain't gotta worry about him. I got this, this is my thang. You wanna fuck, right? It never stopped you before. Besides, look at her, you know the pussy's gonna be good."

Chauncey turned to spot Demi standing off looking like a goddess, noticing the heavy attention she was getting from all the males and even the females in the club. His dick got hard just by sight alone.

"You damn sure know how to pick 'em," he told Brenda.

"I got taste. I'll meet you downstairs in a few. I just wanna talk to my girl alone."

As Chauncey nodded and walked away, Brenda moved through the crowd approaching Demi. "Hey," she uttered, tapping her arm.

"What's up?" Demi asked.

"Come wit' me to the bathroom."

When the ladies walked into the bathroom, Brenda checked to see if they were alone, before she started talking.

"We about to move to the VIP section. It's private and a better party," Brenda stated. She wanted to come at Demi the right way.

"What kind of private party?" Demi asked with a raised eyebrow.

"A party where you can make you some money."

Demi sucked her teeth, knowing where the conversation was leading.

"So, you're saying that you want me to turn a trick for you. I ain't come here for that. Besides, Nico assured me that it wasn't gonna be that type of party," Demi spat.

Brenda looked frustrated with Demi's remark. She glanced at the entrance to make sure it was still clear and then threw Demi a sharp look. "Look, bitch, you gonna make five

157

hundred tonight to suck and fuck a few niggahs, and besides you already agreed to do porn wit' us. So right now, Nico wants me to break you in and see how you handle yourself in the action. He wanna make sure you don't choke when you get in front of the camera, cuz we gonna invent thousands into you. And besides, you think you gotta choice? You got paid in advance, right? If you ain't down, then where the fuck you think you gonna be sleepin' tonight," Brenda threatened.

"So, it's like that? I thought slavery ended a long time ago," Demi retorted.

"Not when you homeless and indebt to us," Brenda shot back.

Demi wanted to fuck Brenda up so bad, but once again, kept her cool.

"Come wit' me to this joint and get your groove on and get paid for it, for once. I guarantee you'll like it. "

Demi reluctantly followed Brenda through the crowded dance floor of people and headed toward a doorway that was in the back and looked off limits to everyone else. There was a heavy set man guarding the door dressed in all black with his arms folded across his chest, obviously keeping a close watch. He stood about six-four and looked intimidating.

Brenda approached him without missing a beat in her stride. As soon as he saw her coming, he nodded his head out of respect and opened the black door. He then watched Demi follow behind Brenda and stared at her backside as she made her way inside.

Demi found herself in a narrow, dim corridor that made her a bit uneasy. They walked a few steps, then turned right and walked down a flight of concrete stairs. When they reached the bottom, Brenda came to another door that looked excluded.

She turned to Demi and said, "This is where all the fun begins."

Brenda opened the door and led Demi into the private party, where just about anything went down. Surprisingly the downstairs party was just as nice as the upstairs, but it looked more exclusive. There were other females present as well, but they were dressed in little to nothing, making Demi feel as if she came overdressed.

The room was dimly lit by candles and low-quality lighting. The bar was stocked with high quality liquor, and the aura of the room looked relaxing and posh with its modern leather chairs, sofas, and marble floors all throughout. The smooth and melodious sounds of Maxwell played at a moderate level, and with the wine drinking and easy mingling, the mood looked blissful.

The men looked wealthy and came in all different shapes and sizes. Some were dressed in their best attire, and some were shirtless and sweaty, looking like they just finished fuckin' a bitch in one of the more private rooms available.

The women were beautiful, high-class and wore lengthy stilettos that made them sound like horses whenever they walked across the floor. The first thing that came to Demi's mind was, it was a swingers club, but no one in the room was a couple. It was just one big freak party for the grown and sexy who had money to burn on some pussy.

Even though Brenda caused some attention to herself as the two men walked to the bar, it was Demi who was the obvious show stopper in the room. The men gawked and drooled over her like the exotic foreign being she was. They knew that she was from out of town and each of them wanted to personally get to know her better in their own unique way.

"What you drinkin'?" Brenda asked her.

"Same thing I had upstairs," Demi replied.

The half naked and voluptuous blond bartender quickly served Brenda her order and Brenda slipped her a fifty dollar bill. Demi didn't take two sips of her drink before she had an older man with aging brown skin and grayish hair approaching her about a one on one.

"She already taken," Brenda chimed.

The man didn't persist. He just backed off looking for the next pretty young thang he could use his Viagra on.

"What was that about?" Demi asked.

"Listen, we already got somthin' goin' on for us down here. Just chill and stick wit' me," Brenda replied.

She looked around for Chauncey and saw him approaching from one of the back rooms with a willing smile. The closer he got, his eyes automatically focused on Demi and her thick, curvaceous figure.

"You ready?" Brenda asked.

Chauncey nodded.

"You got my money?" she asked.

Chauncey passed her a small but bulky brown envelope that was filled with cash. Brenda didn't want to count it while Demi was around, so she told Demi to walk toward the back. When Demi did, Brenda looked at Chauncey and said, "It's all here, right."

"You know I wouldn't cheat you," he replied.

Brenda smiled and stuffed the envelope into her purse.

"So, is your girl ready?" he asked.

"She's down here, ain't she?"

Brenda and Chauncey walked toward the back, where the private rooms were and where the true party would take place. Chauncey walked with a strong, positive posture, with his head up and shoulders upright. The three entered a nice size room with the continuing black marble flooring, leather chairs and custom-made furniture. The room was also dimly lit with sweet scented candles burning. When they entered, there were two more well dressed gentleman who stood as the two ladies arrived.

"Welcome ladies," one of the men greeted.

He was tall and handsome with a trimmed goatee and dark bedroom eyes. He reached out his bejeweled hand and shook Brenda's hand first, then Demi's, with his eyes resting on Demi a little longer.

Demi felt a little uneasy with the situation. But all three men were very handsome and looked to be well built in size under the expensive suits. She thought to herself, *easiest five hundred ever made.*

"Do y'all ladies care for a drink?" Chauncey asked.

Demi raised the drink that she already had in her hand and smiled.

"Well, as you already know Demi, my name is Chauncey, and this is Rodney," Chauncey said pointing to a fellow who stood six-three, with short, dark curly hair and a Coca-Cola smile.

"And this is J-Dub." Chauncey introduced the second man in the room who stood six-one and resembled Morris Chestnut a little with his dark chocolate complexion, deep dimples, and Ceasar haircut.

"You're beautiful," J-Dub complimented as he shook Demi's hand longer than needed.

Staring at him for a second, J-Dub looked very familiar. "Where do I know you from?" Demi asked

He didn't bother playing the incognito role. "Probably on T.V., baby. I gotta lot of hits out there."

As soon as he said that, it finally hit her. J-Dub was a famous West Coast gangsta rapper she'd seen on T.V. plenty of times. "Oh, shit that's right. I love yo' music," Demi lied. She really didn't care for his style, but didn't want to tell him that.

"Thanks," J-Dub replied.

"Don't be getting' no ideas, bitch," Brenda blurted out. "I know you tryna be an actress and all, but you already involved in some other shit now."

Demi was completely irritated and wanted Brenda to shut up. It was her first time around a celebrity since being in L.A. and it made her upset that it had to be under these conditions.

"Oh, really. Well make sure you call me after this, baby. You fine as hell, so you could definitely be in one of my videos," J-Dub said, rubbing Demi's hand again.

Demi downed her drink and was ready for another one, while Brenda was ready to get down to business. She wasn't new to the scene and walked over to Chauncey and pressed herself against him seductively, with her hands massaging his thick chest.

"We need champagne in here," Chauncey said. He walked over to a phone on the table and pushed one button that dialed the house waiter for the room.

With the phone to his ear and Brenda slowly unbuttoning his shirt, Chauncey said into the phone, "Bring two bottles of Moet to the room."

He quickly hung up and began focusing his attention on Brenda. Demi stood to the side, feeling nervous. The two men in the room looked at her with a hunger of lust and desire. They gave off a smile that showed they were ready to get busy. They wanted to see Demi naked and hear her wild moans of passion echoing throughout the room.

"Get comfortable Demi, we gonna be here for a while," Rodney said.

He began to unbutton his suit jacket as his eyes stayed focused on Demi.

"You damn sure look good in that dress," he added.

J-Dub began doing the same. He started to unbuckle his baggy pants and then came out of his Gucci shoes. Demi scanned the room and noticed a small camcorder on the round, mahogany leather top table.

"Yeah, we'll get to that later," Rodney said, approaching Demi.

Rodney pulled Demi into his arms, and began kissing on her neck and squeezing her booty. J-Dub walked up to her and positioned himself closely behind Demi. Both men had her in a tight sandwich position, feeling up her dress and fondling her breasts.

Rodney slid his hands up Demi's smooth, uncovered thighs and began pulling up her dress, exposing her sweet shaven mound. He placed his hand between her thighs and fondled her wet pulsating pussy. He pushed two fingers into her, causing her pussy to constrict, while J-Dub squeezed her ass from the back and kissed Demi on the back of her well shaped neck.

Brenda looked over at her girl getting molested in the sandwich situation and smiled, as Chauncey began undressing her for his own personal gain. But before he could continue, there was a knock at the locked door. He heard someone shout, "Champagne."

Chauncey got up, with his six-pack exposed and solid biceps flexing. He opened the door and took the icy bucket with two large bottles of Moet sticking out. He tipped the house a twenty and quickly closed and locked the door.

"Drinks anyone," Chauncey announced, pulling one bottle from its icy chill.

"Pour me a glass, baby," Brenda said.

Chauncey looked over at his two friends having their way with Demi. Rodney had Demi in a serious lip lock, while J-Dub started to suck and kiss on her right ass cheek, with his hand feeling up her pussy.

"Fellows, y'all drinking?" Chauncey asked.

Rodney pulled away from Demi's sweet tasting lips, savoring the moment. He so badly wanted to thrust his eight inch dick down her throat and have her suck him off. He looked over at Chauncey with this satisfied look and said, "Yeah, dog, pour me a glass."

J-Dub rose from kissing and sucking on Demi's ample ass cheeks and said, "Yo, pour me a glass, too."

Glasses of Moet were soon put into everyone's hand, and Chauncey wanted to make a toast. He stood in the center of the room and said, "Yo, to us in this room right now, 'bout to get it poppin, with money to burn and beautiful ladies under our arms to enjoy for the night. BTP, my niggahs…Big Thangs Poppin."

"BTP," Rodney and J-Dub repeated simultaneously, raising their glasses in the air and clanking them together.

"BTP," Brenda also repeated, looking like a slut with her dress pulled up and tits out.

Demi said nothing, but she did grab a glass.

Everyone downed their drinks and more liquor quickly

163

refilled the empty glasses. Demi followed the others and got her drank on, too. Shit, she needed to if she wanted to perform tonight and make her money. Chauncey promptly refilled her glass and she downed that just as fast.

After the Moet, Rodney began to roll up a blunt. He had an urge to get high and fuck, the right combinations for a really good night. He rolled the weed, while Chauncey continued getting his freak on with Brenda. He poured Moet across her sweet looking breasts, then licked every last drop off of her. She giggled as she pushed his face deeper into her chest, lying on her back with Chauncey on top of her. He licked every inch of her and more.

Demi started to loosen up a bit, feeling the Moet going through her system and the weed making her feel nonchalant. J-Dub pressed himself against Demi from the back, running his hands up her thighs and cupping her tits. He began sucking on her neck and moved her near the leather chair.

He bent Demi over the chair and lifted up her dress again and pulled out her tits. He spread Demi's legs in a downward V position and hunkered down behind her and then pressed his face between her ass cheeks and began eating her out from the back. Demi gripped the armrest tightly and cried out, feeling J-Dub's long tongue dig into her like a drill tip. J-Dub squeezed her cheeks together and circled his tongue into her and began sucking on her lips and consuming the pussy juice that flowed from her pussy.

"Yeah, boy…that's what I'm talkin' 'bout," Rodney moaned.

He had the camcorder in his hand and filmed both his peoples doing their thang. He took a long pull from the burning weed and felt his dick growing harder by the second. He continued to film, zooming in on the intense action that was happening while being captured clearly on camera.

Rodney became extremely hard and it was showing through his slacks. He passed Chauncey the weed and then placed his hand down his pants and slowly masturbated while still filming.

J-Dub had Demi still bent over the chair and ate her out for a good moment until he became so hard that he needed to fuck. He pulled his face away from the pussy, stood up and got butt naked. He was hung like a horse and ready to make a movie.

The weed was passed around the room and Demi took a long pull before J-Dub was ready to fuck her. She felt so nice and horny, that her pussy was wet like water. J-Dub took a long pull and then passed it back to Rodney. He then stepped near the pussy with his dick hard like a rock and thrust it into Demi, causing her to clench the chair for dear life and bite down on her bottom lip.

"Damn, this bitch got some good pussy," J-Dub cried out, gripping Demi's ass cheeks and finding his rhythm.

J-Dub put in work and pulled her hair and slapped her ass red, while looking into the camera. Brenda was sprawled out on the bed riding Chauncey's lengthy size and feeling it in her stomach. Both ladies could be heard loudly from the hallway as the men held back nothing.

Rodney needed to get into the action so he positioned the camera for it to capture the entire room while he could get into the action. He went over to where J-Dub was fucking Demi from the back and he moved in front of her with his dick out and ready. He sat in the chair with Demi situated over him. She got down on her knees and took all of Rodney into her mouth, deep-throating him and chewing on his nuts.

"Shit, girl…that's right, take all that dick in," Rodney said, with his hand tangled in her long hair.

Soon partners were exchanged, finding Chauncey fucking Demi on her back, while Rodney and J-Dub had a threesome with Brenda. Then it would be all four men with Demi, while Brenda would film. Then it would it be Brenda filming Demi getting high again followed by her sucking all three men off and then Chauncey fucking Demi in the ass which hurt her a lot. But it was worth the money, Demi thought.

Most of the shit on film was caught by Brenda with Demi mostly doing all of the dirty work. She watched Demi suck and fuck niggahs for hours while getting her drink on continuously and smoking weed that was laced with PCP.

It was some good coverage. All three men fucked Demi six ways from Sunday and had their way with her in every direction and every position they could think of, even with double penetration happening—for Chauncey, it was five grand well spent.

When it was all said and done, Demi was so high and twisted, she couldn't even move. She was sprawled out on the bed, her body feeling numbed, with her eyes closed and having Chauncey eat out her pussy just for the fun of it. The men were very well sexually satisfied and definitely wanted a round two with Demi really soon.

Brenda was already dressed and still looked to be somewhat sober. She tapped Demi on the shoulder, trying to wake her up from her comatose looking state. Chauncey was out of it, and looked like he planned on staying the night in the private room. He was asshole naked and looked to be in the same condition that Demi was in.

"Bitch, get up…we out," Brenda said, trying to pull Demi off the bed by her arm.

Brenda pulled Demi off the bed wit one good heave and Demi dropped, with a loud thud.

"Fuck!" Demi cried out.

"Bitch, we out," Brenda repeated, looking frustrated with Demi.

Brenda looked at the time. It was almost five in the morning. She wanted to hurry and leave. She was hungry and wanted to catch a twenty-four hour diner and get some breakfast before they went home. She was paid and had the bitch Demi on film wilding out with three known Crips who, with the exception of J-Dub were O.G's from Long Beach. The film would be leverage over Demi in case the bitch wanted to get stupid and go against her for any reason at all. She knew Nico would disapprove of Demi fuckin' niggahs outside of the film industry, but Brenda had to get hers and if shit popped off, she could either put the blame on Demi or Chauncey, but after she edited herself out.

 Seventeen

Demi staggered out the backdoor of the club, falling over the bouncer who assisted her to the car. Brenda walked ahead of them, looking for the valet. The sun was about to make it's appearance, and the cool morning air made Brenda even hungrier and tired.

"Damn B, what you do to this bitch?" the six-one, beefy bouncer in the tight black shirt asked. He had to pick Demi up in the threshold position, because she kept stumbling over him.

"She good, she just drunk," Brenda replied.

The last valet on hand quickly pulled Brenda's Benz around and handed her the keys. Brenda tipped him a twenty and jumped into the drivers' seat. As the bouncer helped Demi into the passenger seat, he couldn't help but to stare as her dress started to ride up her thighs revealing that she had no panties on.

Brenda noticed him staring at Demi exposed crotch. "You know for the right amount, you can have her for the night," Brenda offered with a conniving smile.

The man smiled and licked his lips, but he knew Brenda wanted him to come out heavy from his pockets, which he couldn't afford. "Nah, I'm cool. I got my lil' show," he replied.

Brenda shrugged and said, "Your loss, cuz she's a good fuck."

The man closed the door and allowed the two to be on their way. Brenda sped off, en-route to the nearest open diner.

Forty-five minutes later, Brenda was ordering some breakfast, while Demi was slouched in the booth, trying to get her head right. Her pussy was still throbbing from the abuse it endured from the three well-endowed men she fucked. Her body felt like it got hit by a Mack truck. She wasn't hungry. She just wanted to go home and sleep the effects off.

"Eat somthin', it'll make you feel better," Brenda suggested.

Still looking in a daze somewhat, Demi sipped a little bit of water, but soon after felt like throwing it up. Her stomach was doin' flips since she left the club and her heart felt like it was about to beat out of her chest from the PCP she unknowingly smoked. It was a feeling she'd never experienced before.

Before the waiter could come back with the meals, Brenda went into her purse and pulled out five crisp hundred dollar bills. She passed it over the table to Demi.

"Here, that's for you. You did good tonight. You definitely did your thang."

Demi took the money, but was still too fucked up to count it.

"Put it away," Brenda said.

Demi stuffed the money into the small purse she carried, just before placing her head down on the table.

"See, I just got you paid. A few more fucks like that, and you and me could run this town wit' the money we make," Brenda stated.

Demi looked like she didn't care. Her only concern at that moment was sleep and becoming herself again. Moments later, the waitress came with Brenda's meal which consisted of scrambled eggs, French toast, hash browns, and bacon, with a cup of coffee.

"You sure you ain't hungry, Demi?" Brenda asked.

Demi waved her off sluggishly, trying to rest up.

Brenda shook her head before began digging into her meal. She thought it was crazy how someone from New York could be so naïve and dumb. But then again, maybe Demi had everybody fooled. Maybe she'd come to L.A. to really be a paid hoe, and if that was the case she really was gonna take the city by storm.

After breakfast, Brenda and Demi went back to the house, and Demi quickly passed out on the couch in her wrinkled dress and tousled hair.

"Drunk bitch," Brenda cursed.

She watched Demi for a moment and was happy to turn a sizable profit from her. Brenda breathed greed and lust, and she always wanted to make top dollar as fast as possible. Brenda watched Demi sleep, as her mind raced about how to make more money. She soon came up with a devilish idea. Brenda stood over Demi and shoved her, waiting to see if she would wake from her trance, but Demi was out cold.

Brenda walked over to her phone and made a quick phone call. She needed to take advantage of Demi's drug induced state. After her phone call, she went into her bedroom to change clothes and put on a white Terry cloth bath robe and her furry slippers. She then made herself another cup of coffee and waited for her company to show up. She would glance over at Demi every now and then, who looked damn dear dead and hoped she would stay that way.

Half-hour later there was a knock at Brenda's door. When she went to answer it. Lyfe and Mist were standing there looking high as usual.

"What's poppin', B," Lyfe greeted.

"You know we came here for business and that thang you promised us," Mist said.

"Look, y'all niggahs need to make it quick. She's sleep on the couch." Brenda pointed over to Demi.

Mist and Lyfe smiled and gave each other dap. "That's what I'm talkin' 'bout, B. You looks out for your set," Lyfe said, rubbing his hands together. He was ready to put in work. Besides, this was the perfect payback for Demi always coming out of her mouth wrong to him.

But before the two thugs could step any further into her house, Brenda pushed them back. "No pay, no play." She held her hand out and waited for the cash.

"B, you really gonna charge us to fuck some drugged up drunk bitch? Lyfe questioned with a baffled look.

"Yup…cuz y'all niggahs is thirsty and besides, look at her. Can y'all both tell me that y'all ever had better?" Brenda asked.

Mist laughed. "Yeah, you right. All my bitches been ugly."

"What she on anyway?" Lyfe asked.

"That bitch been smokin' weed laced with some PCP and she been drinkin'," Brenda informed.

"Oh, word," Lyfe replied with a devious smile.

"Yup, she so fucked up right now, that a fuckin' train could run through here and she wouldn't know any better," Brenda said.

"Hold up. Do Nico know we here?" Mist asked.

"Now, why you gon' ask a dumb-ass question like that? Would you be here if he did?" Brenda responded.

Lyfe was thirsty for the pussy, along with Mist, so both men reached into their pockets and passed Brenda a hundred dollars each. She charged them a cheap price because they were her homeboys, and Demi looked lifeless.

After the transaction, Brenda stepped aside, indicating that it was now cool for them to proceed with their actions. Walking all the way inside, Mist took a huge gulp from the 40oz he carried, wiped his mouth and proceeded to unzip his pants, feeling his dick getting harder by the second.

"Nah, blood. I got first dibs on that ass," Lyfe said, pushing Mist to the side. "I been waitin' to get this bitch back."

Mist didn't care if he got sloppy seconds, as long as he was still getting his. And out of respect for Lyfe being Nico's right hand man, he passed the torch to him, saying, "Just save some for me, blood."

Lyfe wasted no time. He stood over Demi with his pants down and dick already out ready for action. Demi was sprawled across the couch looking tempting with her butt slightly exposed, arm dangling off the couch and face pushed into the

172

cushion. He moved in closer and then turned her over on her back. Crouching down, Lyfe pulled up her dress even more, seeing her shaved pussy come into his view.

"Hurry up, niggah. I'm tryin' to get my fuck on, too," Mist blurted out.

Lyfe gently parted her legs and then pressed himself against her, dipping between her smooth thighs and smoothly pushed his dick into Demi. With his shaft rooted into her, Demi didn't budge a bit; she still looked lifeless as Lyfe fucked her on the couch.

He then turned to look at Brenda, but never stopped stroking. "You sure this bitch ain't dead?"

Brenda took a long pull from a freshly lit Newport. "Its good, ain't it."

Lyfe continued to go to work on Demi, sliding in and out of her with forceful strokes. He sucked on her nipples and kissed her on her neck and when he felt himself about to explode, he pulled out and let it lose all over her thighs and stomach. The duration was only about five minutes, but it was money well spent for him. When Lyfe finally pulled out, he wasn't even back on his feet good, before Mist was already naked from the waist down and climbing on top of Demi, thrusting his short dick. He gripped her legs and fucked her slowly, savoring the moment.

Mist ran his wet tongue down the side of Demi's neck onto her thick chocolate nipples and continued to push himself into her. He looked Demi in her face as he fucked, and imagined that she wasn't passed out…that she was enjoying every moment. He knew that PCP mixed with that liquor would have her out cold for a while and have her detached from anything that was happening, but he wanted her to wake up. Mist even thought about violating her even more by penetrating her asshole, but the pussy already had him in bliss.

He ran his black hands all over her body, moaning and grunting, and then grabbed her ass, sinking himself deeper between her thighs. Demi's body moved like a rag doll underneath

Mist's bulky frame, and her expression remained unresponsive.

"Shit, I'm gonna cum in this bitch!" Mist yelled.

The couch looked sunken with Mist having Demi pressed against him. He began to put in work and when he felt himself about to cum, unlike Lyfe, he didn't pull out. Instead, he shot his huge thick load into Demi's pussy, then began to quiver. Seconds later, he looked thoroughly pleased as he rolled off Demi and onto the floor.

"Damn, that bitch got some good pussy. Next time, I wanna fuck her while she awake," Mist said with a serious smile.

Brenda took one last pull from her cigarette and stood up. She towered over Mist as he lay across his back. "Niggah, please. You know she wouldn't normally fuck your ugly-ass. Now, get dressed. I ain't tryin' to see your lil' dick."

Mist laughed and then stood up. "B, you know you like my tool. When I'm gonna have some time wit' you?" he asked.

Brenda showed off a smirk. "You wish, niggah. You gotta come wit' at least eight inches to get at me."

Mist began fixing his pants, then looked over at Demi, who still looked comatose "Damn, B, you a foul bitch. You know she would trip if she found out."

"That's why she ain't gonna find out. Y'all got yours, right…and besides, she's about to do porn, so it's good that y'all break her in."

"Best pussy yet," Mist stated, buttoning up his pants.

The three shared a laugh, got high, and started to drink. Mist and Lyfe lingered over at Brenda's place till the morning sun reached its peak and left feeling good that they'd finally fucked the bitch who'd tried to play them.

 # Eighteen

Demi felt like death several hours later as she slowly opened her eyes from a prolonged sleep. It was apparent that she had a severe hangover by the way her head throbbed like there was someone knocking from the inside out. Massaging her temples in a sluggish circular motion, Demi lifted herself up off the couch and realized that she'd slept in her dress. It looked tousled and torn, and from what she noticed, there was a large amount of sperm staining the bottom. A dress that had cost Perry eight-hundred dollars back in the day was now ruined. Trying her best to figure out what happened, Demi had no recollection of the night before. The only thing she remembered was getting felt up by J-Dub and his friends at the club, smoking weed, and after that it all went blank.

When she stood up, she suddenly felt her knees wobble and grabbed the arm-rest of the couch tightly to prevent from collapsing on the floor. A sharp pain shot from within her thighs, and hit her like a ton of bricks.

"What the fuck?" she muttered, bending over.

Feeling between her legs, she noticed that her thongs were no where to be found, and her inner thighs were sticky from God knows what. Not to mention, her lips had never been so sore. Demi knew that whatever happened the night before, could not have been good. She felt frightened that she couldn't remember a single thing, and hoped that Brenda could help her figure it out. She stood up slowly for the second time, wanting to get out of her dress and scrape herself clean.

She looked around the room, and noticed the house was

empty and completely quiet for a change, which was extremely odd. Normally, there were at least five niggahs in the house at all times. Demi slowly walked down the hallway toward Brenda's bedroom to see if she was inside. But when she reached for the knob and slowly turned, it was locked.

Her ass don't trust no one, Demi thought to herself.

She went back into the living room and went for her suitcase. It was hard for her to move, because the lower half of her body ached with an unexplainable pain, including her head that felt like a beating drum.

Demi sat on the couch and pulled her suitcase close to her. She then noticed her small purse near her feet and picked it up. She opened it and checked her stash, which she did a few times a day, just to make sure it was still there. Counting the bills, Demi made sure it added up to the five hundred dollar advance Nico had given her before stuffing it back in her purse. This time, instead of leaving it on the floor, she placed the purse at the bottom of her luggage. Demi then grabbed a few toiletry items and slowly walked toward the bathroom trying not to make any sudden moves.

She locked the bathroom door and immediately stripped herself naked. At that moment, several crisp hundred dollar bills fell out of her bra and onto the floor. Picking up the money, Demi quickly counted the bills, and realized it was five hundred dollars. She scratched her head, trying to figure out how she'd managed to get the cash. She had no recollection. However, how and why didn't matter. It was hers to keep now.

Wrapping the money up in her tainted dress, Demi approached the mirror and tried to examine her body closely; making sure that there wasn't any visible marks or bruises. She looked clean from the outside, but on the inside she didn't feel right. She leaned over the sink and splashed her face with water, and then suddenly had the urge to throw up. She rushed for the toilet. Dropping down to her knees, she stuck her head down the white porcelain bowl. The vomit seemed to last forever. Demi definitely felt like she looked. After throwing up a few more times, she slowly stood up, gripping whatever was around her for support.

She gazed at her image in the mirror again and shook her head "What the fuck is wrong with me?"

Demi needed to get her head right. She leaned in closer to the mirror with her hands flat against the sink and studied herself closely. It wasn't like her to feel this way after just smoking some weed. Hell, growing up she'd smoked more blunts than Snoop and Lil' Wayne put together, so she knew something wasn't right. Demi couldn't wait for Brenda to open the door, so she could drill her with questions.

After getting another sharp pain from her vaginal area, Demi felt between her thighs again realizing that her lips seemed extremely swollen.

"Shit," Demi said, touching her delicate tissue. "Maybe some warm water will help."

She turned on the shower, making it warm and comfortable and slowly stepped inside. She let the lukewarm shower cascade off her naked skin and lowered her head to the floor. Since coming to L.A., Demi was starting to become someone she didn't want to be. Having sex with random men and allowing them to take advantage of her was the last thing she thought she'd ever be doing in order to get ahead. It wasn't a good feeling. It wasn't something Demi was proud of, and she started to question if it was all worth it, especially after the way she was feeling now. She took the washcloth and tried to cleanse herself thoroughly. She scrubbed most places with force, and then dabbed between her legs gently, still cringing from the slightest touch. She wanted so badly for her pain to run down the drain like the rest of the water.

Demi stepped out of the shower about twenty minutes later feeling somewhat clean, but still troubled. She wrapped a large towel around her body and then started combing her fingers through her wet hair, which was a tangled mess, but she didn't care. Walking out of the bathroom, again she was surprised that the house was still surprisingly quiet. With the numerous empty 40 oz bottles and ashtrays filled with leftover weed, the living room looked a mess. She wished Brenda would've made whoever had the small party clean the shit up.

She took a seat back on the couch and just chilled for a moment. Picking up the remote, Demi turned on the Plasma T.V. and stopped on VH1 when she saw her favorite show, *The Fabulous Life,* doing a special on the wealthy and fabulous Kimora Lee Simmons. Demi turned the volume up and started to watch, wishing she could trade places with Kimora for just a day. The money, the fame, the glamour, the exotic vacations, it was all exciting.

Then again, Demi knew that in due time, she would become just like the famous mogul. She knew that you had to sacrifice something in order to make it to the top. Some celebrities gave up their childhoods, or spending time with family, but for Demi, she had to give up her morality. It wasn't the best sacrifice, but for now she would do what she had to do.

As Demi sat on the couch, collecting her thoughts, she suddenly remembered that a week was about to pass since she'd left home and she hadn't spoken to her family since she left. Her daughter, Aliyah, came to mind. But without access to a phone, it was hard to call anyone. The only phone in the house was in Brenda's room, which she didn't allow anybody to use, so Demi knew she would have to start going back to the payphones if she wanted to talk.

"I need to get out of here," Demi said to herself.

After applying some lotion to her body, she opened her suitcase to look for something to wear. She quickly got dressed in a pair of sweat pants, a Victoria's Secret PINK T-shirt, flip flops, then put her hair into a bun before walking out the door. Demi threw her purse on her shoulder then looked at Brenda's car that was still in the driveway. She wished that Brenda was cool enough to let her drive her car. Demi knew that shit would never happen; even on a good day.

Demi walked two blocks up Crenshaw Boulevard looking for the nearest payphone. She wanted to make a few phone

calls, starting with home. By now, she knew her family was calling her every name in the book, and even though she didn't
want to hear it, it was time to face reality. Besides, Demi needed
to hear her daughter's voice and make sure everything was okay.

She came to the nearest working phone at a small corner
convenience store about three blocks away. After going into the
store and realizing they didn't have calling cards, Demi knew
that she would have to call collect. Knowing how mad her family probably was, she prayed that someone would accept the
call.

Picking up the phone, Demi informed the operator that
she wanted to make a collect phone call, then nervously bit her
bottom lip as the call connected. Demi became even more nervous when she heard Dennis finally answer.

"You have a collect call from, Demi. Will you accept the
charges?" the operator asked.

"Hell, no. We ain't acceptin' shit," Dennis replied.

"Dennis…please. Hear me out," Demi quickly said.

The operator asked if he would accept the charges again
and after pausing for a brief moment, Dennis finally agreed.
When the call went through, Dennis didn't hesitate going off.

"Bitch, how the fuck you gonna go to L.A wit' out tellin'
somebody and then leave Lee Lee here for us to fuckin' take
care of?"

Demi didn't even bother responding to his disrespectful
name calling. "Dennis, I'm so sorry, but I needed to do it. Don't
you understand, I needed to take a chance and try to make some
real money!"

"You a fuckin' selfish-ass bitch. You don't call here in
damn near a week. What the fuck is wrong wit' you? We ain't
yo' fuckin' personal babysitter, Demi. You better bring yo' ass
back to Harlem and get yo' daughter. Ma is pissed." Dennis said.

"Like I said…I'm sorry."

"Damn right, you sorry."

Demi was tired of the insults, but had to take one for the
team. "Where's Aliyah?"

"She in the room watchin' TV."

"Where's Ma?"

"Out doin' her, you know how she is. She ain't got time to baby sit yo' daughter. So, my girl, Renita been takin' care of her."

"Who the hell is Renita?" Demi asked.

"What difference do it make?"

Demi sighed heavily.

"I know you ain't catchin' no attitude over my girl lookin' after Lee Lee. If so, then hop yo' ass on the next plane and come get yo' daughter if you gotta problem wit' it. Shit, if it wasn't for Renita, then I don't know what would'a happened. I don't know how to do no hair and shit, and you know Ma don't give a fuck."

Demi didn't have anything personally against whoever Renita was. In actuality she was grateful that somebody had stepped up and helped her out.

"No, I don't have a problem at all. Is she okay?" Demi asked, referring to Aliyah.

"Yeah, Lee Lee good," Dennis replied.

"Let me talk to her."

Dennis didn't want to put Aliyah on the phone at first. He was still angry with his baby sister for going to L.A. and leaving her child behind like some animal.

"Dennis, please, let me talk to my child. I miss her," Demi pleaded. "I'm sorry for what I did, but I needed to do this. I needed somthin' better."

"So, leavin' Lee Lee wit' us is sumthin' better."

"Dennis, I'm gonna make it up to everyone…believe me. Things will get better for me, 'cause I got somethin' big happenin' for me out here. I'ma lace yo' pockets when I get back."

"Demi, you need to cut the bullshit, seriously. I mean I already know what's gon' end up happenin' wit' you anyway. You gon' fuck some niggah who *was* gonna put you on, get played, then end up feelin' sorry for yo' self. We already got one hoe in the family. We don't need other one. You need to quit wit' that Hollywood shit and wake up to the real world. Snap back into reality and shit. You need to come home and take care of yo' fuckin' daughter, that's what yo' big plan needs to be and stop chasin' that other stupid shit, fo' real."

Dennis' words hurt severely. Demi gripped the phone tightly as she heard her brother's negativity toward her continue. However, just when she didn't think things could get any worse, she heard her mother yelling in the background.

"Niggah, I heard what the fuck you just said. Who you tryna call a hoe? You must be talkin' about that fat-ass girl, Renita you fuckin'."

"No, Ma, I ain't even callin' you no hoe," Dennis lied. "Oh, you ain't gonna believe Demi on the phone," he said trying to get the heat off him.

"What?" A split second later, Janet grabbed the phone and went in for the kill. "Bitch, you better stay in L.A. 'cuz if I see yo' ass on the street it's on."

"She called here collect, too," Dennis continued to snitch from the background.

"Collect? Oh, bitch you gon' pay me back. Yo' ass in California and we stuck here keepin' that crazy-ass daughter of yours. As a matter of fact, come and get this damn girl!" Janet yelled.

"Ma, please. Things are about to happen for me. Just give me a little bit more time," Demi begged.

"I ain't givin' you shit. You gon' write us some damn letter, turn off yo' phone then roll out to California. Bitch, you ain't no Beyonce, so you might as well pack yo' shit."

With tears trickling down her face and her eyes pointed to the ground, Demi took a deep breath. "Ma, I promise. I'm gonna start makin' some money, so I can send for Aliyah."

"Yeah, speakin' of money, that lil' ass two hundred dollars you left me wit' done ran out," Janet said.

Demi just shook her head. "Ma, it's only been a week. How much y'all spend on Aliyah?"

"Don't be questionin' my financial decisions. All you

181

need to know is that the shit is gone."

"Ma, I'll send some more money tomorrow."

"How much?" Janet asked.

Demi knew any mention of the word money would calm her mother down. "All I have is three hundred for now." With the bad luck Demi had in L.A. so far, she couldn't give up her entire stash. Not even half.

"Send me four hundred and I might keep Lee Lee another week," Janet said.

"But you ain't even doin' nothin'. Dennis and Renita doin' all the work."

"So what, bitch. Them muthafucka's live up in my crib. They eat my food, and they watchin' my fuckin' T.V.," Janet retorted.

Demi didn't want to go back and forth anymore, she didn't have the energy. "Fine, Ma," she said defeated. "Can you just put Aliyah on the phone now, so I can talk to her? Please."

Janet sucked her teeth and said, "Hold on."

"Lee Lee," she heard her mother call out. "Lee Lee, come to the damn phone."

Demi stood there patiently waiting for her daughter to respond. She dried her tears with the back of her hand and tried to sound a bit more joyful.

"Hello…hello. Hello," she heard Aliyah answer.

"Aliyah baby, hi," Demi cried out, trying to muster up a smile.

"Mommy!" Aliyah shouted.

"Hey, boo…you miss me?"

"Mommy. You not here. Where you at?" her daughter asked with a heartfelt question.

"I'm far away right now, tryin' to take care of some business," Demi replied.

"Mommy! Come back. Come get me!"

Demi damn near broke down. She didn't want to lie to her daughter. "When things get right for Mommy, Aliyah, I'm definitely comin' to get you. You hear me, baby…its gonna be just you and me, okay?"

"Okay. Popsicle Mommy. Popsicle!"

"How they treatin' my baby?" Demi asked.

"Renita gave me three popsicles."

"That's good, baby. When I get back, I'ma buy you all the popsicles you want."

"Can you come get me?"

"No, not right now. Mommy's at work. But when I get myself situated and have my own place, you're gonna come stay with me, okay?"

"Okay."

"You been a good girl?" Demi asked.

"Yessss. Yes!" Aliyah chanted.

"I miss you. I love you."

At that moment, Aliyah started to scream and Dennis immediately grabbed the phone and told her to go sit down. He then came at Demi with the same negative and harsh attitude from before.

"You need to say fuck what you doin' out there, 'cuz it ain't gonna work anyway and come get yo' daughter. I ain't the father, and Renita ain't the fuckin' mother. Stupid-ass bitch."

CLICK

Demi slammed the phone down, and cried like a baby on the corner. She wanted to fall to the ground, but kept herself steady. Her tears seemed endless, as she replayed Aliyah's sweet voice over and over in her head. Regardless of what her family thought about her, she loved Aliayh and only wanted the best for her.

Thinking about her headshots, she placed a quarter into the payphone and dialed Alex's number. But once again, his cell phone went straight to voice mail, which was a clear indication that she'd gotten fucked once again…literally.

 **Nineteen**

Needing some time alone for a while, Demi didn't want to go back to Brenda's right away, so she decided to go somewhere to grab something to eat, clearing her head in the process. Maybe even rethink the whole situation with Nico and Brenda. After walking a few minutes, she made a right on the busy W. Century Blvd. and decided to go to In-N-Out Burger.

Taking pleasure in a cheeseburger, fries and a large chocolate shake, Demi enjoyed the peaceful moment she had alone. Reflecting back on her situation, Demi knew that she only had two options. Either she could stay and continue to make it as an actress or go back home to be with her daughter. With things going so bad, the easiest option would be to hop on a plane back to New York, but she had to admit the potential fame and money was calling her.

However, by doing porn, fears of her being blacklisted or typecast in the industry was something Demi was concerned about. She'd gone through too much to be unable to get legitimate work in the film business. Then suddenly, a helpful thought came to her when thoughts of Traci Lords, a one time porn star who'd started doing adult film in her teen years, eventually worked her way up to becoming a television and B-list movie actress. Although she wanted to be an A-list actress and not a B, Traci's success gave Demi some hope that she could eventually expand.

The time passed quickly as Demi sat staring off at a distance most times, or playing with the straw in her cup. Before she knew it, she'd spent over two hours in the fast food restaurant, and the day was soon making way for dusk to settle over the calm and warm sky of the hood. She checked the time and saw that it was almost seven o' clock. Demi didn't want to be hanging around when dusk finally blanketed the sky and the bona fide trouble started to come out. After only being in the rough neighborhood for a short time, she knew what Inglewood was about after hours and was wise enough to know that a woman like her could become an easy target on the streets. Demi stretched before standing up, placing her uneaten food in the trash can, then walked outside.

Making her way back down Century Boulevard, Demi hadn't even gotten that far before she noticed a black Yukon truck racing toward her. With her eyes fixated on the speeding vehicle, Demi's heart began to race and her intuition instantly told her to run. But for some reason, she couldn't move. Instead, Demi just stood there and watched the truck come to a screeching stop right in front of her. Suddenly doors flew open and out jumped two men dressed in all red, and approached her with an unpleasant demeanor. They both grabbed her forcefully.

"What the fuck? Get off me!" Demi shouted, trying to free herself from their grip.

But both men held onto her tightly, dragging her back to the truck. By that time, Demi noticed another figure step out from the backseat. She stared closely and was surprised to see that it was Brenda.

"Demi what fuck is wrong wit' you? How you gonna disappear like that?" Brenda yelled.

Demi glared at her. "Are you fuckin' serious?"

"Look, bitch, you just can't be walkin' off by yourself like that, especially in this hood. You gonna end up shot or raped on some dirty-ass street corner," Brenda said like she was concerned.

"So, you think you my master now?" Demi shouted. "I just took a walk."

"Put her in the car," Brenda commanded the two goons.

"Are you fuckin' serious?" Demi said again.

Her question was never answered as the two men pulled

Demi to the truck and tossed her in the backseat, closing the door behind her. The goons waited for Brenda to get into the backseat as well before they jumped in the front seat and quickly pulled off.

"Brenda, don't fuck wit' me," Demi warned.

"No bitch, don't fuck wit' me," Brenda replied angrily. "Nico already paid you in advance, so how the fuck you just gonna run off. You are already paid for."

"I didn't fuckin' run off. I went to go use the fuckin' phone to call my daughter," Demi shot back with fire burning in her eyes.

"Whateva. You shouldn't have just left like that. I'm responsible for you."

"Responsible? So, I'm yo' child now?"

Brenda didn't respond. She just sat back and ignored Demi.

"Bitch is yo' dumb-ass hard of hearin'? I said I'm not yo' child!" Demi cursed.

Without warning, Demi caught a hard back hand slap from Brenda that forced her into the door. Brenda glared at her and then said, "I told you, don't fuck wit' me!"

The two goons in the front seat started laughing.

Demi held her face, looking pissed off. There was no way she was going to let Brenda disrespect her like that. "Bitch!" Demi yelled then lunged forward to whip Brenda's ass.

However, Brenda stopped all that when she quickly revealed a 9mm and pointed it toward Demi's face. "You better chill, bitch!"

Demi sat frozen in her seat. She couldn't believe what was happening. Staring down the barrel of a gun, she knew she'd probably bit off more than she could chew.

The rest of the ride back to the house was in silence. While Brenda remained calm and casual, on the other hand, Demi was fuming on the inside.

"So I'm yo' property now, I see," Demi said with attitude in her voice.

Brenda continued to ignore her.

"Is this shit funny to you?" Demi added.

"Shut the fuck up. I'm not in the mood for your shit," Brenda retorted, with the gun still gripped in her hand.

"What happened last night, Brenda? What the fuck did y'all do to me? Did you let them niggahs at the club do some foul shit?" Demi asked.

"You got paid, right?"

Demi was heated at Brenda's nonchalant attitude. "If you ain't have that gun in yo' hand, I swear…"

"You gon' do what, bitch! I told you before, you a long way from home. This ain't Harlem, Demi, so don't get it twisted."

"You right, this ain't Harlem. It's so many pussy-ass niggahs and bitches out here, that I lost count," Demi responded.

"You need to save all that mouth for when you suckin' dick on camera. You ain't gotta make shit difficult for yourself, just do what you told and we gonna be good."

"Whateva bitch…go fuck yourself!" Demi shouted.

"You really wanna test me, I see." Brenda let out a chuckle. "Let me tell you sumthin. Don't ever bite the hand that fuckin' feeds you. I'm the one who helped yo' broke-ass out. I put shelter over yo' head. I'm the one who helped put a lil' cash in yo' pockets. So keep fuckin' tryin' me and see what happens to you."

Demi nodded. "If you gotta keep throwin' that shit up in my face, then you shouldn't have done it. When I get my shit straight, you ain't gotta fuckin' worry about me. But trust me, I ain't gonna forget what you did. I'll definitely be back around to settle this shit."

"Bitch, don't ever threaten me. I don't give a fuck what Nico thinks about you, I'll fuckin' kill you," Brenda retorted, with a hard glare.

The two men in the front seat found their confrontation amusing. They both were listening carefully, but remained quiet.

A few moments later, the truck pulled into Brenda's

driveway. "We here, B," the driver said.

Brenda got out of the truck, followed by everyone else. When Demi walked inside, she noticed Lyfe and Mist seated on the couch, getting high as usual and drinking. Both men looked at each other with a peculiar smile, like they shared a private secret between them.

"Welcome back," Lyfe joked.

"Fuck you," Demi cursed.

"Hey, just let me know when and where, for a…"

Before Lyfe could continue his statement, Brenda shot him a look that said, 'shut the fuck up.'

Lyfe took a long pull from the black tar weed he was smoking and just sat back against the couch with a mocking gaze on Demi. He knew he had to fuck her again, this time with her aware of it.

Thirty minutes passed before Nico walked into Brenda's house with a look of disappointment spread across his face. He'd obviously heard about Demi's long walk around town, and the tension that was building between the two women. Nico was strictly about business, so he wanted to hurry up and squash the beef.

Nico walked into Brenda' living room with an aura that said authority. Demi couldn't help but notice how good Nico looked to her, but she disguised her desire for him with a scowl expressed across her face, and distaste for what Brenda had done.

Nico looked over at Demi who looked unhappy and pissed off. He then turned to look at Brenda. "Ay, B, I need to holla at you for a minute….walk wit' me outside," he instructed.

As the two walked outside, Brenda knew Nico hated when their girls posed any types of problems to his business, so she couldn't wait to hear Nico tell her to get rid of Demi. It would be her pleasure.

"What's good, Nico?" Brenda asked.

"You pulled a gun out on her?" Nico asked calmly.

"Yeah, I did. The bitch wouldn't shut the fuck up. First,

she leaves off wit' out letting me know and then she came at me sideways. She lucky I ain't shoot her fuckin' ass," Brenda explained.

Nico towered over Brenda under the dark sky. He looked nonchalant for a moment and then suddenly back handed Brenda with his right fist. Brenda flew back against her parked Benz like the wind had lifted her off her feet. She held her face and looked up at Nico with a wicked stare.

"Ay, let me tell you somthin', B. You don't point a gun at any one of my bitches that will be workin' for me, unless I tell you to do so. That bitch is about to get me paid. I got production already lined up for that young tasty thang in there. She's marketable and I don't want you fuckin' that up for me. So you handle Demi and you handle her right. I want you to make her feel at home in this bitch. I want her comfortable and I want her ready to work," Nico stated angrily.

Brenda just stood there in disbelief. He'd never hit her over one of the girls before, and it pissed her off a great deal. She thought that she'd done her job right handling Demi, but obviously she hadn't. Brenda didn't understand why she had Nico so upset. She just knew Demi was gonna be the one in trouble, but it was her who was in hot water. It pissed Brenda off knowing that Nico had Demi's back instead of hers. She wondered if it would become more than business between the two of them, and at that moment, jealousy started to overtake her body.

"I'm sorry, Nico. I fucked up. It won't happen again," Brenda said submissively.

"It better not."

Brenda walked away, leaving Nico standing alone in the driveway. When Brenda walked back inside, she threw a furious glance at Demi and kept it moving toward her bedroom.

Realizing that Brenda was damn near bipolar, Demi ignored her. Still tired from the night before, she was ready to get some rest, but with Lyfe and Mist still lingering in the room, she knew it wasn't happening anytime soon. She was ready to violate Brenda's rule and retreat to one of the bedrooms for some peace and quiet. She hated the way Lyfe and Mist stared at her, like they knew something about her that they weren't telling. They continued to get high and drunk and watched rap videos on cable.

Shortly after that, Nico walked in with his normal cool and relaxed demeanor. He looked over at Demi and knew he had to smooth her over in order to undo what Brenda had created.

"Demi, c'mere, let me talk to you in private," Nico called out to her.

Following his orders like everybody else, Demi stood up and followed him outside. Nico took in her beauty for a moment, loving how she filled out even in a pair of sweat pants, and how her eyes twinkled in certain lighting. He knew tons of niggahs who would pay handsomely to see Demi doing porn. She had a look about her that was unexplainable—beautiful, sassy, sexy, but still hood and most important…a banging body.

Nico himself wanted to fuck her, but he always put money over pussy.

"You okay, Demi?" he asked with a concerned tone.

"No, you need to check that bitch before shit get ugly. How the fuck she gonna pull out a gun then tell me I need to come back to the house, like she got fuckin papers on me," Demi said.

"Ay, first off, she knows better and second off, you ain't gotta worry about Brenda anymore. I already handled that. You gonna be good from now on. But I need to know, you ready to get to work? I'm startin' production on you in the next couple of days, and I need your full attention into this film. I don't want you gettin' distracted."

Demi was silent. Doing porn made her nervous, but it was work, and she knew it would be impossible to back out now.

"Yeah, I'm ready," she answered reluctantly.

Nico smiled. "Let me look at you," Nico said, taking Demi by her hand gently and having her twirl around for him.

"You like?" Demi teased.

"Are all New York ladies as fine as you?"

"I'm one of a kind, boo…there ain't no other like me, ya heard," she replied.

"I see."

"But what's up wit' you…I mean, I see you king of shit out here. You got a lady?" she asked.

"Fuck a woman. I'm about my business, shorti."

"Yeah, but you gonna need a right hand bitch to hold you down someday."

"Brenda holds me down, a'ight."

"You think so? The bitch keeps hatin' on me. I'm just sayin', she be havin' problems sometimes, and right now, you look like the type of niggah who don't need any problems in yo' life right now."

Nico stepped to Demi a little closer. "I can deal wit' a problem. I just need you to do me right so we can make shit happen."

"Believe me, Nico, you and me, we can definitely get sumthin' poppin. I see the way you be lookin' at me, thinking about it," Demi continued to tease.

Nico chuckled. "You need to stay focused on business."

"I am," she replied with a smile.

Nico then took Demi by her arms and held her tightly in his grip. He looked at her with a hard gaze. "Let me tell you sumthin, Demi. I'm not Brenda, so if you fuck me, you'll end up wit' your head cut the fuck off."

Demi nodded.

"A'ight, ay, you do good by me, and I'll do good by you. But I want you to start by kickin' all that bullshit-ass drama to the curb. You and Brenda need to make this a happy fuckin' home."

Demi continued with her smile. "I definitely wanna be very good to you. Believe me, whateva you need, I'm there."

It was war now, she said to herself. Demi knew how strongly Brenda felt about Nico, and now she wanted to hit Brenda where it would hurt the most—her heart. She knew get-

192

ting close to Nico would nearly kill her, and Demi wanted to see the bitch crumble. So she would play Nico closely, and fuck him when the time came.

In her mind, she was ready to put in work—get down right nasty and turn L.A. the fuck out. She felt that now was the right time for the world to know her—see her in fuckin' action. First it would be porn, then a successful career in Hollywood and from there on, the sky was the limit.

Brenda didn't know it, but when she pulled that gun out on Demi, and threatened her life, it created a monster. Demi could become very vindictive and had that hate for Brenda settling in her heart. She was already pissed off at the world. Her brothers ridiculed her and showed her no support, and her mother gave up on everything a long time ago. And she was determined not to become that bitch that was bitter in life, knowing she missed out on her chance.

Nico continued to talk to Demi about a few other things and Demi listened carefully, taking in everything that he was saying. When it was all said and done, Demi went up to him and hugged him tightly. A hug that assured him that she was there for him.

Nico gave Demi his cell number to call him if she had any other problems.

As the two continued to talk, little did they know, Brenda stood quietly and watched everything from a darkened bedroom window. She hated to see Demi up on Nico so closely, touching him in ways that made Brenda's eyes flare up and fists tighten. Brenda knew that Demi was pushing up on Nico for only one reason—to take her out of the picture. And Brenda would be damned if that shit was going to happen.

 Twenty

Three days later, Demi was in an Econo Lodge hotel bathroom out in Carson, California getting ready to perform her first act on film. The bathroom door was locked as she took in a deep breath, while staring at her image in the mirror. Her first shoot wasn't exactly what she expected. There were no lights, cameras, action with a quality director on a sound stage or nice studio. Instead, it was in a small shabby hotel room, with one hand-held camera and several of Nico's homeboys lingering around to watch the show. Demi found out that Nico ran an underground website for his blood homies and put out raunchy DVD's for sale on the streets that were very profitable.

Looking at herself in the mirror, Demi fluffed her long hair, which Nico wanted in loose curls. He'd also gone out and purchased white lace lingerie, a long string of pearls and a fedora type hat, specifically for the shoot. It wasn't exactly Demi's style, and she wasn't sure what was up with the sexy gangsta look, but it was what Nico wanted, so she had to cooperate. Nico also informed her that she didn't need to wear panties. He wanted easy access.

Demi glanced over at the outfit that was hanging up on the back of the door, and took herself a quick sip from her fourth Hennessy and Coke that rested on the bathroom sink. In her mind, if she was getting ready to fuck a few strangers in front of a camera, getting drunk was the best way to get through it.

Sliding on the tasteless attire, Demi downed the rest of her drink and then slid into some six inch clear stilettos shoes. She definitely looked like a porn star with her long defined legs and clear glossy lips which looked like ice itself. After looking at herself in the mirror one last time, Demi walked out of the bathroom and into a room full of lustful thugs who were eager to see how nasty she was willing to get for a buck. She scanned the room for Nico and saw him by the bed talking to the guy holding the digital camera.

"There we go, I like that… ay, that's what I'm talkin' about. You ready to ride?" Nico asked, staring at Demi with lustful eyes.

Demi nodded.

"Damn!" she heard someone say.

"I got next, right?" another thug joked.

"I'll buy that for a dollar," another goon said, creating laughter in the room.

Demi moved through the thugs and approached Nico in a timid gesture. She had her arms folded across her chest. She felt like a piece of shit for a moment. It wasn't an unfamiliar scene to her, but it felt like she'd hit her lowest point in life. She started to remember her experience with a few niggahs she'd fucked for the come up before Perry came into the picture. And to keep herself from feeling like shit, Demi kept reminding herself that it was just a job. If she was going to be an actress, Demi would have to do sex scenes with other actors anyway, so this could just account for practice.

"What I gotta do?" Demi asked.

"You just gotta do you. Enjoy the shit and wild out on my homies like it ain't a thang for you," Nico explained.

"Homies?" she questioned.

"Ay, the more on film, the better," Nico added.

Demi's heart began to race. She looked around the room not knowing who would be the lucky one to pop her cherry on film. Some of the guys standing around looked half way decent, but the others ones made her want to throw up in her mouth.

"Ay, Demi, you good right?" Nico asked, like she had a choice.

Demi lied. "Yeah."

"Ay, homies, y'all niggahs come over here and let's make

this movie. I know none of y'all niggahs ain't scared of pussy!" Nico shouted.

"Hell, no," someone shouted back.

"Niggah, just tell that bitch to get on her fuckin' knees, open wide and I'll do the fuckin' rest," another man yelled. He stirred the room up with laughter.

"You a funny niggah, Monk," someone added.

Demi watched three men come up to her with big smirks on their faces. They were all in red gear of course, showing off their blood colors for all to see. They crowded around Demi and waited for Nico to give the word. Nico was telling the camera guy something and then he turned to his homies.

"Ay yo, let's get this shot right, y'all niggahs know how we do, give our homies their monies worth. Blood In-Blood Out Entertainment, Crenshaw Mafia, my niggahs!"

They nodded, and shouted out their sets, tossing their gang signs in the air and becoming hype off the moment. Demi watched the gang signs go up, but kept quiet as niggahs showed off for the camera, almost forgetting that she was in the room. Everyone started stacking, which was announcing their affiliations to their gangs, cliques or just spelling out their sets or bonds in a non-verbal communication way, with a rapid movement of fingers moving, twisting or dancing about for everyone to see on the DVD.

Demi looked over at Nico and yelled, "What are they doin?"

"Stackin'...showin' our loyalty for all to see what we about and how we do."

Nico smiled. It was what he wanted to see. His business was thriving and he was at the centerfold of it all, running shit and making serious ends from it all. Blood In-Blood Out Entertainment was into everything from producing hardcore underground rap albums to promoting low rider car shows, and of course porn. They were all ruthless entrepreneurs that had money to burn and a reputation to uphold.

But Nico's porn websites and DVD's were the most profitable legal service he had. His porn sight had over one million viewers and his DVDs were pushing up to fifty thousand copies and reaching out all over the Unites States. Nico was ruthless in the world of his legit business ventures just like he was ruthless in the streets, in the dope game, banging and murdering.

"A'ight, let's go niggahs. Quiet on the fuckin' set," Nico yelled like a real director.

Demi positioned herself toward the bed and braced herself for what was to happen.

When everybody got in position, Nico called out, "Action."

Within seconds, Demi was overcome by the three goons who were all on her like prey. Quickly taking off her hat, lingerie, and breaking the fake pearls, they tossed her on the bed and began fondling her, licking her everywhere, sucking on her breast and sticking fingers into her wet pussy with no hesitation at all.

With everything happening so fast, one goon was able to get naked without her even knowing. He squatted over Demi's face and forced his dick down her throat as she was sprawled on her back with another man eating her pussy out. The third man devoured her breast like candy. Demi didn't understand why Nico even wanted her to wear any clothes, if everything was going to be ripped off so quickly.

The camera began zooming in, capturing Demi sucking the niggah's dick eagerly. However, she had to stop suckin' for a minute, and twisted her face into a pleasurable moan as the second man ate out her pussy with conviction. She dug her manicured nails into the back of his head and wrapped her legs around him. The liquor in her system had definitely taken affect.

Like the top porn star, Jenna Jameson, she wanted to be the best on film and definitely had no limits. She wanted to impress Nico, and let him know that she had skills.

The trio went to work on Demi, moving her here, sucking her there and sticking their dicks into every hole available. Each was having their way with her and she didn't reject. She went with the flow. The other men in the room looked on with excitement, having the camera man capture the look on their faces as they got high and drunk and enjoyed the show.

The three men constantly threw up gang signs as they tore into Demi, either hitting it from the back or getting their dick sucked. Nico stood to the side, loving the show that was being put on and knowing that the sales for his DVD would hit the roof.

They ran the train on Demi like she was the track itself. The first man came across her face, making his semen look like lotion dripping off her chin. When the second man came, he exploded on her stomach and the third wanted to take it to the next level and forced Demi to swallow his nut, which she did. It had the other thugs in the room going crazy, and dying for next with her.

The camera man focused on everything closely, and zoomed in on the money shots, capturing Demi in a few very unimaginable positions. It was definitely hardcore porn performed to the fullest. Nico knew that his customers would be very happy with the footage.

A long two and a half hours later, it was all over. After Nico made everyone leave, Demi remained naked on the stained and wrinkled bed looking like she'd been through hell and back. With her hair a mess and wearing a smirk across her face, she locked eyes with Nico, and tried to hold a decent attitude about herself. She wasn't going to cry, bitch, or complain about it—what was done, was done. She held her own with the three men and knew that there was no turning back. She wasn't going to feel violated, and she wasn't gonna be ashamed of herself. Demi knew that she did what she had to do. In her mind, it was called survival.

"You good?" Nico asked.

Demi stood up, not bothering to cover herself. "You impressed?" she asked with this ill-disciplined grin.

Nico laughed. "You definitely held your own."

He walked up to her and tossed a wad of bills at her side.

The stack was appealing in Demi eyes, and she knew by the sight of the cash, it was a lot. Demi picked up the money and quickly went through the bills.

"I got another shoot that I want you to do next week. It's in a more classy environment, wit' a better class of homies," Nico informed her.

Demi wanted Nico to be impressed by her performance, but she didn't want to do another film anytime soon. She was also bothered that this all just seemed like business to him.

"I can't get a thank you, a least," she said.

"Bitch, for what…you got paid right," Nico replied with a serious stare. "Just get dressed and I'll take you back to the crib."

He walked out of the room with a nonchalant attitude, leaving Demi alone to get dressed and feeling like a commodity. She picked up the money again and counted fifteen hundred dollars. At that moment, all of the mixed feelings she had were completely gone. She was happy. Now she could try and find another photographer and get some decent headshots. After headshots, the next thing was to start mingling around the city. She had to network with the elite. Demi knew that if Nico continued to pay her the same amount or even more, then she would be knocking on the doors of Hollywood real soon.

 # Twenty-One

The camera man zoomed in on Demi sucking dick on the hood of a white 1970 Chevy Monte Carlo inside one of the deserted warehouses next to the Blood In-Blood Out warehouse. The man she was blessing with her sweet lips was lying against the hood of the car with a wide smile as Demi deep-throated him like her mouth was a bottomless pit. Nico stood by and watched as Demi put in work. Forty days had passed since Demi stepped foot in L.A. She seemed to be an instant hit.

Nico watched Demi closely, yet he also watched his boy Lyfe, whose dick was hard from watching Demi perform. Nico was on his cell-phone talking but seemed to have his eyes and ears on everything. He was about business and nodded towards Demi agreeing with how she was performing.

"Damn, Nico, you need to put me in there too wit' the bitch," Lyfe suggested. "I need to hit that again."

Nico shot him a glance and told the person on the phone to hold on. "What the fuck did you just say, niggah? Hit what again?"

Lyfe cursed himself for running his big mouth. He knew Nico would be pissed if he ever found out what him and Mist did. Nico was overprotective when it came to his investments, and didn't like his girls to have sex with anybody without his permission.

"Oh, no… my bad. I didn't mean again. I just meant when you gonna let me hit. You know…for the first time," Lyfe said.

Nico continued to stare at Lyfe with cold eyes but didn't say anything. He knew something wasn't right, which meant he'd ask questions later. Somebody would eventually break, so he turned around and continued with his call. It was obvious that his phone call was more important than his boy running his mouth. Lyfe on the other hand quickly brushed it off and continued watching Demi give the performance of a lifetime. He reached his hand down into his pants and fantasized about Demi doing him the same way.

The past three weeks had been really busy for Demi. She was on the grind trying to get her money right. Nico had her in a porn film at least three times a week. They'd shot in Athens, Pasadena, and even Santa Monica. He'd put Demi up on the website quickly, and her performance had gotten over two million hits within the first week. Word was spreading like wild fire and Demi was becoming the next biggest thing in porn, with a fan base growing by the thousands, both east coast and west coast. She was the next Superhead...yet even better.

Demi's exotic look and extreme freakiness on camera was becoming very profitable for Blood In-Blood Out Entertainment. She was making good money from her sins and was finally feeling comfortable with her situation to do her thing. She was definitely becoming a big star, even though it wasn't exactly the type of star she dreamed of.

"Shit, I'm cumin'!" the man Demi was sucking off yelled.

Demi continued to slob him down, not missing a beat. She had her hands gripped around his nine and a half inch hard dick as she ran her tuneful lips rapidly up and down his shaft. Suddenly, the young thug jerked, only to grab a fist full of her hair that made the camera man smile. Demi's co-star trembled against the cold, hard metal hood of the car, and made wild noises that had the camera man excited once again.

"Shit! Oh shit! Damn...oh shit...damn!" he cried out, as Demi's lips felt like a strong vacuum.

Demi felt his dick harden in her mouth, which turned her on even more. In her mind, she was now known as Mz. Lush, and it was no holds barred with the young thug she tasted. Getting into the character would help her performances on film. She had to bury Demi deep down somewhere and bring out a woman who just didn't give a fuck.

The camera man tried to focus in on Demi's expression. He decided to zoom in on her eyes again. He wanted to capture that deep neurotic look she held while sexing her prey. He focused on her, then panned out; capturing Demi's thick lips wrapped around the nice piece of black dick.

"Oh shit, I'm cumin'," the guy shouted again.

He lifted his butt cheeks and held his dick steady in Demi's mouth, feeling himself about to go off. Demi sucked him till the end and felt the nut burst into her mouth, but she still didn't miss a beat as his load dripped down her chin.

The guy looked exhausted and Demi had a smile about her that said it all. The camera man was satisfied with the shots he'd gotten and called it quits. At that moment, Demi got down off the hood of the car looking sexy as hell in her pumps and birthday suit. Pretending to be her alter ego, Mz. Lush, Demi felt comfortable and right at home.

She pranced up to Nico in all her glory. "You like?"

But it was Lyfe who responded. "Yeah, I like. Let me get a round wit' yo' fine-ass."

Demi sucked her teeth and rolled her eyes, which made him upset. "Fuck you!" She focused back on Nico.

"So, it's like that," Lyfe replied. He was ready to go upside Demi's head, but with Nico around, he knew better.

"Lyfe, step the fuck off!" Nico instructed.

Lyfe shot Demi a wicked stare and then slowly walked away.

"Hurry up and get dressed, so we can go," Nico ordered to Demi, then walked away.

Demi watched as Nico pimped over to the camera man and gave him some dap. She also heard him say that they had another shoot in two more days. All Demi could do was sigh. She wanted her porn career to come to an end soon, but didn't know how to bring the subject up. With the taste of cum still in her mouth, Demi knew she didn't want to suck dicks for the rest of her life, even if the money was good. By Nico raising her pay from fifteen to eighteen hundred a film, she'd saved over ten thousand dollars. She'd even sent a thousand dollars home to her mother in order to buy her some time with Aliyah. Janet, in turn, told Demi since her money was coming in more frequently she could stay in California as long as she wanted, but the minute the money stopped, it was a wrap. However, Demi didn't have plans on letting Aliyah stay in New York too much longer. Ten thousand wasn't a lot, but it was time to move on from porn.

Two hours later, Nico and Demi were sitting inside a premier restaurant in West Hollywood called the O-Bar. It was a hot spot known for great comfort food, with a contemporary setting. It was also Nico's favorite place to go when he was celebrating. With all the money Demi was making him, he definitely had tons to celebrate about.

During dinner, Demi found out that Nico had three boys, ages ranging from ten to fifteen months, with three different baby mothers. She wasn't surprised though. Nico was a very handsome man with a credible street reputation so what woman wouldn't want to be with him physically? Demi, herself, found him very attractive and wanted to bed him down when she first met him. Now, it seemed as if they strictly had a business relationship.

But with Demi overhearing some things about Nico from some people on the shoots, it also made her question her business relationship with him. Supposedly, he was ruthless with his partners and crazy to the point that if you were making him enough money, he kept you on lock down. You became like a slave in his business and if you threatened his money, then he had killers coming for you. Word has it, he'd killed a few of his actresses before. Basically getting paid from him came with a price.

Demi didn't want the rumors about Nico to trouble her. All she knew was that by working for him, she was better off than before. Nico had her full attention, and so far he was keeping his word and for Demi, that's all that mattered.

Demi took a bite of her ginger glazed sea bass. "No disrespect, but how did you get yourself involved wit' a bitch like Brenda?" For some reason, she felt comfortable enough to finally ask him that.

"What is it between y'all two?"

"The bitch is a hater, that's all. She's threatened by me, and I know it. Are you fuckin' her?"

"That's really none of your business," Nico replied in a casual but stern tone.

"Dag, I was just askin'."

Nico frowned. "Well, don't ask."

"Well, what kind of ladies do you like?"

"You ask a lot of questions. But to answer you, I like the ones that can get me money. I love a bitch that hustles hard and makes her ends."

"And what you think I'm doing," Demi said.

Nico stared at her. "You makin' some noise for yourself now… I like that. But in this game, you gotta know how to hold your own, and never bite the hand that feeds you. Remember that Demi. And this thang wit' Brenda…the beef wit' ya'll, I don't want it escalatin'. She's a G, and she's makin' me some good money and I don't want you fuckin' that up. I've known her for a long time, you understand?"

Demi nodded.

"Cool, now finish your food so we can get the fuck outta here," Nico added.

Demi glanced at Nico and didn't say a word. She just kept reminding herself that her situation was only temporary.

After dinner, Demi got into Nico's truck, but he hesitated in starting the engine. He just sat there with a blank stare. Demi looked at him and asked, "What's wrong?"

Nico turned and looked at her with an evil smirk. "Suck my dick."

"What?" Demi questioned with a baffled gaze.

"I said suck my dick right now," he repeated in a commanding manner.

Demi was shocked by the way he suddenly came at her. She felt disrespected and used. It was bad enough she had to suck random dicks for a living, now she had to do her boss. "Where is all this comin' from?"

"Shut the fuck up. You suck dicks all the time, and now you wanna question why you gotta suck this one. Don't get cute, bitch!"

Nico began unbuttoning his jeans and pulled out his dick that looked like a long, thick black sausage. Holding his manhood with a tight grip, he looked over at Demi with a mocking stare. "Ay, I ain't got all fuckin' night."

Demi knew that she had to do what she was told. Nico's vulgar mood was killing her willingness. She wondered why the change in attitude, thinking that she probably said something to offend him; maybe it was her bringing up Brenda and questioning his relationship with her. The look Nico had said that he was upset about something.

Following his command, Demi kept her mouth shut and leaned downward into his lap and slowly took Nico's nicely sized tool into her mouth. She began bobbing her head up and down, salivating all over his dick as she sucked him off. Nico leaned back in his seat and gripped her long black hair, tangling it up into his fist.

She had rhythm and technique to her, circling the tip of his dick with her tongue—coiling and twisting. She ran her fist up and down his shaft causing a satisfying moan to escape from his lips. Demi went to work after hearing him moan and shudder the way he did. She licked slowly down his shaft and swept her sweet tongue across his nuts, tasting all of him bit by bit.

"Damn, bitch. You definitely got skills," Nico said

faintly.

He had his eyes closed and released his grip from her tangled hair. Demi sucked, licked, and chewed on his nuts and all in between his thighs. Nico had his legs spread widely, giving Demi better access to the dick as he clutched the back of the passenger headrest tightly. With Demi's glossy lips wrapped around his manhood and tongue curled around the base, she sucked him off rapidly, feeling Nico about to explode into her mouth. She was ready for him. After all, he was the boss man.

She heard Nico panting, as he thrust his hips upward. He rammed his long dick further down her throat. But Demi kept her rhythm and continued to keep him in her mouth, with her hands and lips covered in saliva. She knew it wasn't long before he came. Demi felt Nico's thick meat harden in her mouth and within seconds, he began quivering. He almost ripped the headrest apart with his tight grip. Demi continued to suck on it and then abruptly felt Nico burst his creamy white juices into her mouth. Demi didn't miss a beat as she continued to suck him off, and then swallowed every last drop of him. She moved back into her seat and wiped her mouth. She knew he was pleased, actions spoke louder than words. And his actions said it all.

"You happy?" Demi asked sarcastically. She was so tired of men taking advantage of her.

Nico looked nonchalant for a moment. He buttoned up his jeans and then turned to look over at Demi. He then said in a very soft and casual tone, "That is what I pay you for, to suck and fuck niggahs, not to question me about anything…Mz. Lush."

Demi just looked at Nico with a hard stare that could slice through concrete. But she kept her mouth shut and her opinion to herself. At that point, Demi knew more than ever that she had to find a way to leave. In the meantime, she would continue to save her money. She had to be smart about it. Mistakes were not optional.

After Nico dropped Demi back off at Brenda's, she sat in

the living room with her mind running a mile a minute. That was until Brenda walked out of her bedroom and saw Demi lounging on her couch. Both ladies exchanged hard glares at each other for a few seconds before Brenda spoke up.

"Why you on my couch? Nico told me to let you sleep in a bedroom now, so I shouldn't have to see your ass every time I get home from work."

Demi just rolled her eyes.

"Look, this is still my place, so don't get too fuckin' comfortable. Little do you know once that pussy gets dried up and Nico get tired of you, you'll see what's up."

With everything that had just gone down with Nico, Demi wasn't in the mood for anymore drama. "Whateva."

Brenda didn't like Demi's attitude and stepped closer. "Bitch, you ain't all that!"

"Why the fuck are you in here botherin' me? Don't you have somethin' else to do? Go get high or some shit !" Demi shouted then quickly stood up.

Brenda laughed. "You think Nico gonna have yo' back, bitch? You just some hoe he makin' money off of, and then after you, he'll bring the next hoe around to make money off of."

Demi didn't give Brenda the satisfaction of knowing how Nico had just treated her.

"Well, you should'a seen that niggahs' face tonight when I was suckin' his dick after we came from the O-Bar. He was lovin' that shit." She mocked Brenda with a sinful smile knowing the words would hit home. "Then I fucked him…thanking him for the star treatment."

It pissed Brenda off even more to find out that Nico had taken Demi to a nice restaurant. She'd known Nico for a long time, and he never took a girl anywhere, especially not alone. Brenda didn't want to admit that Demi was definitely becoming a threat to her. She refused to be replaced by anyone.

Demi continued. "Yeah, bitch, he took me there and he was loving the way I sexed him in his truck. He promised me all kinds of shit. See, I know how to make money for him, but you…you just washed the fuck up."

Demi added more lines perfecting her lie, and never cracked a smile.

Brenda was ready to beat the shit out Demi, and show her how a true bitch got down, but then she thought about Nico and how he wanted them to keep the peace in the house. It almost killed Brenda not to punch the shit out of her.

"You better step the fuck off, fo' real bitch!" Brenda warned through clenched teeth. "When Nico's gone from yo' side and through wit' you, that's when I'm gonna get off my leash and let you know what time it is."

"Yo' ass ain't nuthin' but all bark wit' no bite!" Demi yelled.

Brenda didn't return with her response, she just glared at Demi and backed off, knowing her time would come and that Demi's dreams of Hollywood would soon come to a dreadful end.

When Brenda walked off, Demi knew that it was time to step her game up and get from under Nico and Brenda's wing. She didn't know how long her role in porn would last. *Shit was gettin' hectic*, she thought to herself.

# Twenty-Two

"Demi Rodriquez," the short, stout man called out in the waiting area where Demi sat.

"I'm here," Demi called out.

Her heart immediately began to race. *This is it*, she thought. She stood up in her brand new cream, Tracy Reese silk shirt and black pencil skirt. A classy and sophisticated outfit that she'd just purchased the day before. Besides, sending money back home for Aliyah, and buying a new pre-paid cell phone, the outfit was the third important thing she'd bought with her money.

Demi had also opened up a checking account for herself at Bank of America. With now close to ten grand in her account, she had to make sure the money was safe. She knew from her hotel experience that just hiding money in odd places wasn't cool, so she figured it would be more professional to just do it the right way and put it into a bank where no one could touch it. Demi knew that hiding money around Brenda was a no-no, especially with all the goons constantly in and out of her place.

Demi tried to erase any recollection of Brenda as she followed the gentleman down a long hallway. She put on her best smile, hoping her cheerful attitude would help with the meeting she was about to attend with Mr. Robert Hampton, a very well known franchised agent in the business.

Over the past week, Demi had done her homework and researched several different agencies in the Los Angeles area. When she had a small break from spreading her legs, she would take a cab down to the local library and get on the internet. She would spend hours reading, and studying the acting business, mostly focusing her attention on agents and casting calls. This time she wanted to be educated. Taking matters into her own hands, Demi had done the research on attaining an agent and found out that there were commercial agents, theatrical agents, a legitimate agent, a voice–over agent, modeling agents, variety agents and full service agents. If that wasn't enough and very overwhelming, she also found out that agents were franchised, or not franchised, which was good to know in her kind of work.

After reading up on franchised agents and finding out that they were the ones who were licensed to represent union performers, Demi learned that it would probably be to her advantage to get a franchised agent. She became aware that union pay was much better than non-union pay and that she would get benefits and some work environment controls that prevented directors and producers from making a slave out of her.

Also, franchised agents were required under their franchise agreements to conduct their business with you in certain ways. This would give Demi a certain level of protection and an outlet to register grievances.

Mr. Hampton was a franchise agent with a well-known roster of familiar clients. He dealt with mostly theatrics and commercials, and was known throughout Sundance for putting actors into well-known films that got nationwide attention. Demi would hit him up every day by phone, dying for a meet and greet with him. But Mr. Hampton was very selective with who he signed onto his agency as a client. He only wanted to work with the best and talented, and those that had their shit together, meaning that they were willing to work hard. Mr. Hampton took nothing less and wanted his clients to always give their all. He only agreed to see Demi because he saw that after several days of being persistent with phone calls, he saw that Demi was relentless, which certainly was a good quality to have.

Demi followed Mr. Hampton into his office and took a seat in one of the chairs positioned by his desk. His office looked cool with the photos of some of his clients hanging on the walls, a flat-screen television mounted behind his desk, and a wonderful view of Wilshire Boulevard from his tenth floor corner window.

Demi was ready, even though she didn't have the one page resume or headshot that most agencies required. In this case, she was just gonna have to sell herself and hope that it would work.

Demi sat opposite Mr. Hampton and tried to look relaxed. Mr. Hampton stood about five-seven, and wore clear wire rimmed glasses that looked expensive. He was also a funny looking white man with a receding hairline, a busy goatee, and chubby fingers.

He shuffled through some papers that were spread across his desk and then leaned back in his leather chair, locked his fingers around each other and focused on Demi, staring over the rim of his glasses. He was already captured by how beautiful she was, but chose to keep his comments to himself. Besides, he'd seen tons of beautiful women coming into his office with dreams of becoming the next Angelina Jolie; they came in different shapes, races and sizes. The big question was did they have talent. So even though Demi was beautiful, he wasn't impressed. To him, it was the character of the person that he was sold on, not the look.

"Demi, is it?" he asked.

"Yes. And thank you so much for takin' the time out to meet wit' me," Demi replied.

She hadn't even been in the office five minutes and he was already asking her questions that would probably reduce her chances of benefitting from his services.

"Actually Mr. Hampton, I don't have any acting experience."

Mr. Hampton stared at her for a brief moment.

"Oh boy…here we go. Ms. Rodriquez, I don't have time for this. You can't expect anybody in this business to take you serious if you don't have any experience. Where is your resume…your headshots?"

"Mr. Hampton, I'm gonna be completely honest with

you. I've had a rough time since coming to Los Angeles almost two months ago. I met a well-known photographer who was supposed to do my headshots along with managing me, but things didn't quite work out as planned. Look, I don't wanna bore you with another sob story because I'm sure you've heard tons of them. But I'm a hard worker. I promise if you take me on as a client, I won't disappoint you.

Mr. Hampton let out a long sigh. "Are you working now?"

Demi didn't think it was best to be one hundred percent truthful. "I'm flexible right now. I do have a job, but it's only temporary."

"And what is that you do?" he wanted to know.

Demi began to sweat on her forehead a little bit. "I do odd jobs. I bartend here and there, and I'm also doing a little babysitting."

He threw his pencil down then nodded. "Where are you from?"

"New York, the upper west side," she lied again.

"New York, huh…great city. I worked there for years before coming out here," he said.

Demi displayed a warm smile.

"So, you wanna become an actress, huh? Tell me about yourself and what are you looking to find here with this agency?"

This was where Demi had to sell herself to him. She took a deep breath, locked eyes with him and began.

"First off, I've heard a lot of good things about you." Demi made sure to articulate every word, and definitely no slang. "Mr. Hampton, after all I've been through, I only want to deal with the best. I came here from New York trying to find something better for myself."

"So, why didn't you try this in New York? Why didn't you try and land some small roles there before coming across the country?"

Demi didn't want him to think she was stupid, even

though believing a complete stranger really was. "Actually sir, I really wanted to take a chance out here. L.A. just has a better vibe."

"Well, I don't think that was the smartest decision young lady. Little do you know, this is a tough business, and it's not easy to break into. Some experience would've helped," he informed.

"I understand. I sacrificed a lot by coming out here, so like I said before, I'm willing to work hard. I have a young daughter back home that I support, and I want a better life for her. I want to show her that you can do whatever you want as long as you put your mind to it. I came to Los Angeles with almost nothing to my name, but I worked hard and refused to quit."

Mr. Hampton didn't respond, but continued to study her.

"No disrespect Mr. Hampton, but believe me, I'm gonna make it big with or without you. Even if nobody else does, I believe in myself. Hell, I feel that my life is a movie within itself."

He reclined in his leather chair, staring at Demi. He was somewhat impressed with her character and loved her rawness. Not to mention, even without the headshot, it was obvious that she was very photogenic.

"I'm not gonna lie to you Demi, you do need more experience in this business just for an agency like us to even consider taking you on. You have character and I like that, and you have a very appealing look to you, but the lack of experience still bothers me. What kind of work are you looking to get into anyway? Commercials, stage plays, motion pictures? Do you wanna play the desperate house wife next door, or the deranged Glenn Close in Fatal Attraction?"

"It doesn't matter. I'm very diverse. I just know, if you set me up with any auditions, I'll definitely leave an impression. I just need a chance to build on something," Demi stated with conviction.

Mr. Hampton studied her for a moment. He couldn't lie…he did see some potential in Demi, and decided that it wouldn't hurt giving her a chance. He knew that in Hollywood it was seventy percent your look, ten percent personality, and twenty percent skills, until you became seasoned.

"Here's what I'm gonna do for you. I'll keep an ear open for anything I hear that may be a fit for you. I'm gonna give you a month trial and send you out on a few casting calls, then we'll see what happens from there," he said. "If all goes well, I'll sign you to a contract with my agency. But before the trial starts, you've gotta enroll in some acting classes, and get some head-shots done. I can recommend several photographers."

Demi smiled so hard her cheeks began to hurt. "Are any of those photographers named Alex Trend?"

Mr. Hampton shook his head. "No, not at all."

"Great," Demi said. "Thank you so much. All I'm askin' for is a chance."

"You got it," Mr. Hampton said walking toward the door. "Now here is some information on acting classes, along with two photographer's phone numbers. I'll be in touch," he ended as Demi turned around to leave.

She left his office with so much confidence, nothing could ruin her day. That was until her cell phone started to ring. Demi looked at the caller I.D and saw it was Nico. She sighed, knowing his calls were always about business, and business with Nico meant more sucking and fucking if she wanted to continue getting paid and having shelter over her head.

But Demi ignored his calls, stuffed her phone in her purse and kept it moving, saying to herself, "Not today, boo."

It showed on her face, knowing that her life needed to change for the better. She was determined not to go backwards. She needed to move forward and start making better decisions for herself. Her first decision was to say, "Fuck Nico for the day. It's time to work on my new life."

# Twenty-Three

Demi walked down Wilshire Boulevard with a radiant smile. It was her time to shine and she was ready to make her move in this game called life. It finally felt like all her hard work was finally going to pay off. Even though she didn't sign any official paper work with Mr. Hampton to become her agent, she had a good feeling about him and the auditions he would set up for her. Demi already had it embedded in her mind that whatever auditions she took, she would kill it.

Demi needed a break from Nico, Brenda, the house and the porn industry. She needed some time out for herself and decided to stay away from everyone for the day. Nico had been blowing up her cell phone non stop since she left the meeting, but she refused to answer the calls. In the past weeks, she had busted her ass for him, so in Demi's mind she could use the day off. Nico was definitely acting like her pimp. He ran his business like a fucking plantation, and treated her as a commodity, not as a woman or a person. She was sick of it all.

The sun shone heavily over the city, with the hot air feeling good to Demi as she strutted down the busy L.A. street. It was mid-afternoon and the city seemed so alive. Where Demi was, looked like a mini Times Square somewhat—with the tall buildings, billboards, the traffic, and the stores that lined the street. Not to mention with people coming and going, it kind of reminded her of home.

Demi walked into a jazzy coffee spot to get herself a nice cup of coffee, which she suddenly had a taste for. She wanted to be around strangers to get her mind right so she could focus on the opportunities that had just been presented to her. After standing in a fairly long line, Demi paid for her Cappuccino and looked for the nearest available table. Once she found a single bar stool type-seat facing the window, Demi placed her cup down then began to watch different people walk by. Taking a sip of her coffee, she smiled when she noticed an older man attempting to cross the busy street.

At that moment, Demi immediately thought about the only friend who'd been true to her since she'd come to California. Demi hadn't spoken to Benny since the day he dropped her off at Brenda's house. She missed him and wanted to hear his voice. Every time Benny came around, he had some assuring words for her, and at a time like this she needed someone with an inspirational influence.

She pulled out her cell phone and quickly dialed Benny's number hoping that he hadn't changed it over the past couple of weeks. The phone rang once, then twice, then a third time. When it reached the fourth ring, Demi was about to give up hope, but then heard someone say, "Hello."

She knew by the voice that it was Benny. The strong West Indian accent made her smile. "Benny," she called out with enthusiasm.

"Pretty gal, me know that voice anywhere," Benny replied. "How ya been?"

"Oh my God Benny, I missed you," Demi cried out.

"Me missed ya too? How's Hollywood treatin' ya?" he asked.

"Benny, guess what, I met with this agent today and he's well-known and is willin' to work wit' me. He's gonna represent me, Benny…do you believe that? I'm gonna have an agent," Demi stated with joy.

"Ya see that pretty gal, you're on ya way. Ya just gotta keep believing in yourself and keep pushing forward."

"Benny, where are you? I wanna see you so we can go out and celebrate. You busy?" she asked.

"Yes. Me so sorry pretty gal. It's me and my wife's anniversary today, and we're spending the day together. Do you think me can get a rain check?"

Demi smiled. "Sure, Benny. Happy Anniversary. Even though I've never what yo' wife tell her…" Demi stopped when someone tapped her on the shoulder. She was shocked to see him standing there.

"Hello, pretty gal. Are ya there?" Benny asked.

"Umm…yeah Benny I'm here. Tell yo' wife I said Happy Anniversary. I'll call you tomorrow to see how everything went."

"Okay."

It was all Demi heard before quickly hanging up the phone and locking eyes with Rasheed. She wondered what he was doing all the way out in California. Demi remembered their last conversation in the club back in Harlem, but also remembered giving him the cold shoulder.

Demi smiled. Even though they'd met once, it didn't go so smoothly. Yet, it felt good to see a familiar face for once, someone from Harlem. "What are you doin' out here?"

Rasheed leaned down and hugged her like they'd known each other for years. "I came to L.A. about a week after we met," he replied.

He was dressed in loose fitted denim jeans that looked like hand me downs, a regular white T-shirt and some aged, white air-force ones. Demi still wasn't feeling his style, but he was cute as always.

"For what?" Demi asked.

"Basically on business." Rasheed looked around the coffee shop. "There's a table for two over there. You wanna join me?"

"Sure." Demi grabbed her cup along with her purse, and followed Rasheed to a nearby table. "How's yo' friend Malik?" she asked taking a seat.

"I ain't talked to him in a while, but I'm sure he still following yo' friend around." When Demi grinned, Rasheed didn't hesitate complimenting her. "You're still beautiful as ever."

Demi blushed.

"Thanks. So, what business are you on all the way out

here. Should I even be sittin' here wit' yo' ass? Are the Feds watchin' us?"

"Funny…real funny. You must not have a good memory. I told you that night at the club that I was a writer."

Demi nodded then took another sip of coffee. "Oh, yeah that's right. So, did you come out here to get some inspiration?"

"No. Remember that script I told that I was workin' on, about the dude from the Bronx who was misguided and lost in life, and came up in the streets. He sold drugs, shot people, and just didn't give a fuck."

Demi nodded. "Yeah, I remember, I kinda dissed it, right?"

Rasheed grinned. "Yeah, you did."

"I'm sorry for the way I treated you when we first met. I shouldn't have talked to you like that."

"Nah, it's cool, no sweat. But just to let you know, that shit I wrote, it was about my life. I've been through it, Demi. I did six years in an upstate prison for drugs and violence. I've been on the streets since I was eight. My moms loved her drugs and boyfriends more than she did her own son."

"Sounds a little like my life," Demi interrupted.

"Yo, I used to be animal out there and had that same frame of mind as all these other niggahs on these streets. It was all about the money, the women, the clothes, and cars. But I opened my eyes to reality when I was twenty-five. Shit, I even got shot five times by my own cousin over fifty dollars."

"Damn, that's deep. I had no idea."

"Well, I'm out here because an independent film company finally bought my script," Rasheed explained.

Demi was impressed. "Really? Now, that's what's up."

"Yeah, when I got the news, I packed up some of my shit and flew out here, so I could seal the deal," Rasheed said. "They actually loved the script so much that they wanted to put it into production right away."

Demi's face lit up. "Really? So, how does that work?"

"Well, believe it or not, I didn't expect the process to go

so fast. By the time I got out here and the deal was finally done, they already had some Z-list actors in mind." He started laughing. "Why couldn't they have gotten Denzel to play me and shit? Anyway…a few weeks after that, they informed me that they were about to start filmin' a few scenes. The movie will more than likely go straight to DVD, but it's a start. Maybe my next script will be picked up by a major studio.

"Congratulations."

"Thanks. I been chillin' wit my fam until I see a few scenes bein' shot, then I'll probably go back home," he paused. "Then again, it's so beautiful out here I just might stay."

"Oh, so you got family out here?" Demi asked.

"Yeah, I got an aunt and lil' cousin who live out in Pasadena. That's where I been posted up at."

"Wow. I'm so happy for you."

"Thanks. I told you I liked hard work," Rasheed responded with a huge smile. "So, what are you doin' out here? Well, besides being in Blood In-Blood Out movies?"

Demi almost fell out of her chair. "What? Who told you that?" She'd talked to Michelle once or twice after she first starting doing porn, but didn't realize her friend was blasting the news.

"Oh, don't worry, your girl didn't tell me because she didn't have to. Your movies all over the place. They real hot on the street out here. Even Malik told me he bought one back at home."

"They selling them back home?"

"Yep. A few vendors got'em on 125th street."

Demi was not only speechless but embarrassed and humiliated.

"Listen, I'm not here to judge you. Obviously, you had to do what you had to do," Rasheed continued.

"Yeah, but now I feel so fuckin' dirty and guilty." Demi cleared her throat. "Did you watch one of the films?"

Rasheed smiled. "I ain't gonna lie. My lil' nineteen year old cousin had a copy, and I watched some of it. Let me ask you somethin', though."

"What is it?"

"Do you enjoy doin' that type of shit?"

Demi looked down toward the table. "No, not at all."

"Then I would say you are a pretty good actress. You just need to put yourself in a more positive environment. You're too pretty to be doin' that type of shit anyway, Demi. Don't play yourself like that."

Rasheed's advice made Demi feel even worse, but she appreciated his honesty. "I'm workin' on some positive things. I actually just had a meetin' wit' a top franchised agent, and he said he would possibly put me on his roster. I just gotta take some actin' classes and get some headshots. It's a step in the right direction...I think."

"You right, that is a step in the right direction. I wanna see you do well Demi, but not with your legs in the air, or your ass bent over. That's not a good look, luv."

Demi nodded. "I feel you."

Rasheed paused for a few moments. "Come take a ride wit' me," he suggested.

"What?"

"Come take a ride with me. I have my aunt's car outside."

Demi was extremely hesitant. She hadn't known Rasheed for very long, and for all she knew he could've been a serial killer.

"Look, I see the look of concern on your face, but all I ask is that you please trust me. Hell, why don't you call Michelle and tell her you're with me, so in case something happens she can call the police." He laughed slightly, then reached into his back pocket and pulled out his wallet. "Here...this is my license. You can even give her that information."

"Where we going?" Demi asked.

"It's a surprise."

"Oh, hell no."

"Demi...please just trust me," Rasheed pleaded.

The look on his face read sincere as he handed her his license. After contemplating a few minutes, Demi finally spoke up.

"A'ight let me call Michelle and give her yo' information though. I've been bamboozled too many times out this motherfucker. Shit, give me yo' aunts information out here, too."

All Rasheed could do was laugh as Demi pulled out her phone to call her friend. It rang six times before going to voicemail. Strangely, it had some crazy message on there about if you were an old fling of hers, lose her number. Demi just shook her head.

A few minutes later, she and Rasheed were driving in his aunt's black Pontiac Bonneville headed north on the I-110 expressway. She was quiet on the way to the unknown destination, but kept her hand on her cell phone that already had the numbers, 911 on the screen. After getting jerked around by so many people, Demi wasn't taking any chances. Rasheed tried to make her feel comfortable a few times by talking about things back in New York, but after several unsuccessful tries, he too became quiet, until they arrived at The First Baptist Church, twenty minutes later.

Demi was completely confused. "Why are we here?"

Rasheed turned off the car and looked over at her. "It's my surprise."

Demi became even more confused. "What?" she asked in a baffled tone. She stared up at the church's tall brick structure and huge stone steps that led to the doorway. "Why is comin' to a church my surprise?"

"What? You don't like surprises?"

Demi chuckled. "I can't go in there. What am I'm supposed to do?"

"Nothin' at all. You can just sit there and watch."

Demi sighed. She was extremely nervous—more nervous than the day of her first porno shoot. At least she was familiar with sex, but she knew nothing about going to church or God. Janet had never taken the time to instill the works of the Lord in her as a child, nor did Demi discover Him on her own as an adult.

Rasheed continued to encourage Demi to take that first step inside. He took her hand into his and looked at her with such confidence that Demi suddenly felt out of harm's way.

"Trust me," Rasheed said.

That was the problem. Demi didn't really trust anybody. But nevertheless, she nodded and followed him inside of the church. When they stepped in, they stood quietly in one spot, which Demi didn't understand, but she was so overwhelmed with the twenty-four member choir singing, that it didn't matter. Their voices echoed throughout the church and sent chills throughout the congregation that made some members jump for joy and shout out hallelujah. The choir members were all draped in beautiful yellow and blue robes that covered them with a glow and glory, as they stood in front of the congregation, swaying from left to right and singing in tune with the band and pianist.

However, Demi's confusion all became clear when she saw an entire film crew filming the choir singing. She was floored. This crew didn't look anything like the set of her porn movies that consisted of just one camera guy. No, this was different. There were at least three cameras with operators, a boom operator for sound, a director of photography, lighting technicians, a film editor, and a key grip who was in charge of the set. They even had a wardrobe person there.

Rasheed waited until the director yelled, "Cut," before he turned to look at Demi.

"I hope you like my surprise. This is my aunt's church. The film company is on location and is in the process of filming the scene where the main character gets his life together. It's funny because it's the end of the movie, but they're filming that particular scene first."

Demi continued to look around. "Yes, I mean this is all really nice, but I guess I still don't understand why you brought me here."

"Well, for one, something led me to you. Maybe because someone knew you needed to see what a real role is like. See, the congregation is in the movie…basically they're all extras. Secondly, I was wondering if you wanted to be in the movie as well."

Demi looked like a happy child on Christmas day. "Are you serious?"

He smiled. "Yes, I am. I'm gonna play a congregation member too, but as you can see I'm a little late to the set. I had an important meeting today with an agent that couldn't be missed." When Demi looked confused, Rasheed continued. "Yeah, I need an agent too if I'm gonna stay in the screenwriting business. I need someone who's gonna shop my scripts around, or tell me what kind of scripts film companies are looking for."

"It looks like you really got yo' stuff together," Demi said.

"I'm trying," Rasheed responded. "Now, I'm gonna go over and tell the director that you're gonna be here as an extra as well. Trust me, none of the extras are getting paid, so he could care less how many people play the congregation members," he laughed. "I know it's not some big role or anything, but like I said earlier, it's a start. Plus you can keep your clothes on for this shoot."

Demi shot him a look. "Real funny."

She stood there as Rasheed quickly ran over to the director to give him a heads up. After waiting for less than a minute he ran back over to her.

"Okay, let's go and take our seats. They are about to start rolling again."

Demi followed behind Rasheed, as they walked down the center aisle. Even though it was movie set, that didn't hide the fact that it was still a church. She'd never been so nervous in her life. Church was always something she'd seen on television, or heard about through other people, but she never took the time out to attend any services or went to anything related to it. Her life was the streets, and her family definitely didn't have time to take her to church. On Sundays in her house, her mother was always prancing around drunk, or laid up with some dude she'd met the night before.

Rasheed stopped at the fourth row and sat next to a beautiful dark skin woman dressed nicely in a yellow and black sundress. The lady smiled at Rasheed and kissed him gently on the cheek before patting him on the arm.

After Demi sat down next to him, he looked at her then said, "Aunt Trish this is my friend Demi. She's from Harlem."

Demi smiled and said, "Nice to meet you."

"It's a blessing to meet you too. Welcome," Trish replied with a warm smile. "Are you excited?"

"Yes…yes I am," Demi replied.

At that moment, someone yelled out, "Places everyone…and remember when the pastor makes his approach to the podium, I need for everyone to clap loudly!"

"Sir, we do that anyway, he's our *real* pastor remember?" someone else yelled out.

The congregation started laughing, including Trish.

"Quiet on the set," the first voice yelled. "And…action!"

Exactly on cue, everyone started clapping wildly as the pastor stood up and approached the podium. He was a tall and sturdy looking man with a long, distinguished black robe which made him look like a judge.

He stared out into the congregation with a fulfilling gaze and strong posture. "God is good."

The congregation returned with, "All the time."

Rasheed and his aunt both returned the saying as well with wide smiles. Demi however had no clue what they were talking about.

"My young generation, it is a blessing to see this church occupied with the youth. With so many of our children astray with the gangs, the drugs, the violence or into prostitution, we want our youth to know that despite their past, there is still hope." The pastor's voice deepened as he allowed his tone to lengthen the ending of a few syllables as he preached in typical

Baptist fashion. "That regardless of where you been in life, Godddddddddd still loves you. People you need to know that what you do in the dark, will come to light and that there is always a home to come to with Jesus. Oh yes, He loves us. He loved us so much that he died for our sins. Oh yes, He did!" the pastor shouted.

The church went on hollering and agreeing with the pastor, as Rasheed nodded his head. He clutched Demi's hand tightly as she sat stiffly trying to take everything in. In all, she still felt like a fish out of water.

The pastor preached on, "If you're not changing for the positive, then you're not growing." He went on to talk about the youth again.

Demi's skin cringed at the thought of how she hadn't changed for the better.

The pastor continued, "Our youth need help out there, folks. They need guidance and wisdom. They need direction and prayer. They need an understanding that God is the way and that we are put here on earth for God's purpose. His will to live through us. He has a plan for all of us…oh yes he does. His plans outshine any plan that we think we have for ourselves, but when you follow God's plan…oh Lord, there is no such thing as failure. There is no such thing as disappointment and malfunction, but only greatness and prosperity to come when we do it God's way. Oh the youth, we need to love them and teach them," the preacher continued on.

The pastor went on to preach for another minute or so until he ended by saying, "To our young ladies and gentlemen sitting here this evening, accept Lord Jesus into your lives and know that knowing is power and understanding is wisdom. Be with Him, talk to Him and walk by faith not by sight. Come…come to the alter and accept him as your Lord and savior."

At that moment a young man, who was sitting in the front row stood up and slowly walked to the alter. He then fell to his knees. The young woman who sat beside him quickly

227

jumped up and wrapped her arms around his shoulders. As the pastor made his way down, the man's shoulders began to hunch up and down, which looked as if he was crying. Seconds later, the pastor placed his hand on the young man's head, just before someone yelled out, "Cut!"

Everyone started clapping as the young man on the floor quickly jumped up. "Let's take ten ladies and gentlemen," another person yelled.

As the congregation began to rise, Rasheed looked over at Demi. "That's supposed to be me on that floor." Demi examined the actor from head to toe. "It seemed so real."

"Hey, y'all get up so I can get out this pew. I want to go say something to my pastor," Trish said excitedly. "Y'all come, too."

With not much of a say so, Demi nervously moved out of the way, then followed behind Trish as she made her way up to the front.

"Pastor Adams, even though the sermon was made for the movie, it was still well taught," Trish praised.

Pastor Adams turned to greet Trish with a gracious smile then shook her hand. "Thank you, Sister Trish." He then looked at Demi who stood tensely next to Rasheed.

"Pastor Adams, you remember my nephew, Rasheed. He's the one this movie is based on, and this is his friend, Demi," Trish turned to Demi. "I'm sorry, honey. Other than being here are you involved in the film at all?"

Rasheed cleared his throat then jumped into the conversation. "Umm…well Demi is not really involved with this particular film too much, but she is an aspiring actress."

"Well, it's good to see you as always Rasheed, and nice to meet you young lady," the pastor said extending his hand. "Like Sister Trish said, even though the sermon was meant directly for the movie, I still meant every word. You all need to take what I preached about to heart. We need both young and old to step up and make Jesus the Lord of your life."

Both Rasheed and Demi shook their heads.

Pastor Adams smiled. "So, Demi you want to become an actress. Have you done anything besides this? I'm a big supporter of black folk who do positive things."

Demi knew she couldn't tell the pastor of a prominent church that she was doing porn. She didn't want to embarrass herself and have everyone look down at her in shame. So, like the same lie she'd told the agent, she also told Pastor Adams that she was between odd jobs, among other things, and now had an agent possibly representing her.

"You know, Demi, God is the best agent anyone can have in their lives. He will never lead you wrong way. He is always watching over you," Pastor Adams informed.

Demi nodded. She was still new to church and religion, but she felt the warm hospitality coming from everyone. The pastor said a few more kind and inspiring words to her before attending to other matters.

Demi and Rasheed continued to talk until was it was time for the shoot to resume. After the scene finally wrapped, Rasheed introduced Demi to the director and a few other people before they all left the church. Even though it wasn't some big production and Demi knew no one would probably never know she was even in the movie, she still felt proud that Rasheed had allowed her to be a part of such a wonderful experience. Demi also felt good about him trying to help her out…like a real friend. After all she'd endured she was grateful for his kindness and his genuine spirit. By being around him and Trish, for the first time in her life, it felt like she was around family.

When they got into the car, Demi's cell phone started to ring again. She looked at the caller I.D and saw that it was Nico, but quickly ignored the call. It had been a good day for her and she wanted to enjoy the moment with Rasheed and his aunt as long as she could. Besides, they'd asked her to join them for dinner at Trish's and she happily accepted. Demi wasn't in any rush to return back to Brenda's hostile environment, which she now regretted calling her home. She closed her eyes, blocked out anything dealing with Nico or Brenda and savored the moment. It was peaceful for once.

"Good morning," Demi heard someone say.

When she opened her eyes, she saw Rasheed standing over top of her with a silly kind of grin. She also awakened to the good smelling breakfast being made. Looking around, Demi realized that she was on a couch but it wasn't Brenda's. She rubbed her eyes as panic started to seep in.

"Please don't tell me I spent the night over here." She quickly sat up, realizing that she was still in Pasadena.

"Of course. I'm not sure what happened after dinner and that movie last night, but you fell asleep so quickly. We decided not to bother you because you were resting so peacefully. You looked so worn out, we just figured you needed the rest," Rasheed stated.

"Oh my goodness. Can you please take me back Wilshire Boulevard? I can catch a cab home from there," Demi said, then hopped up.

Rasheed frowned. "Why don't I just take you all the way home?"

"No...no, that's not a good idea. Just take me back to the coffee shop."

Rasheed knew that Demi was panicking about something. "Are you sure?"

But before Demi could answer, she rushed toward the bathroom and did a nose dive toward the toilet. It was a same routine that she'd been doing for the past week. She knew something was wrong.

"Are you okay?" Rasheed asked with concern.

Demi continued to throw up, feeling extremely nauseous and sick. She clutched her stomach and held her face over the toilet feeling the urge to throw up again.

"I'm fine," she lied.

After lingering over the toilet for a few more minutes, Demi stood up, looked at herself in the mirror and began rinsing off her face. Her eyes were red and her legs felt somewhat numb. She didn't want to look sick, so she doused her face with water again, then collected herself before walking back into the living room. Rasheed had already poured her a glass of Ginger Ale.

"I really need to go," Demi stated.

"Are you sure? I mean, you don't have to be in a rush," Rasheed replied. He handed her the glass.

Demi nodded. "I just wanna go."

After talking a few sips of soda, Demi walked back over to the couch and started to gather her things. She picked up her cell phone and noticed ten missed calls. Six had come from Nico while the other four were from Brenda. Knowing she had several threatening messages, Demi shook her head and stuffed the phone into her purse.

Ten minutes later, Demi was getting into Trish's car with a distressed signal on her face. It was difficult having to go back to reality. On the way back to L.A., Rasheed tried to talk to Demi to give her some comfort, but she seemed distant from any conversation and just stared out the window.

When Rasheed pulled up to the same coffee shop, Demi was still quiet and let out a low sigh. He looked over at her and said with concern, "You know, I'm sure my aunt won't mind if you stay with us for a while, especially if you're not comfortable where you're staying. She actually enjoyed your company. Plus my lil' cousin was over his father's house last night. I'm sure once he comes home and realizes that you're the girl from his favorite movie, he won't mind if you stay."

Rasheed smiled. He wasn't sure if Demi would find his comment funny, but it was worth a shot.

Demi turned to face him, but didn't smile back. "I wish it was that easy. I can't inconvenience you and yo' family wit' my troubles. Y'all are good people and don't need to get caught up in my mess."

"Are you in trouble, Demi?" Rasheed asked.

"I can handle myself." She leaned toward him and kissed him on the cheek. "Thanks for everything. You have no idea what it means to me." She was grateful for the special connection they'd made.

Demi started to step out the car, when she heard Rasheed say, "Demi, sometimes we have to deal with the stigma of poor choices, but remember to always keep your head up high, luv. Nobody is perfect."

Demi let out a half-hearted smile and nodded. She felt a warm and caring vibe from Rasheed, which ironically, reminded her of Benny. They both always knew the right words to say.

She knew that one day she would do a movie with Rasheed, a respectable movie. He was about his word, and probably the dude she should've got with back in Harlem. Her lesson; never judge a book by its cover-priceless.

 # Twenty-Four

When Demi walked into Brenda's house, she noticed Lyfe slumped on the couch and staring aimlessly at the T.V. getting high from some Hawaiian pink weed. He glanced at Demi when she walked by instantly finding major humor.

"You're so fucked, dumb bitch," he snapped.

"Shut the hell up," Demi replied.

She walked in the back room where she slept and put down her purse. She then walked into the kitchen to see if Brenda had anything that would help with her nauseated feeling.

However, she didn't make it too far because as soon as she came out the room, Brenda met her in the hallway.

They both glared at each other and then Brenda broke the silence by saying, "Where the fuck was you at bitch?"

Demi rolled her eyes and tried to walk pass Brenda, but Brenda stood in front of Demi blocking her path with a malicious stare.

"You heard me talkin' to you. Where the fuck was you at?" Brenda strongly repeated. She looked Demi up and down. "You walkin' around here all dolled up like you goin' to a fuckin' board meetin' or somethin.'"

"Brenda, get the fuck out my way. I'm in no mood for yo' shit right now," Demi warned. Her stomach was still churning.

"Bitch, you under fuckin' contract. You ain't supposed to leave this house without permission, and you damn sure ain't supposed to be stayin' out all damn night. Nico's been lookin' for your ass. You don't fuckin' know how to return a phone call?" Brenda shouted.

Demi closed her eyes and tried to calm down, but it was-
n't doing her any good. She was getting fed up with everything,
her living conditions, the porn, the gangs…everything. Enough
was enough.

Slouching down on the couch, Lyfe continued taking
pulls from the weed and waited for something to jump off.
Brenda continued with her verbal attack. She was up in Demi's
face so close that Demi could feel several spit balls hitting her
nose, which pissed her off even more.

"You in my fuckin' crib, so don't ever forget that, you
slut bitch. You ain't nobody. Who the fuck is you?" she shouted
while moving her forefinger back and forth in Demi's face. " I
already told you, I'll fuck you up." Brenda went on, trying to
break Demi's spirit.

Demi finally brushed past her. "You don't own me. None
of y'all fuckin own me…fuck you," Demi retorted.

"Bitch, I owned you since the day your dumb-ass walked
into that office lookin' for Jorel," Brenda stated with a chuckle.

Demi had a baffled look on her face. She stopped in her
tracks. "What?"

Brenda continued. "You think Jorel was the brains behind this operation. Bitch, I set you up. I brought you here," she
bragged. "Jorel works for me. I pay him to find me fresh pussy,
and since you wanna go hard, I'll drop you dead just like I did
that bitch in Watts for fuckin' wit' me."

Demi was so mad, her body began to tremble.

"You sent Jorel to look for me?"

"No stupid. I send him to find hard up chicks like you!
The ones that be tryin' to be somebody that they not," she
barked.

"Fuck you Brenda! You ain't shit."

"You ain't shit either, bitch. And you not even smart, or
you woulda known that I was the one who had your room broken into. I had you followed, bitch," she admitted with pride on
her face. "I knew you would be callin' me. It was only a matter
of time before your dumb-ass came runnin' to look for a shoul-

der to lean on. You can't out-smart me, bitch. I'm the fuckin' queen bee in this city. I'm the one who set your ass up in the club that night, too. I let J-Dub and them give you PCP then take your pussy. They paid me well for that shit too. Not Nico…they paid me, five thousand big ones. See, I got my own lil' operation goin' on the side. That muthafucka think he gon' make all the money, but he's wrong." Brenda then began to laugh. "Oh, speakin' of money, I also let Mist and Lyfe fuck you raw that morning as well. Shit, I made a lot of money off you that day."

Demi quickly turned her head and looked at Lyfe who was laughing his ass off.

"Yeah that pussy was good, too," he boasted.

"I guess all muthafuckas from New York is stupid cuz Nico told us that your brother got a hold of one of your porno tapes back in Harlem." Brenda's voice deepened as she dug in for the kill. "Your dumb-ass mother called the office number on the back of the tape which goes directly to our warehouse. Get this," she laughed. "She talkin' 'bout you owe her money so now Blood In-Blood Out entertainment now owes her. She said she on her way out here to get hers."

Lyfe and Brenda laughed like crazy.

"She think she gon' go to the address on the back of the tape and collect a check, or maybe even find you. The bitch gon' collect a bullet."

Brenda burst out into laughter again. But Demi immediately tightened her fist. Not only was she still pissed at Brenda about putting a gun in her face, but now after hearing her shocking confessions, Demi lost all sanity. As Brenda continued to rant, Demi unexpectedly punched Brenda in the side of her face with such force that Brenda stumbled and damn near hit the floor. By the look on Brenda's face, she was completely caught off guard by the sudden attack.

"Keep talkin' shit!" Demi screamed.

Brenda regrouped quickly and charged Demi ready to take her out. Demi stood her ground and when Brenda came close enough, she three-pieced Brenda with a combination of

235

punches, striking her in the face and side. Brenda stumbled again and was stunned that Demi had some hand skills in boxing.

"What now, bitch?" Demi asked.

"Oh, shit!" Lyfe uttered, as he jumped off the couch and ran toward the scuffle.

Demi and Brenda were locked in on each other, tossing, and spiraling viciously near the hallway. Brenda threw Demi against the wall and caught her with a swift punch to the body. However, she was no match for Demi, who kept punching Brenda in the face. Before Brenda knew it; her face oozed blood.

Brenda became furious, but it was obvious who the better warrior was. Both girls went blow for blow at each other like niggahs fighting on the block, until Lyfe stepped in and gave Brenda the advantage. He held Demi from behind, pulling her off of Brenda and left her exposed for attack.

"Niggah, get the fuck off me!" Demi screamed, as she fought aggressively to free herself from Lyfe's grip.

She started to bite at his wrist and moved wildly in his arms. Lyfe saw that it was becoming hard to hold her, as Demi stirred around like a rodeo bull in his grasp.

"What you doin' Brenda? Fuck this bitch up!" he shouted.

Brenda moved in for the attack with her face red from all the blood, but Demi wasn't gonna let it be that easy. She kicked about madly, screaming and cursing, and trying to free herself from Lyfe's hold.

"Fuck y'all," Demi cursed frantically.

As the tussle continued, Demi found herself on the floor being kicked and stomped by both parties, with Brenda trying to go in on Demi's pretty face. She wanted to scar the bitch, but Demi found herself in the fetal position, trying to protect herself. Demi tried to get up and run for cover, but was knocked back down by Lyfe, who hit her in the back with a broomstick.

"Fuck her up!" Brenda shouted, as she punched Demi in

the back of her head.

Demi was under attack like a lone soldier in Iraq. Still, she fought back. She turned and swiftly kicked Brenda in the knee, which made her fall down next to her. When Brenda was down, Demi was on her like flies on shit. She took a fist full of Brenda's braids and knotted them in her fist tightly, which caused Brenda to cry out in agony. Then Demi leaned over and took a chunk out of Brenda's face by sinking her teeth into her skin, crushing down on flesh and bone like vice-grips. Brenda screamed out in pain, with Lyfe once again trying to pull Demi off.

Demi was ready to take it to the extreme and even fight to kill if necessary. She was strictly fed up. She took all that pain she felt, the hurt she suffered, the constant betrayals she tolerated, and the challenges and hardships she endured throughout her life, and poured it all out with her fight against Brenda.

Demi felt the taste of blood in her mouth as her jaws were sunken into Brenda's face like a pit-bull's lock. She still had Brenda's hair tangled in her fist and wanted to tear every single braid from her head. Lyfe tried to pull her away, but the strength and power that Demi mustered up would've been like him trying to pull a truck up a hill. Demi was locked in and ready to kill.

Brenda screamed out loudly and felt like she was about to pass out from the pain.

"Get the fuck off her, Demi!" Lyfe shouted.

But Demi refused. She wanted to kill the bitch. Sitting back up, Demi quickly snuck in a few punches into Brenda's open face. Before she knew it, more than one person was now trying to pull her off. The hallway was suddenly covered with other niggahs grabbing away at Demi and trying to help Brenda. After several attempts, it took the effort of three dudes to finally pry Demi away.

When they were finally separated, Brenda clutched her face, and squirmed around on the ground screaming and cursing. Her face was covered in blood.

When the goons stood Demi up, she continued to stare at Brenda like a raging bull. She was proud of her handiwork. "I told you not to fuck wit' me!"

"What the fuck happened?" Mist asked with a baffled look on his face.

The room was thick with commotion, and everyone was in awe at what Demi had done. When the third homie tried to help Brenda to her feet, she almost collapsed in their arms.

"Damn, she fucked B up," Mist commented.

Soon, Nico showed up at the front door with a look that could kill. Everyone parted like the red sea when he stepped through the living room area.

Demi locked eyes with him, but didn't say a word. She just didn't give a shit anymore. Whatever was going to happen would just have to happen. She was ready for Nico too if he came at her with the bullshit.

"Ay, take that bitch into the bedroom," Nico ordered.

Lyfe and Mist pulled Demi into the back bedroom where she'd been staying, and locked her inside until Nico and his crew could sort everything out. Nico looked at the damage done to Brenda's face and knew she was gonna need medical attention. Brenda looked like she wanted to pass out as the third goon walked her over to the couch.

"Take Brenda to our spot," Nico instructed to Mist.

Mist gave off a funny look before picking her back up. The goon along with Mist carried Brenda outside to Mist's car and placed her in the back seat. Little did Demi know that Brenda would never receive medical attention. She'd stolen from Nico, bit the hand that fed her, and had shown the ultimate disrespect.

Lyfe had obviously ran his mouth to his boys about Brenda allowing him to fuck Demi. Once Nico started his investigation, all kinds of foul shit Brenda had done came out. Nico had decided to spare Lyfe's life but Brenda had to go.

As soon as the car pulled off, Nico knew it was time to handle Demi. He was fuming. She'd cost him time and money, so now there would be hell to pay.

He ordered Lyfe to wait outside while he went to see about Demi. He walked into the back bedroom to find her sitting on the edge of the bed with a scowl still on her face. Her mouth was still covered in Brenda's blood and it looked as if she was ready for round two. Demi turned to look at Nico and didn't even budge when he came toward her.

Nico stood over Demi with an enraged scowl. He was silent for a moment. All of a sudden, he back-handed Demi with a direct hit to her face. She flew off the bed and landed flat on the floor.

"You stupid bitch! What the fuck is wrong wit' you?" Nico barked. He stood over her as she gripped the floor. "I should fuckin' kill you for what you did!"

Demi looked up at him with daring eyes. "Do it then, niggah! I don't give a fuck anymore. It's better than bein' a slave for you."

"You don't give a fuck anymore! Bitch, don't fuck wit' me, I'll spread your fuckin' brains all over this carpet."

To make his threat even more believable, Nico pulled a .45 from his waistband and pushed the tip of it against Demi's temple as he yanked her hair back and forth. Demi didn't resist, but almost accepted her fate like she was willing to die.

"Where the fuck was you? I've been callin' you," Nico said.

Demi was silent as tears welled up in her eyes. Nico pressed the gun harder to her temple and demanded an answer. But Demi still remained silent as tears fell to the floor.

"Let me tell you somthin', forget 'bout them Hollywood dreams. I own your ass now…you hear me bitch! You locked down from here on out, and if you even try and get out, trust me, I'll kill you," Nico strongly said." Your mother called to the warehouse. I know how to get at your daughter if I need to."

He stuffed the gun back down inside his pants and glared at Demi as her tears flowed even more. She looked like she would never stop crying.

"You fucked Brenda's face up bad, so believe me bitch, you gone work that fuckin' hospital bill off!"

Demi remained silent. She thought about her daughter and wondered if she would ever get to see her baby girl again. She thought about Harlem and now wished she was back at home.

"I can't believe you. I can't believe you have so much loyalty to a bitch who playin' you. Brenda makin' her own money off yo' girls on the side, and you don't even know about it."

"Oh, shit got back to me."

"Did you know she took me to a club and allowed some rapper named J-Dub and his friends Chauncey and Rodney run a train on me? She even let Mist and Lyfe fuck me for some money. Why would you want somebody like that in yo' corner?"

The mention of the Crip, Chauncey's name instantly pissed Nico off, but he didn't show his emotions. Demi needed to be taught a lesson for stayin' out all night. Brenda would be handled, head split down to the white meat.

"Ay, dry your tears and fix yourself up. We got a shoot to do in two hours. And I want you lookin' fresh," Nico barked.

Even with the chaos that erupted in the house, Nico was still about his business. His only obvious concerns were getting back to business and making his money.

He turned to leave the bedroom, when he suddenly heard Demi burst out, "I'm pregnant!"

Nico turned toward her. He showed no emotion.

"I can't keep doin' this shit wit' a baby on the way," Demi announced. She hoped that he would have some type of compassion for her.

Nico walked up to her like he was ready to strike her again. Demi braced herself for the blow, but it never came. It was a gamble for her to say that she was pregnant without really knowing, but Demi had a good feeling she was. By throwing up every morning, she remembered having the same symptoms when she was pregnant with Aliyah. She knew her body well.

However, the sad part about it was that she didn't know who the father actually was.

"Bitch, we gettin' rid of that shit. I'll make you an appointment at the abortion clinic tomorrow. Ain't no way a baby gon' fuck up my money," Nico said, and kept moving out the door.

Demi sighed heavily and listened to the sound of the door locking from the other side. She felt trapped in an on-going nightmare without any real chances of ever becoming an A-list actress. Demi just wanted an escape, but it felt like she was sinking deeper into the quicksand without a rope or vine to pull herself out to safety.

She cried inside for help. "Somebody, anybody," she chanted.

Twenty-Five

An hour later, Demi heard the last watch dog leave the house. She knew she had to get out of the house before Nico came back to get her with his crazy-ass goons. Demi had come too far to be stuck doing porn for the rest of her life. She also knew that when Brenda came back home, her life would be endangered. She knew that if she stayed any longer she would either be dead or in jail, so she had to make a move.

However, before making any moves she had to call Michelle first. For Demi, it was a better safe than sorry type of call that had to be made immediately.

Pacing the floor, Demi dialed Michelle's number and waited for her friend to answer. She hoped that Michelle wasn't off somewhere fucking because that would've thrown a small detour in her plans. Plans that couldn't warrant mistakes or any second chances.

Demi was about to hang up and dial the number again when she finally heard someone answer, "Michelle," she called out. It felt so good to hear her friend's voice.

"You in a movie yet, bitch?" Michelle asked teasingly.

Demi didn't have time for jokes. "Not yet. Look…"

Michelle cut her off. "You know I been meanin' to ask you. Yo' ass been out there almost two months and I ain't seen you in no videos, commercials …nothin'. Bitch, you must not be suckin' the right dick."

"Michelle listen, I called because I just wanted to tell you that if somethin' happens to me, please take care of Aliyah. I don't want her with my mother."

"Girl, what the hell you talkin' about?" Michelle asked.

"Please, Michelle. Can you just make me that promise?" Demi shouted in an impatient tone. "She's scandalous and might be coming out here."

"Yeah…yeah sure. I promise. What the hell is wrong wit' you?"

Demi didn't want to alarm her friend too much about all that was going on. "Umm…nothin'. I just got some issues goin' on out here, with Nico and Brenda that's all."

"Shit who you tellin'. I got some real issues too 'cuz I'm pregnant," Michelle uttered.

Demi almost dropped the phone. "Pregnant, Oh my God, you serious?" "As many abortions as I done had over the years you ever known me to joke about 'dat shit?"

"Yeah you right. Who's the father? Wait, don't tell me it's Malik."

"Yup," Michelle answered happily.

"You still fuckin' wit' him? That's a record for you."

Michelle laughed. "Yeah, we been kickin' it extra hard since you left. Shit, Malik be doin' his thang in and outside the bedroom, which might make him a keeper. I'ma keep the baby, too." She paused. "And I cut off all my other nigghas. I told them not to even call me no more. I gotta get serious about life."

Demi was happy for her friend's plans to settle down. It was a clear indication that anyone was definitely capable of change. For a quick moment, Demi had forgotten about her own troubles, especially the fact that she was probably pregnant with a stranger's child.

"What happened wit' you and Rasheed yesterday?"

Demi really didn't have time for a lengthy conversation. "Everything went well. He's really a nice guy. I just wish I had-n't dissed him that night. I've learned a lot from him."

"Dats cool. Maybe we all can do the corny-ass double date shit when you come back. Hell, when Rasheed come back too, I guess. Malik said 'dat niggah might stay out there in L.A. I heard he makin' cheddar."

"Okay, look I need to make another call. I'll talk to you

later," Demi said.

"Bet. Hurry up and make some money, bitch. Damn! My baby is gonna need milk, pampers and a Gucci diaper bag."

Demi smiled. "Don't forget what I said about Aliyah."

"You know what, get the hell off my phone talkin' 'dat nonsense," Michelle replied just before hanging up.

Demi walked over to the mirror on the dresser and studied her bruised face. It wasn't that bad, but it definitely showed her black and blue eye, and her swollen lips. However, she still didn't look as bad as Brenda. She then walked over to the door and stared at it for a few seconds. It was her first time realizing that the regular lock had been switched for a shiny new deadbolt, which locked from the outside. Knowing it wasn't like that before, Demi knew Brenda or Nico had planned that while she was gone. They really were trying to keep her hostage.

Demi instantly became frustrated. She scanned the room trying to find something for her escape. She picked up her cell phone and was ready to dial 911, but thought against it. She then went over to the window and pulled it up. When it went up with ease, she realized how stupid Nico and Brenda really were. They'd locked the bedroom door, but hadn't even bothered to check the window. With the house being on one floor, it was an easy jump, which was what Demi had to do if she ever wanted her freedom back.

She quickly put on a pair of tennis shoes and some jeans then began packing her things in the suitcase, taking everything with her before making a phone call to Benny. She knew he would come to pick her up and take her somewhere safe.

"Hello."

"Benny?" Demi called out.

"Hey, pretty gal," Benny greeted.

"Benny, I need you to come get me. I'm leavin' Inglewood," Demi informed.

"Ya okay?"

"Not really, I got into a fight and if I don't leave here soon, it's gonna be more trouble for me."

"Oh, no. Me come get ya right away."

"Not to the house Benny. It's too dangerous for you to come get me here. I'll meet you somewhere."

"Where?"

After informing Benny where to go, Demi immediately hung up and made sure that her shit was in order. She knew if she didn't leave rapidly, chances would be slim later. Lifting up the bedroom window a little more, Demi could hear music blasting and niggahs yelling at each other from a close distance. Knowing how most of the dudes in the neighborhood rolled, she knew they were more than likely right in front of the house, which was a good thing because the bedroom was situated on the side of the house.

After dragging her bag to the window, she peeked her head out to make sure everything was clear. When she didn't see anyone, Demi tossed her bag outside then quickly perched herself on the window ledge and leaped off. Moving like a crackhead on a stealing spree, she quickly grabbed her bag and dashed toward the back of the house.

Between the houses was a small passageway littered with empty beer bottles, trash cans and old chairs, which Demi made sure not to bump into so nothing would make any noise. She tossed her luggage over the neighbor's rusted fence and then pulled herself over, gripping whatever she could to give her leverage. When she was on the other side of the neighbor's yard, she looked back to make sure nobody was following her, then did a quick sigh of relief. Now all she had to do was make it to the corner of 2nd Ave and West Hardy, which was six, long blocks away.

She moved discreetly through the yard until she came out on the other side of the block. She took off running, carrying her bag in hand. Even though, she'd made it out, Demi knew that she was far from being safe. Running for her life, the blocks seemed quiet and the traffic was sparse. But Demi never stopped until she made it to her destination. As she waited for Benny to show up, she constantly kept a keen eye out for anything unusual, especially for any of Nico's goons coming through. She had to keep her guard up so she watched the area closely.

She waited for Benny for about fifteen minutes, then quickly thanked God when she finally saw his cab coming toward her. Demi grabbed her suitcase when Benny pulled up and quickly threw it in the backseat before jumping in the front. There were no time for a formal hello.

"Benny, please just drive. We need to get out of here!" Demi yelled.

He knew something was wrong when he saw the terrified look on her face, not to mention the black eye sent up a red flag as well.

"Pretty gal, what kind of trouble ya in?" he asked in a worried tone.

"I fucked up, Benny," she admitted.

"What's going on?"

Demi looked around nervously. She just wanted to get out of Inglewood.

"I'll fill you in. I'm just so relieved that I made it outta there alive. I don't care where I go, just somewhere safe."

She knew Nico had eyes and ears all around, and that she wouldn't be protected in the area, or anywhere in L.A probably. She thought about going back to New York, knowing that was one place where Nico couldn't fuck with her.

Benny tried talking to Demi. He knew something was wrong and wanted Demi to be honest with him. He continued to drive down W. Hardy Street and when they were at least four blocks away, Demi finally decided to come clean. She looked at Benny and told him everything, even the porn. She also admitted that she was probably pregnant, and then mentioned the fight she had with Brenda.

"I really don't wanna put you in danger, Benny. You're a good friend and a family man," she said.

Benny did his best to comfort Demi, knowing that she was in trouble. "Nonsense, pretty gal…ya need help, and me here to help ya. Ya can come and stay with my family until ya get yourself settled in somewhere nice. But ya gotta get your life right. Don't let this dream of becoming an actress change ya for the worst," he stated.

Demi nodded.

While waiting for a light to change, Demi was listening to Benny talk about family when she noticed a black Yukon pull up closely on Benny's side. At first she didn't think anything of it, but when the windows rolled down, a lump formed in her throat. She sat up straight, eyed the vehicle, and gazed at the malicious grin on Nico's face. Simultaneously, the back right door opened and a body was pushed to the ground.

Demi's heart throbbed recognizing her mother's bloody face before it hit the ground. Demi yelled, "Pull off!"

Instantly, two automatic weapons became clearly visible. Demi screamed again. "Bennyyyyyyyyyyy!"

At once, Demi dropped to the floor then managed to pop open the passenger door. Abruptly, heavy gun fire erupted never giving Benny a chance to step on the gas. Bullets tore into the cab at top speed, just as Demi made it out of the cab onto the ground. She screamed for help, taking cover beneath the car.

Bullets riddled the car everywhere causing Benny to be hit several times. When the gun fire came to a halt, the truck quickly sped off and turned the corner sharply. Demi was hysterical. She didn't know if she was injured or not, and was about to take off running when she noticed Benny slumped over in the driver's seat. She wanted to faint. She ran over to the driver's side of the car and grabbed Benny, pulling him out of the riddled car, and just two yards away from her lifeless mother. She held Benny in her arms as she rocked back and forth in the middle of the street.

"Benny, please...no, this is not happenin'. God, please don't take him...please, don't take him!" she cried.

Bystanders rushed to assist her, and police sirens could be heard from a distance. Demi continued to hold Benny in her arms, until one of the bystanders said to her, "Oh my God, miss, I think the lady next to you is already dead."

When Demi looked down at her mother, she noticed a calming spirit across her face. It was a look she'd never seen on her mother before. She thought about leaving the embrace of Benny, and rushing to be with her mother. Within seconds, she'd completely decided against it. She'd pay her respects at the funeral.

She glanced back over at Benny who was now completely lifeless. Tears began to trickle down her cheeks and her heart raced. She was to blame for his death and it hurt like hell to know that.

A few minutes later, the police and ambulance were pulling up and rushing over to the victims. Demi felt herself becoming ill. She saw the EMS workers standing over her, trying to move Benny to the ground. One of the guys uttered, "Hey, I know you. You're an actress, right?"

Demi let out a half-ass smile. Maybe he'd seen one of her porn movies. Demi closed her eyes slightly, wishing she was just filming a movie, wishing she could finally hear some famous director yell, "Cut." But Demi couldn't live her fairytale life anymore. After all, Nico made it clear what he would do if she left him. As her eyes closed completely, she finally understood that making it in Hollywood wouldn't be easy...but she had to try for Benny's sake.

COMING SOON

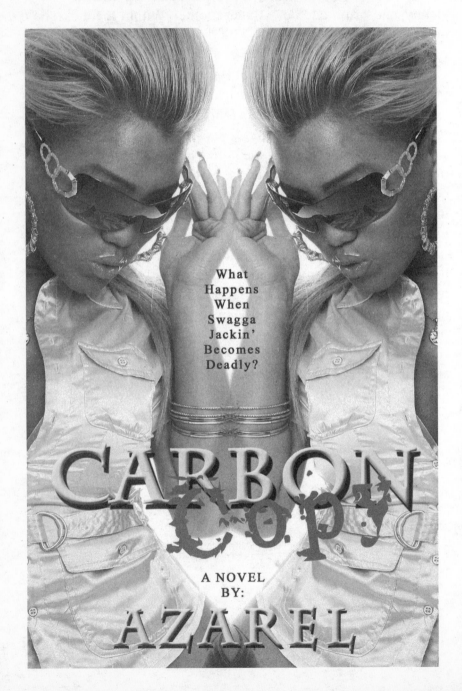

What Happens When Swagga Jackin' Becomes Deadly?

CARBON Cop

A NOVEL BY:

AZAREL

IN STORES NOW!!!
PICK UP YOUR COPY TODAY

Never before has there been a novel that keeps you on edge, drooling at the mouth, and totally satisfied. Good Girl Gone Bad is sure to be a classic.
- Azarel

GOOD Girl
Gone BAD
DANETTE MAJETTE

Most people think when you say, "I do" all problems come to an end. When happily ever after seems impossible, three women transform from good girls to bad women. Just when they think they've made it out of the grimy streets to a more ideal lifestyle in the suburbs, their lavish lives turn sour. Unfortunately, for the sexy threesome they are all suddenly faced with financial hardships that land them between a rock and a hard place.

While Alyse and her husband Lance live paycheck to paycheck with barely any money to make ends meet, Jazmine gets brutally abused daily by her husband Vince, a well respected police officer by day and a drug addicted maniac by night. Then there's Roslynn a compulsive shopper who's used to a pampered life style and seconds away from sending her husband into bankruptcy. Roslynn all of a sudden has to make a change when her big secret destroys her marriage.

With nowhere to turn, they all mastermind an elaborate scheme to get the money they so desperately need. They plunge themselves into a ruthless game of sex, betrayal, and survival. No one suspects them of any wrong doing until their plan goes terribly wrong. Join these three ladies on an exciting journey from the good life to the desperate life.

A Sexy Urban Tale

The Brooklyn Streets Never Been Hotter!!!

BROOKLYN Brothel

A Novel By:
C. STECKO

NOW IN STORES

In Stores Now
A HUSTLER'S WORST
NIGHTMARE
"Newcomer Derrick King Has Claimed His Spot In Urban Lit With A Hustler's Worst Nightmare."
- Shannon Holmes - National Best Selling Author Of B-More Careful & Bad Girlz 4 Life
A NOVEL BY
DERRICK KING
www.kingpenpublications.com

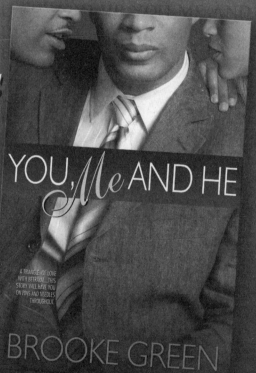

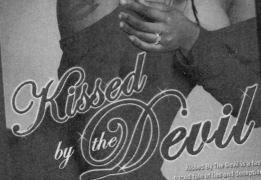

MAIL TO:
PO Box 423
Brandywine, MD 20613
301-362-6508

FAX TO:
301-579-9913

ORDER FORM

Ship to:	
Address:	
City & State:	Zip:
Attention:	

Date:
Phone:
E-mail:

Make all money orders and cashiers checks payable to: **Life Changing Books**

Qty.	ISBN	Title	Release Date	Price
	0-9741394-0-8	A Life To Remember by Azarel	Aug-03	$ 15.00
	0-9741394-1-6	Double Life by Tyrone Wallace	Nov-04	$ 15.00
	0-9741394-5-9	Nothin Personal by Tyrone Wallace	Jul-06	$ 15.00
	0-9741394-2-4	Bruised by Azarel	Jul-05	$ 15.00
	0-9741394-7-5	Bruised 2: The Ultimate Revenge by Azarel	Oct-06	$ 15.00
	0-9741394-3-2	Secrets of a Housewife by J. Tremble	Feb-06	$ 15.00
	0-9724003-5-4	I Shoulda Seen It Comin by Danette Majette	Jan-06	$ 15.00
	0-9741394-4-0	The Take Over by Tonya Ridley	Apr-06	$ 15.00
	0-9741394-6-7	The Millionaire Mistress by Tiphani	Nov-06	$ 15.00
	1-934230-99-5	More Secrets More Lies by J. Tremble	Feb-07	$ 15.00
	1-934230-98-7	Young Assassin by Mike G.	Mar-07	$ 15.00
	1-934230-95-2	A Private Affair by Mike Warren	May-07	$ 15.00
	1-934230-94-4	All That Glitters by Ericka M. Williams	Jul-07	$ 15.00
	1-934230-93-6	Deep by Danette Majette	Jul-07	$ 15.00
	1-934230-96-0	Flexin & Sexin by K'wan, Anna J. & Others	Jun-07	$ 15.00
	1-934230-92-8	Talk of the Town by Tonya Ridley	Jul-07	$ 15.00
	1-934230-89-8	Still a Mistress by Tiphani	Nov-07	$ 15.00
	1-934230-91-X	Daddy's House by Azarel	Nov-07	$ 15.00
	1-934230-87-1-	Reign of a Hustler by Nissa A. Showell	Jan-08	$ 15.00
	1-934230-86-3	Something He Can Feel by Marissa Montelih	Feb-08	$ 15.00
	1-934230-88-X	Naughty Little Angel by J. Tremble	Feb-08	$ 15.00
	1-934230847	In Those Jeans by Chantel Jolie	Jun-08	$ 15.00
	1-934230855	Marked by Capone	Jul-08	$ 15.00
	1-934230820	Rich Girls by Kendall Banks	Oct-08	$ 15.00
	1-934230839	Expensive Taste by Tiphani	Nov-08	$ 15.00
	1-934230782	Brooklyn Brothel by C. Stecko	Dec-08	$ 15.00
			Total for Books	$
		Shipping Charges (add $4.25 for 1-4 books*)		$
		Total Enclosed (add lines)		$

* Prison Orders- Please allow up to three (3) weeks for delivery.

For credit card orders and orders over 30 books, please contact us at orders@lifechaningbooks.net (Cheaper rates for COD orders)

*Shipping and Handling of 5-10 books is $6.25, please contact us if your order is more than 10 books. (301)362-6508